STAR-SPANGLED
SCANDAL

STAR-SPANGLED SCANDAL

A NOVEL

LORI SWERDA

STAR-SPANGLED SCANDAL
A NOVEL

iUniverse books may be ordered through booksellers or by contacting:

iUniverse
1663 Liberty Drive
Bloomington, IN 47403
www.iuniverse.com
1-800-Authors (1-800-288-4677)

Because of the dynamic nature of the Internet, any web addresses or links contained in this book may have changed since publication and may no longer be valid. The views expressed in this work are solely those of the author and do not necessarily reflect the views of the publisher, and the publisher hereby disclaims any responsibility for them.

Any people depicted in stock imagery provided by Getty Images are models, and such images are being used for illustrative purposes only. Certain stock imagery © Getty Images.

ISBN: 978-1-5320-6978-9 (sc)
ISBN: 978-1-5320-6979-6 (e)

Library of Congress Control Number: 2019902271

Print information available on the last page.

iUniverse rev. date: 03/07/2019

ACKNOWLEDGMENTS

To Casey and Lauren, my two daughters, for accompanying me on countless research outings. Thank you for spending summer vacations in spooky old graveyards with your mom.

To my friend Teia, who encouraged this book from the time she read the first draft of the first chapter. Your enthusiasm for finding out what happened next kept me writing and moving forward. Thank you for all your support.

Thank you to my mom, Barb, and my sister, Debbie for being first readers. Thank you to fellow author, Matt Cost, for your feedback and inspiration. Thank you to my brother Wes, my aunt Judy, my friends at Rose Hill, Chris at Mount Olivet, and Dewey for helping me realize it's cool to be a history nerd.

Thank you to Dorothy, Armen, Bob, and Theda for their hospitality and assistance tracking down a mystery. Here, I also thank divine intervention.

INTRODUCTION

The following novel is based on the true story of a torrid love affair and brazen murder that occurred in Washington D.C. in 1859. Most elements of the story are fact and those that are fiction are historically possible. Through meticulous research into the events that occurred, relationships between characters, and the reality of human nature, the fictional elements are also entirely probable. If you find yourself searching the web like mad for what is true and untrue, then I have done my job well. Star-Spangled Scandal is not a textbook meant to teach, but a tale meant to entertain, and if a little learning occurs along the way, then so be it.

CONTENTS

PART THREE
Alicia Key Pendleton

PART ONE

PHILIP BARTON KEY II

Bracing myself for the impact of the fourth bullet, I glanced up at the February sky and down the barrel of a gun. From the corner of my eye, I could see the White House shimmering in the morning sun. In the other direction was the home of the man standing over me now. I would never deny being in love with his wife and even as I lay here in agony, I thought of her and hoped that she was not witnessing this horrific scene. What if he was coming for her next? I had failed to free her from this brute as much as I'd failed to prepare for a moment like this one. There were so many goodbyes unsaid. The faces of my four children flashed through my mind. My sister Alicia would raise them now, wouldn't she? Dan aimed directly at my face, and pulled the trigger, "Click."

Nothing happened, but the blood drained steadily from my body through the existing wounds and began to pool between the cobblestones in the street. I wondered if love always ended in such pain. Perhaps I had known the answer to that most of my life, the first lesson being along the banks of Maryland's Potomac River when I was just four years old.

CHAPTER 1

EARLY GRAVES

Edward, sliding down the muddy bank and disappearing into the raging rapids, was the first in a devastating string of tragedies for my family. The beauty of the Potomac River was undeniable; silver rippled waters flowed calm and flat during most of the year but could turn turbulent and angry during a period of heavy rain. Ships loaded with large wooden barrels stacked three high with commodities like tobacco and sugarcane sailed by, going to the port at Georgetown in the summer of 1822.

My brothers and I lay on the grassy bank making up wild stories for one another about what secret cargo each ship carried and what exotic location it might be venturing to next. A pastime our mother quickly ended after my nine-year-old brother Edward, drowned.

Our childhood home was a brick and stone structure along the Maryland side of the Potomac River, very near the capital of our new nation. It was two stories and rather spacious but after being kept inside by rain for what seemed like weeks, the walls were closing in on us. Edward was silly with the excitement of an especially beautiful day; we all were. After breakfast, my sisters, brothers, and I dashed into the backyard, through the terraced gardens filled with white roses and black-eyed Susans, and straight to the edge of the wild river. We'd watched it from our bedroom windows and couldn't wait to get an up-close look at the brown rapids, but the banks were slick and unstable.

Edward skidded to a halt ahead of the rest of us and edged forward, peering over into the churning water. Suddenly he lost his footing, and we watched in terror, screaming helplessly, as he plunged into the river below. Edward clawed furiously at the muddy wall that separated him from us. "Swim Edward, swim," we shouted at him. He knew *how* to swim, but the current was too strong and within seconds he was swept away. I called his name over and over from the riverbank that day and for many years after that in my dreams. By late afternoon his body was recovered by a fishing boat, two miles downstream, and just like that, he was gone.

The rest of that day is unclear in my mind, but I do remember the devastation my family suffered at the loss of my brother. I remember seeing my father cry, and I remember the silence that seemed to cover our home like a dark cloud for many months.

Before Edward died, my father, Francis, had been making a name for himself in the law profession and he wrote the words to an ever-popular account from the war of 1812 that was being called the "Star-Spangled Banner," and celebrated throughout the country. My mother, Polly, was too busy caring for us children and enduring continual pregnancies to be concerned with much else. It was a decent life in prosperous times.

Being born in Georgetown in 1818 had been a promising start for me as a new baby. The war was over, liberty from England was all but ensured and there was a general cheeriness in the air. The marble foundations of the capital were set as I learned to walk in the parlor of my family home on Bridge Street. As the eighth child born to the Key household, I was only one among an entire brood of young children needing attention daily, so I was fortunate that I received the special attention of my oldest brother Frankie. He was also named Francis Scott Key and my father had already set claim to being called Frank by everyone who knew him well enough. Frankie was twelve years older than me and the most attentive of all my older brothers. The story of the day I was born was legend in our family. Mother and Frankie had been home alone, watching after the youngest children, when one month too soon I'd decided to make my screaming entrance. Frankie had no choice but to help her deliver me into the world and from that moment on, he marveled over my every move. He had even chosen my name, Philip, after our great uncle. I was adored by no person on earth like I was by my brother Frankie.

Gradually after Edward's death, my mother's sweet and even temperament returned, and she went back to running things quite smoothly at home while adding more siblings to our already large family.

Our family prayer time held every evening without fail included a prayer for the soul of my brother. The slaves my parents owned were required to attend this evening ritual as well, though I believe they would not have missed it if given the choice. Most of them were considered by us and themselves to be members of the family. We had been together for so long that no one remembered a time without them. "Uncle" Clem had been brought with mother and father when they moved from Fredericktown and some like Eliza came from the plantation, Terra Rubra, where my father was born. Eliza had known my father as an infant and theirs was a mutual respect and affection that was both detested and envied by others in a time that the nation was becoming deeply divided over the issue of slavery.

Childhood in Georgetown was simple and mostly happy but not still or quiet. It seemed with so many children living under one roof that you were never alone. Outside our front door, it was no different. Horses and people were at all hours passing by on our dusty street. It was a busy town and it seemed fitting that our large family was in the center of it. My father was never bothered by all the commotion. Being calm, practical and patient, he handled his law practice, his family, and his brush with fame with the same humility.

As children, we enjoyed the attention we'd receive when he allowed us to accompany him to a reading of the famous poem he had produced at the battle of Ft. McHenry. We were proud that people seemed to like father so much but were too young to fully understand the significance of the wartime poem. Father wrote poems all the time; poems about us that rhymed our names with nonsense words and made us collapse into fits of laughter. He wrote poems to mother to tell her lame things that he could so much easier have simply said aloud, but that's what he did. He wrote.

He was soft-hearted and we knew that even when he was busy that he could be easily tempted to frolic with us if we asked him in just a way. Mother tried to shoo us away insisting we let him work, but he never did mind. He was full of surprises and one of our favorites was fathers attempt to devise an egg hunt. We'd gone outside to collect the eggs for breakfast and found that father had left us little scrap notes near the spots the chickens normally laid. Each contained a poetic clue as to where we could look next. At the end of our hunt, we were rewarded by discovering a pile of eggs that father had dyed a vibrant shade of blue, along with a few pieces of hard candy that he'd left tied up in a brown paper sack. He'd insisted that a blue chicken had come by and laid the eggs, then wandered on down the road. He claimed he "dropped" the bag of candy there in his astonishment of spotting the odd hen. Father was so believable and convincing that we actually went on searches through the streets in hopes of catching a glimpse of that blue chicken.

As I matured, I admired my father's talent for writing and began to comprehend the bravery that he had conjured up that September of 1814, before I was even born. Apparently, it had been unsettling for everyone during that summer. Father was not particularly invested in the war with the English, but as the stories of the British raiding and plundering became personal and included the homes and businesses of his friends in neighboring cities, father had decided enough was enough and he became determined to do what he could to support the cause. Father joined a neighbor, Mr. Peter, who formed and led a militia on several missions including marching sixty miles to a town along the Patuxent River that had been raided. The folks there needed backup and reassurance if nothing else, once the invaders had gone. With that particular assignment complete, the group made up of farmers, lawyers, and the like, disassembled and returned to their homes after only a few days and father's closest encounter with danger during the mission had involved being thrown headfirst off his horse and into the river. He decided then that he had no desire to know any more about the dangers of war.

Like it or not though, our family had remained amid battle. Rumors swept through the town all summer of an imminent British attack on the capital and Georgetown. As a precaution my brothers and sisters, along with our family's most important possessions, had been promptly sent to our grandparent's home at Terra Rubra in Fredericktown.

Mother insisted on staying with father in Georgetown for as long as possible saying she'd have worried herself sick about him otherwise. Eventually, father convinced her to stay a few days at least with some friends in Montgomery County just outside the city. She reluctantly agreed as Georgetown became more and more desolate by the hour. With her safely away, Mr. Peter asked father to join him on another brief mission. This time not as an enlisted man but as an advisor on the Maryland terrain the militia was headed through. He knew the land well enough and volunteered to offer his services in any way he could be helpful.

The battle of Bladensburg turned out to be a disastrous and embarrassing defeat by the British troops who were far more prepared and equipped. The militia and father had fled the town and managed to save themselves from slaughter but had left the door to Washington wide open.

Father had returned as quickly as he could to stand watch over his family's home. That very day, August 24, 1814 to be exact, Washington was burned and destroyed without defense and father had watched helplessly and nervously from a few miles away in Georgetown as the plumes of smoke rose over the city, and the overpowering burning smell drove anyone left, inside, with the windows closed.

He always paused here in the story and raised his eyebrows to the sky as if saying a silent prayer. "A miracle happened that day," he'd say softly. Going on to tell that among the devastating loss, came a sudden swath of thunderstorms so intense that it could only have been sent by God himself to put out the fires of the capital. The ground had rumbled with thunder and the rain came down in sheets so thick that you could not even see out the window for the nearly twenty minutes that the storm raged. Father had prayed hard during those moments and when it was over, the city was destroyed but the fires were out, and the British had gone. Georgetown had not been touched at all.

Upon victory, several retreating British soldiers unable to resist the temptation of the handsome farm homes they passed had broken off from the group to loot and steal. One such home belonged to Dr. William Beanes. The doctor was a longtime friend of the Key's and father credited him with saving the lives of more than one member of our family.

Not being one to concede, Dr. Beanes, after being robbed, had sent for help, and the thieving soldiers were captured and locked up. One thug had escaped relaying the story of how the doctor had captured his fellow soldiers. Feeling invincible from their current success, retaliation was swiftly ordered. The doctor and several other men, in a most uncivilized manner, were taken prisoner the very next night.

My uncle, being the closest friend to Dr. Beanes had immediately tried to intervene on his behalf, but to no avail. That was when he'd come to father for advice and support. He insisted that father could "talk the hind legs off a donkey," and that he was the doctors best chance at release. It sounded like a lost cause, given the climate of the war, and it was not without risk.

Father said he thought of the time years earlier that the good doctor had come in the dead of night to his home to treat the children who burned with fever and the family doctor seemed unable to do anything more. Father had been terrified at the thought of losing a child or even two and in desperation, he had sent for Dr. Beanes well after midnight and begged him to come to Georgetown right away. He swore never to forget the kindness of the doctor who came at once and stayed, watching over them until the morning when the fevers finally broke.

Upon my Uncle's recommendation and father's renowned reputation as a top-notch lawyer in the city, orders were issued by General Mason and President Madison to both father and to a man called John Skinner. Mr. Skinner was a lawyer as well who had succeeded before in prisoner release negotiations. They were to find the British ship holding the doctor and argue for his release. They were provided a stack of letters attesting to the doctor's character, written by British soldiers who had been cared for along the way by Dr. Beanes and a general idea of where to find the ship called the Tonnent, and nothing more. Father met Mr. Skinner near Baltimore and they took to the water searching the Chesapeake Bay for days to find the fleet.

When they finally spotted the ship, Father's anxiety level had reached an all-time high. He was nearly sick with anticipation of the task at hand. He had argued many things but never on an enemy ship bobbing off the coast of Baltimore. He wondered to himself what he had been thinking by accepting this assignment, he felt utterly unqualified and nervous as they climbed aboard the British ship that September day. Upon seeing the doctor face to face and the deplorable conditions he was being kept in below deck, father was newly motivated to see him released. Father let his animosity toward these British officers fuel his determination. He'd turned on that so-called "Frank Key charm" and after dining, strong drinks and stronger arguments by father and Mr. Skinner, the officers were convinced that the only proper course of action was to release Dr. Beanes.

According to father, part of the manipulation of making a strong case involved indulging the boastful conversation of the officers regarding their repulsion towards anything American and their plans to deal with it. Father and Mr. Skinner had been alarmed at such conversation taking place in front of them but were helpless to protest. Father was soon told what he already suspected, and with great dread agreed to the terms, which meant that he, Mr. Skinner, and Dr. Beanes would not be going anywhere for a few days. They had walked directly into a hornet's nest. The British were about to attack Baltimore and they were now privy to the plans.

The Americans watched helplessly as the British fleet crept closer to Baltimore and into positions that were intended to easily defeat and then destroy the city. Father claimed to never have felt so hopeless in his life. To the attackers, this battle was personal. Baltimore was the home of the shipbuilders responsible for crippling the Royal Navy. Hundreds of British ships containing not only precious cargo, but the lives of brothers and fellow sailors had been rammed and sunken in open seas, by a fleet of armed vessels built in Baltimore just for that purpose. Father heard over and over the anger fueled reference to those detested "Baltimore Clippers."

The tension was palpable when the first explosion rocked the waters in the early morning hours on September 13th. Father and the others were held aboard a smaller craft about a mile behind the line of British Bomb ships but could see the high points of Ft. McHenry in the distance, like a great rock formation standing guard at the entrance to the city. Above the walls father noticed the red, white, and blue flag flying high above the fort and he prayed and wondered how long it could last. At first, father said, the explosions had been jarring and sent a shock through the body, but as the day went on and turned to night the blasts of the rockets and cannon fire were dimmed by both temporary deafness and familiarity. Father had walked from end to end of the boat at least a hundred times, wringing his hands, and keeping his eyes to the fort walls to look for any sign of surrender.

As darkness fell, a violent thunderstorm raged through the harbor only adding to the already chaotic scene, yet somehow to him, it seemed appropriate. Father had tried to rest below deck in the evening but when he did the continuous battle woke him. The commotion took him back to a time in his youth when his drunken father, our grandfather who died when I was just three, would come stumbling home after an evening spent downing whiskey and still singing tavern songs, he crashed his way through the family home, scaring them half to death. He inadvertently heard those songs again in his head and they stuck in his mind like a leech.

It was no use, he'd been unable to sleep, so he joined Mr. Skinner and Dr. Beanes on the deck and together they waited and watched as the break of day slowly approached. They took turns using the spyglass but through the morning mist and smoke, they could see nothing. The explosions abruptly stopped and the trio had glanced at each other wondering if this was good news or bad. Expecting to see the white flag of surrender they shared a moment of sorrow. Father then took his turn peering in the spyglass. The same sudden gust of wind that removed the smoke from his view, caused a flag to ripple weakly. "Stars and Stripes," he cried out, passing the glass for the others to look for themselves. He could scarcely believe his eyes, had we won? He would pause his tale here just long enough to have us begging him to finish, although we'd heard this story hundreds of times and knew the outcome well.

"It seemed impossible. The odds were astronomical," he continued. Confirmation came as the British ships began their retreat and fathers next reaction had been "paper" he needed paper. In his pocket was a letter and he decided that the content of the letter was negligible compared to this moment and so he began scribbling on the back of it. Filled with joy and gratitude, he did what he always did best, he wrote.

Oh, say can you see by the dawn's early light,
What so proudly we hailed at the twilight's last gleaming,
Whose broad stripes and bright stars through the perilous fight,
O'er the ramparts we watched, were so gallantly streaming?
And the rockets' red glare, the bombs bursting in air,
Gave proof through the night that our flag was still there;
Oh say does that star-spangled banner yet wave,
O'er the land of the free and the home of the brave?

That morning in the Chesapeake Bay when he penned the words about the battle he'd just witnessed at Ft. McHenry, his words spilled out in poetry, but the tune that had plagued him throughout the night had nothing to do with patriotism. What happened next was something that father had not expected. He'd been working feverishly on his poem when they'd arrived back to shore. His brother-in-law, Joseph greeted them and was amused at father's deep distraction. He inquired, what was so important that he couldn't lift his head from paper to greet his own family? Father had self-consciously showed him the piece he was working on and instead of kidding him further, Joseph became dead serious. "By all means, finish it," Joseph said. Father did complete his writing that evening and allowed Joseph to read the finished piece. He was impressed at the stunning account of the battle scene and insisted that he should have it printed immediately. The people were hungry in the city of Baltimore, hungry for details and firsthand accounts of the victory that had taken place the day prior and this was exactly the thing to satisfy their hunger.

Joseph knew the owner of a local print shop and presented fathers work to him and by midafternoon the distribution of the "Defence of Fort M'Henry" had begun. The caption mentioned that the tune of the tavern song "To Anacreon in Heaven," had loosely inspired the rhythm of the poem, and anxious to recite the words aloud, the people, being familiar with that tune, gave it an easy transition from poem to song, and it spread among the masses.

The popularity of the "Star-Spangled Banner" as it eventually became known, may have made him famous, but to us, he was just father. He encouraged our learning and he cared immensely about our education. From the youngest age I can recall, he hired tutors for subjects where he felt he lacked expertise. He told us many times, at our request, the story of that night in 1814 at Ft. McHenry. Mother could never stay for the retelling. It upset her too much to think of how much danger her dear husband had faced. We loved his description of how the night sky lit up like day during the bombing and how he'd use the flash to check his pocket watch. Our favorite part of the story was when he realized the British were retreating, beaten. His heart had thumped so hard in his chest, he said, that the only thing he could do to calm himself was to write, scribbling on the back of that letter. This part we could picture in our minds, the rest was unimaginable.

CHAPTER 2

TERRA RUBRA

Frederick County Maryland, roughly forty miles Northwest of Washington was possibly the most serene, beautiful place for a child to spend time. As often as possible my father took us to Terra Rubra, his childhood home just outside Fredericktown. "Look there Philip," father shouted to me over the clip-clop of the horse's hooves, excitedly pointing out the first glimpse of the creek that we followed along the rudimentary carriage road to the estate.

The manor built by my grandfather, John Ross Key, in 1773 was enormous. A covered porch spanned the entire width, nearly 100 feet, of both stories in the front, supported by large plastered columns. The rear wings had been carefully built with bricks brought over from England. Three large dormers protruded from the attic level and Gabled chimneys marked the location of each fireplace. Terra Rubra meant "red earth," and the expansive farmland surrounded the manor for miles in every direction.

There was plenty of space for the families visiting throughout the season. The servants handled the meals and washing, so it was the more the merrier. And it was always merry at the place we also called Pipe Creek. The older children would be allowed to stay for the entire summer, supervised by whichever relatives remained, even when the adults had to take turns returning to the city. If we were fortunate, that would include our most favorite aunt.

Aunt Anne had married one of father's old schoolmates named Roger Brooke Taney. Father was extremely protective of his little sister and Roger was the only man father considered good enough for her. Anne loved children and she had a way of making each of us feel that we were *her* favorites as well. Sweet cakes and new toys would often be waiting for our arrival at the farm if Aunt Anne was there. Uncle Roger was a busy man, but he had endless energy and was usually bouncing, racing or tossing us children around, much to our delight. It was always exciting to look forward to seeing them and our cousins at Terra Rubra.

Even when I was old enough to decide for myself what to do with my leisure time I chose to return with the rest of the family and stay if I could. Here the green pastures dotted with grazing farm animals stretched out in every direction, the trees were taller; healthier, and the water from our abundant spring definitely tasted better. We had the freedom to explore and over the years we'd built so many log bridges over the creeks, and pine tree forts in the woods, that sometimes we forgot, between visits, where to find them. The nearby Catoctin Mountains had waterfalls, swimming holes, and good hunting. It was so different than the noise and bustle outside of our house in Georgetown and the quiet always took some getting used to.

Father's status brought a bit of attention to our quiet country getaway and unexpected guests would often appear, even many years after he'd written his well-known song. As we'd pass other farms and travelers on the day's carriage ride to Fredericktown from Georgetown, families would call out greetings and father was compelled to stop and say hello. It made for a slow trip, and as kids it was torture. All we wanted was to kick off our shoes and walk in pipe creek until our toes were numb from the cold spring water.

Fredericktown was, in many ways, the most important city in the state and next only to Baltimore in growth and population. It was the crossroads of all the major hubs of industry. To get much of anywhere, one usually passed through the prospering town. The grist mills were thriving thanks to access to water power being provided by the Monocacy River and its connecting creeks and streams flowing toward the Potomac. Flour, cornmeal, and grain were being processed and shipped to Baltimore in lines of wagons long enough to lose count of them. Stills were producing cider, brandy, and my grandfather's favorite drink, rye whiskey, in enormous quantities. The iron furnaces were turning out thousands of tons of iron each week. A combination of brick front shops and market stalls lined the cobblestone streets offering goods like fabric, coffee beans, blocks of cheese, and fresh citrus. Even new carriages could be acquired with one trip into town.

Father's friends included an ever-increasing group of dignitaries and statesman, especially after the "Star-Spangled Banner" had been published repeatedly and become famous. It seemed everyone wanted to meet the man behind the song. One of those people was first Maryland Governor Thomas Johnson who lived near Fredericktown as well, on a plantation known as Rose Hill. Governor Johnson was retired from politics and was now living with his daughter Anne and her family. His health was declining, and he'd been living alone in a home several miles North when Anne had asked him to come and live at Rose Hill. He had, after all, originally owned the property and given it to Anne as a gift on her wedding night. Governor Johnson was glad to have the company of his family. He was extremely fond of his grandson Thomas and granddaughter Ann. He tutored young Thomas in his studies sharing his knowledge of law and politics, and Thomas was molded into a fine and well-spoken young man of which his grandfather was most proud. Between building a new nation, owning an iron furnace in the mountains, serving for three years as Governor, and becoming a Supreme Court justice, Thomas Johnson had somehow missed the growing up of his own children and it was one of his biggest regrets. He became reflective when his good friend General Washington passed away unexpectedly from illness in 1799. After delivering a eulogy at a memorial service held in Fredericktown, he fully embraced the decision to devote the rest of his life to his family and enjoying his precious grandchildren.

I didn't have the privilege of knowing Governor Johnson personally, although I'm told I met him once. Unfortunately, I was an infant, and don't remember the encounter. My brother Frankie, however, had gotten to know the man and his family very well. Father was invited to Rose Hill for a banquet and to present a reading of his famous account of the defense of Ft. McHenry. Naturally, everyone at Rose Hill Manor wanted to meet the famous Francis Scott Key. They were nearly our neighbors after all. Frankie was eight years old when he first visited there with father. Upon his introduction to Governor Johnson, he'd called Frankie, "the poet's son," something he continued to call him for several years before passing away in 1819. It wasn't a term Frankie particularly welcomed but Governor Johnson was kind and jovial and Frankie decided that he could call him whatever he'd like. While engaged in conversations in the parlor with father, Governor Johnson had asked his grandchildren to entertain Frankie by showing him around the grounds. Being young adults at the time they weren't sure exactly what to do with an eight-year-old boy. Thomas asked if Frankie liked fishing to which he had replied with a definite yes. Ann was not interested, to say the least, and insisted on fetching refreshments instead.

The boys walked past the gardens beginning to wilt for the season, through the orchards picked clean of fruit and followed the gentle slope of the farm until they came to a creek that reminded Frankie exactly of Pipe Creek at Terra Rubra. He was immediately at ease; this was his element. He was great at catching fish and Thomas was soon impressed with his skills. Frankie told Thomas all about Pipe Creek and how he would spend summers and the holidays at Terra Rubra. He told him about his home in Georgetown and about his brothers and sisters and about how his father had come to write the Star-Spangled Banner. Frankie was the oldest boy in my family and hadn't ever had an older brother to look up to and Thomas only had a sister, so the two were fast friends despite somewhat of an age difference.

Frankie had asked Thomas, "is it true what they say about your grandfather?"

He replied, "I guess that depends what they say."

Frankie told Thomas what he heard, "They say he's a hero of the revolution, and that he made all the cannonballs used in the war, and that he was best friends with George Washington!"

Thomas laughed, "part true," he said. Frankie sat in wide-eyed amazement as Thomas described his grandfather and George Washington's close friendship. His grandfather had been behind nominating his friend as the first commander and chief of the new nation. He described the iron furnace owned by the Johnson brothers where they *had* made cannon balls for the war, though not all of them. Thomas offered to take Frankie to the Catoctin Mountains to see the furnaces for himself very soon.

"Wow, you must be proud to be named after him," said Frankie.

Thomas replied, "That I am; and you must be proud to be named Francis Scott Key."

This had puzzled Frankie for a moment. He'd never thought of it that way before but yes, it was true, he had every reason to be proud to be called Francis Scott Key.

As the sun set on the beautiful orchards and fields of Rose Hill, Thomas promised to come to Terra Rubra to see Frankie's Pipe creek. The two were as good as brothers and Thomas was true to his words. Rose Hill was very similar to Terra Rubra in many ways and so were the two families who lived at them. It was a natural fit, and the Governor's family and the Key family grew closer while entertaining each other many times over the next few summers.

No family is immune to tragedy and sadly, young Ann, Thomas' sister died in 1816 a few years before I was born, and I never knew her. Nobody felt much like celebrating for a time after that. Thomas however, had known me from the time I was a baby and I grew up thinking of him as not so much my brother, but as Frankie's older brother.

Rose Hill was also the first place I saw Virginia Timberlake. Our family had arrived at Terra Rubra for the summer and Frankie and I rode the few miles to say hello and pass on greetings from mother. "C'mon Philip, I'll race you," Frankie teased as we started out. The summer heat had arrived early in western Maryland and as we rode, the foggy sky predicted the humid and hot day that was already beginning. We were sweaty and soaked by the time our horses reached the long driveway leading to the manor.

Virginia was sprawled out on a blanket in the grass with Ann Rebecca. The two girls were giggling as if they had the most amusing secret. She was probably not yet at an age that would be considered appropriate for a teenage boy to court her, but I thought she was the most beautiful thing I had ever laid eyes on. Blond curls hung nearly to her waist and her eyes sparkled in the June sunshine.

Ann Rebecca, Becca for short, was the daughter of Thomas, who's friendship with Frankie had remained close through the years. When Becca was just a baby, Thomas had suddenly taken ill and passed away. His family was shattered of course, and so was Frankie. Anne Johnson had barely recovered from her daughter's death and now her only other child, her son, was gone too. A young but always noble Frankie promised Thomas in his last moments to look out for Becca always. Tragically Becca's mother passed away not much longer after her father and she had gone to live permanently with her grandmother at Rose Hill.

Frankie kept his word and he took special care to visit and check in on Becca as often as possible, though he never found her in need of anything more than what her grandmother was providing. Becca resembled Thomas with the same big green eyes and wavy brown hair. It was bittersweet for Frankie, and he was always melancholy after visiting her. Oftentimes, on the way home, he rode alone out to the cemetery to visit Thomas' grave.

For having lost both parents, Becca was still as pleasant of a child as any, and she was excited to have a friend visiting the plantation. Virginia seemed much older than Becca though they were close to the same age. Virginia was taller and had already begun to turn into a young lady while Becca still had the look of a child. Virginia was also more outgoing than Becca and the first thing she said to me was "you're not going inside looking like that are you?" I looked down at the sweat-soaked shirt and smoothed my shoulder length hair flat against my head, hoping to improve my appearance. She was lovely and full of sass, but I had no idea who she was or why she was there.

As it turns out, we lived very close to each other in Washington as well and were both visiting Fredericktown regularly during this time. Becca's grandmother knew Virginia's grandmother. Something unpleasant was brewing in Washington and Anne had offered Rose Hill as both a retreat for Virginia from city gossip and to be a companion for her orphaned granddaughter Becca. The invitation was gladly accepted, and arrangements were made for Virginia to travel to Maryland where she could be free of the stink of the city.

It seemed everyone in Washington had something to say about Virginia's mother and new stepfather. Virginia had been lost somewhere in the middle of the controversy, not really understanding the magnitude of what was happening in the world of her mother. She did understand that people were being cruel and that she was no longer invited to the events and homes of some of her playmates. It was a miserable time for her in Washington and Virginia had been glad to escape to the country where no one would know her.

It was easy to forget the ugliness of the city in a place as beautiful as Rose Hill. Walnut and Sycamore trees lined the property and the thick jungle of rose bushes behind the manor fascinated the girl from the city. Although her fascination had quickly turned to frustration as she soon found that the rose bushes were best admired with her eyes and not with her fingers. The thorny branches were not as beautiful as the roses that grew from them and this was how Virginia thought of her mother, a beautiful rose on top of the prickly thorn branches of Washington.

Virginia was happiest in Fredericktown. She was treated well, easily becoming part of the family. She and Becca had so much in common and quickly, they were inseparable friends. They made daisy chains from the flowers growing wild near the well. They took long walks and skipped rope and helped Cook make tea with mint leaves collected from the garden. It was quiet and peaceful and although she missed her mother, she sometimes wished that her family would forget to send for her and she'd stay forever at Rose Hill.

She had no such luck. When summer ended, she would always have to leave, and she'd watch behind the carriage as the world she thought of in greens and blues and whites, turned brown and grey and thorny, as they approached Washington.

By the time I met Virginia that day on the front lawn, she had visited Rose Hill a few times already and seemed so mature to me that I doubted her when she told me her age. I was nearly six years older than her, but it didn't matter; I was smitten. I found any excuse I could to come by and see her. I'm sure my mother found it strange that I was suddenly offering to deliver notes or asking if she needed me to pick anything up in town.

Frankie, however, knew right away. I couldn't have kept anything from Frankie if I tried. He knew me better than I knew myself and when we'd left Rose Hill that very first day, he was shaking his head and laughing at me. I tried to act like I had no idea what he was talking about.

Frankie had married his wife Elizabeth years ago and he knew love when he saw it. He never mentioned it to mother, but he must have told father because there was a poem written that very summer about the beautiful *Virginia,* which father insisted on reading at every gathering. Frankie and I were the only ones who knew he was not gushing about the beauty of our neighboring state, but merrily tormenting me. I took it in stride and even though I'd glare at him from across the table as he recited the poem again and again, I secretly enjoyed the poem and it didn't displease me to hear her name. I panicked a little when Virginia was among the guests invited to Terra Rubra for a summer party. I approached my father and reluctantly acknowledged that he was right about my love interest. He feigned surprise, and I begged him not to read that particular piece of poetry in front of her. He had replied, "in that case, I most definitely will!" He didn't embarrass me that day, and I knew he wouldn't, but it was clear he understood. I had fallen head over heels in love with Miss Virginia Timberlake.

When I first heard of it, father had already been involved in the so-called "petticoat affair" for some time. I wondered if he'd played any part in getting Virginia out of Washington and into the peace of Frederick County. Either way, the division within President Andrew Jackson's cabinet had everything to do with Virginia's mother. It seemed the President had a fierce loyalty to those he considered his friends, which included Virginia's family. Disgusted by the backlash of Virginia's mother and now stepfather becoming married, President Jackson secured legal help from father in the ongoing battle to defend them.

My Uncle Roger was an excellent lawyer in Fredericktown, besides being father's closest friend and brother-in-law. He and Uncle Roger shared similar political views and had agreed on almost everything since childhood. Roger had been a senator with some political connections but could never convince father to enter politics himself. However, upon the announcement of their acquaintance Andrew Jackson running for President, the two had finally taken a strong interest in politics. They admired Jackson greatly and father worked on his campaign in full force in 1828. Father worked diligently, as always, for President Jackson and by allowing me to apprentice I worked hard on behalf of Virginia. That sealed my professional fate. I would be following in my father's footsteps as a lawyer. This case involved Virginia and so to me, this was personal.

When eventually the President all but started over with a new administration, he asked for father's assistance in convincing Uncle Roger to accept the position of Attorney General. Both were now deeply embedded in the Jackson administration and though they had gained recognition, respect and the trust of our seventh President, it had also gained them political enemies. Hence, my formal introduction to the world of politics.

During her last summer in Fredericktown, I proposed to Virginia. We had spent every day together either sitting near the river with a picnic or walking through the markets or catching the latest show passing through town. It was clear to us both that we were more than just friends. Of course, Virginia had no family nearby to ask permission from, and they would have said she was too young anyway, so when I asked her to marry me, it was just her and I.

We rode horses into the Catoctin Mountains to our favorite spot at a waterfall we knew as McAfee Falls. We could climb the rocks to the top and sit on a flat warm ledge watching the crystal-clear water cascading over the side. We kissed, among other misbehaviors at the top of that waterfall. It was the best summer of my life. We spent that last beautiful August day by the water being in love and imagining our future together. Knowing the summer would be coming to an end, I couldn't stand the idea of letting her go again without knowing for certain that I'd get her back. So, I asked her if she would marry me. Side by side, I held my breath and waited as what I had asked registered in her mind. After what seemed like an eternity, her soft pink lips parted and with an adorable smile she said, "Yes, I'll marry you!" I let out my breath and out with it came a "woo-hoo," which made her giggle, and I fell in love with her even more.

On impulse, she shimmied to the edge of the rock where we sat and daringly plunged into the swimming hole below. Catching me completely off guard, my jaw dropped, and it was my turn to have a laugh. I followed her lead and hopped into the water. With most of our clothes still on, we explored one another's body for the first time. The mixed sensations of hot skin and cold water sent shivers up my back. I was in paradise with the girl I loved, and I longed for time to stand still. We finally emerged from the water, still soaking wet and a bit weak in the knees. Quickly, we readied the horses and took off across the field in the direction of Fredericktown. Without a word, we raced as fast as we could until we got to the main road. The galloping of the horse was the only thing covering up the sound of my thumping chest and I was glad for that distraction.

When we arrived back at Rose Hill Manor that day, it was anything but celebrating and deciding how to share our news. The entire place was in upheaval and it took asking several times to finally piece the story together that Becca's grandmother, Anne had died. She laid down for an afternoon nap and Becca had been unable to wake her. A doctor was sent for from town, but there was nothing he could do, she was gone. Anne had managed the estate so well on her own, that without her, no one seemed to know what to do next. I gave Virginia a quick peck on the cheek and told her that I was riding home to Terra Rubra to tell my mother and father the news. Father would know what to do.

I did not realize that was the last time I'd ever see my Virginia. If I had known, I'd have stolen her away with me to Terra Rubra that very day. If I'd made her my wife, with or without permission, she could not have been sent away.

Virginia had been collected before evening and was returned to Washington and to her family. She had no way of knowing that her declaration of engagement to me, Philip Barton Key, would be disregarded as silly nonsense of a girl too young to marry. She'd waited anxiously, expecting to hear from me. She was aware that members of my family would be coming back to the city in a few days. Surely someone would be bringing a message by for her.

I did send ahead a message, but her grandmother had gotten to it first, and when she realized the serious nature of the engagement, she was afraid of her granddaughter eloping, and she burned the letter. Virginia's mother had moved to the new Florida territory with her husband to escape the hostility toward them. The recent events had done serious damage to her mother's reputation. She wanted Virginia to have nothing to do with the people and politics of Washington. Before her trunks were fully unpacked from her Summer at Rose Hill, she was packed again and sent to join her mother and Stepfather in Florida. We sent letters constantly and tried to find a way, but the distance was too great, and the obstacles too many, for young love to survive. It broke my heart, but it was not to be. I would never forget my first love, Virginia.

CHAPTER 3

ANNAPOLIS

To distract myself from my aching heart, I'd gone directly from Terra Rubra, away to school in Annapolis, and focused on studying to become a lawyer. It was all I had that gave me the will to press on with my life. Upon returning to Washington, I'd moped around our home until father literally dragged me from bed one morning and said, "time to get to business." We'd moved to a larger home on C Street nearer the capital and not far from our old address in Georgetown, which we now used as a law office. We'd walk the several blocks in the mornings together. The city of Washington had gone from swamps and mud to marble and streetscapes complete with planned roads and sidewalks. Father marveled daily over these changes that had occurred in the years just since he had come to live in the city.

"Look there Philip," he'd say. "A rank smelling swamp was in that beautiful lawn beyond those hedges. A rut deep enough to tip carriages was here at this corner. We are walking on a canal of filth."

He described so well the way the city looked back then, and I tried diligently to picture it myself. I didn't remember it looking like anything but meticulously planned squares and it took quite some imagination to visualize it in any of the ways he described. "That building was burned to the ground when the British went through here," he said with a hint of frustration in his voice. It still made him angry to think of the evening many years ago that he'd watched this city burn from his home on Bridge Street. "Such a senseless waste and unnecessary evil deed," he recounted.

But it was peaceful now during our morning walks and those became some of my fondest memories. The cities inhabitants were not yet awake, and it felt as though we had the entire place to ourselves. The street lamps had been recently extinguished and the faint smell of smothered flame could still be detected in the fresh morning air. I came to associate this smell with my father and our mornings together. When he passed away years later, I thought of the scent as a sign from him. I'd smell it in the most unusual places where fire ought not to be. I imagined it as his way of saying that he was thinking of me and it was a great comfort.

I had pictured things playing out quaintly with Virginia. We'd marry and live in the city, near my family and the law office. We'd have beautiful children, a dog, and a home with columns framed by a perfectly manicured lawn. We'd be a deliriously joyful little family and live a charmed life together. It was taking some time for my mind to accept those losses. It was as though I was mourning a life I'd never actually had. A year had passed since I'd lost her, and I was nowhere near ready to start thinking of other possible options. In the six months since I turned twenty, I had somehow grown into my adult form and it was impossible to ignore the attention that I was getting from the ladies and eligible daughters of my family's social circle. At first, through my sorrows, I hadn't noticed. I'd always been called a "handsome boy" and didn't think much of it, but apparently, I'd become a handsome man and was beginning to attract some serious interest.

Annapolis was where everything changed for me. I'd lived with my brother Frankie and his wife, Elizabeth while attending St. John's University there. I tried to get back to visit them as often as possible. Annapolis was a charming waterfront town on the pristine Chesapeake Bay. Seeing hundreds of sailing ships, the squawking seagulls, and the Liberty Tree on campus gave me the same warm feelings that I had thinking about Pipe Creek. Except that I couldn't return to Terra Rubra just yet, too many memories, so Annapolis was my first choice when I felt I needed a break from Washington.

Frankie's family was perfect. One clever son named after Frankie, and one darling daughter, named Lizzie after her mother, both adored their father immensely. His wife, Elizabeth, was like a second mother to me and I adored *her* immensely. She was pretty and quick-witted and made me laugh more than anyone else I knew. Frankie and Elizabeth epitomized everything I wanted my life to become. They did things together, as a family, and included me as well, when possible. Frankie had served a year in the Navy before realizing that he was not suited for the life of a midshipman. He wanted to be home with his wife and raise a family and so he ended his Naval career and took a job at the Farmers Bank where his father-in-law was president. Frankie who had taught me to fish and hunt and ride horses, now clean-cut and clean-shaved wore fancy clothes and counted money for a living, to my amusement. To me, it seemed as if someone had put a child in adult clothing and cast him playing a banker in a skit. It never seemed real in my mind, but Frankie was the responsible kind and he did whatever it took to provide for his family. They did not own servants or live in a mansion, but they were happy and so to me they were rich.

My oldest brother was also my best friend and I usually told him everything, so when I mulled over what had happened with Virginia in Fredericktown, he empathized. "She was the one Frankie," I said to him sitting on a fishing pier near his row house along the waterfront. We were crabbing off the dock hoping to catch enough blue crabs to be dinner for five. The water was choppy, and the crabs were not biting.

"Forget this," said Frankie. He offered a hand and pulled me up. "You need to loosen up, have some fun."

We rounded the corner of Church Street and Reynolds Tavern came into view. I'd seen the place before of course but had never been inside. Probably because father would not have liked hearing that his teenage son, who was supposed to be studying hard in school had gone out drinking on his "responsible" older brother's watch. Nor did father approve of the activities of pubs in general. But I was a grown man now, not a schoolboy and I could make my own decisions. Frankie stopped me just before we walked inside and asked, "what name do you want to give?"

I looked at him, puzzled, and he said, "Trust me, kid. Don't use your real name."

I thought it was odd, but what did I know, this was not my area of expertise. "I suppose I'll use Barton," I said coming up quickly with my middle name.

"And for your last name?" he continued.

"Philips?" I grinned.

"Very original." Frankie laughed.

I asked what his name was going to be, but of course, I should have known. He used the name Thomas, Thomas Johnson.

Though it was still daylight outside, inside was like night. It took my eyes several minutes to adjust and when they finally did, I felt like I was in a whole different world. Most of the light was coming from the fireplace and candles situated atop the mantle. The one oil lamp that burned was behind the bar where it couldn't be spilled by the staggering patrons. I heard music coming from somewhere but couldn't see what was creating it. Mostly I just followed Frankie. We seated ourselves at a table and he ordered pints. It wasn't my first drink, but it was the first time that I got drunk. Frankie kept the ale coming and after the second one, I stopped counting. I remember feeling content and warm and carefree and it was a much-needed feeling. The other much-needed feeling came to me by the way of a woman.

Ella introduced herself to us and I can recall Frankie telling her my name, Barton Philips. She was sitting on my side of our table and although Frankie was doing most of the talking, I was getting the entertainment. A sensation came over me and it took me a second to realize that Ella's dainty, soft hand was rubbing my thigh and inching closer and closer to my groin. She was talking to Frankie but rubbing on me and she was just as attentive in each way to both of us. She smelled good, like citrus, sweet, and I wondered if she tasted the way she smelled. I liberated myself from trying to keep up with the conversation and slouched down slightly in my chair to let her hand fall exactly where I wanted it. I gave in to being drunk and happy and closed my eyes for a minute. When I opened them, Frankie was putting away his billfold and I did not comprehend exactly who or exactly what he had just paid for. Next thing I knew, I was outside the tavern door and Ella and I were descending a set of stone stairs around the backside of the building. I remember a cool room, skin, sweat, and the way she moved on top of me. So many of my senses were on high that I couldn't separate what I heard from what I saw, or what I smelled from what I tasted. But it didn't matter because it all felt good.

Ella delivered me drunk and satiated back to my brother inside the tavern a while later, and I draped my arm around his neck and declared that I loved him and that he would always be my best friend. He responded by standing us both up and helping me walk back to the house where Elizabeth immediately tore into him for going missing so long. We had scared her half to death, and she was somewhere between relieved and furious when she realized the state I was in.

"Oh Philip, what did you let him do to you?" She snickered as I repeated to her how much I loved Frankie and that he would always be my best friend.

"Off to bed with you then. You won't be loving him come morning," Elizabeth replied as she helped me out of my boots.

I climbed into bed and finally, for the first time in over a year, it was not Virginia Timberlake who was on my mind as I drifted off to sleep.

The tryst with Miss Ella had cured me of my depression and aversion to getting involved with another woman. So, I took full advantage of my God-given gift and I began to repay the attentions of the ladies who had been so anxious to spend time with me. I took new pride in my manly six-foot-tall body and gained a confidence with women that I had never felt before. My unruly straight brown hair was cut short now, and I intentionally shaved my face only every other day, because I liked the rugged look of the day-old stubble. Our family could afford the finest leather shoes and tailored clothing, and shopping quickly became one of my favorite activities. I enjoyed walking about the streets of Washington dressed dashingly, showing off my wares, and turning heads.

Father had just entered his sixty-first year and was perhaps feeling a bit sentimental. He asked me to accompany him on a business trip West for company. We put our law practice on hold and set off for New York City where we began our journey. Staying one night at the Astor House Hotel, we dined with a fellow named Daniel Edgar Sickles. He and I were both in our early twenties and he too was following in his father's footsteps and becoming a lawyer, he practiced in New York, and I in Washington. Oddly, we even resembled each other in appearance. We discussed politics and the weather and parted ways. Father, who never said anything ill of anyone, surprised me as we were leaving the dining room saying, "that man is as red as the devil himself." I shrugged it off. Dan Sickles was no one to me and I had no reason to believe I'd ever see the man again.

We traveled by boat and carriage during the weeks that we adventured into the frontier. I was entirely unprepared for the lessons

I was about to learn. I knew very little of the rigors of extended travel. For one thing, it was cold. Most of the journey to Cincinnati on the riverboat was so frigid that we had nothing much to do but stay below deck. Fortunately, our traveling companions were entirely pleasant, and it was at least good company and lively conversation. Our stateroom was absurdly small, and father and I had a good laugh when we first saw it. It was adequate for our needs, but such close quarters taught me much more about my father than I ever needed to know. He wrote home to mother and reported the grandeur of our accommodations with an unusual sarcasm that I found highly amusing.

Our destination was St. Louis and upon arriving we were pleased to find that the scenarios we had created en route, of a scanty, dismal, poor excuse for a city were completely wrong. Our dining and accommodations rivaled that of the Astor House in New York City. St. Louis was remarkable, and I wished we had longer to explore it. I was aware from the beginning that we were heading for St. Louis and that father had a bit of business to attend to. I was not aware that it was not the ending destination of our journey. I imagined we'd begin the return trip and was surprised when father announced casually that we'd be traveling South next, destined for Alabama.

I recalled he had been assigned a mission by his friend and then President, Andrew Jackson to Alabama years ago. He was sent to help find a resolution to a land quarrel between the government, the settlers, and the Indians. He had managed to sort out the matter and made many friends. I knew that he thought fondly of his time there. "Who shall we be visiting first father," I inquired.

With a flush of redness in his face, he mumbled, "an old friend."

I don't believe I had ever seen father flustered before so immediately I knew that there was something else going on here. "Father, are you blushing? Alright, let's hear it, the truth, who are we visiting in Alabama?"

"It's not so much a who, anymore," he started to explain. "When I went to Alabama years ago, I made a very good friend there, and I was in touch with her even after I returned home"

"HER?" What on earth was happening here? I suddenly had the sinking feeling that I was about to want to hold my hands over my ears and make noises like a five-year-old child who didn't want to listen. It never crossed my mind in twenty-two years that father was anything but completely dedicated and devoted to my mother. I sat dumbfounded and waited for him to continue.

"It isn't what you think, she is dead now. Her name is Sarah, was… Sarah Ann Gayle and she was the governor's wife when I last saw her," he began. "Now Philip, I know you may find this hard to hear but I am a man after all and I was quite taken with this young lady. She is the only woman who ever wrote me a bit of poetry in return. We connected on a level that I hadn't experienced before. I love your mother dearly of course, but that doesn't make me impervious to the enchantment of an interesting woman. We spent many hours together, along with her children. The governor was away much of the time and seemed a bit detached in my opinion. We had such fun, she was beautiful and brilliant and had the most remarkable knack for linking words and rhymes. The children too were a joy. Smart and funny just like their mother. Nothing inappropriate transpired there. I am a gentleman. Nevertheless, I was tempted. I don't deny that the poems and words we exchanged were approaching the line of adulterous."

I'd heard enough and I needed to think and get some air. "So, if she's dead, why are we going back?" I asked without a bit of gentleness that I probably should have tried to convey. I saw the hurt in his eyes and I immediately understood that I had just experienced a great unveiling. The childlike admiration I had for my father had just evolved into a trusted partnership between men and I knew then that I was wrong to be so quick to judge.

"I promised her I would come back someday," he said quietly. "Of course, I thought that would be a reunion between living people but obviously God had other plans for Sarah." He stood and faced me. "I enjoyed her as a person. I had no intentions of acting on my feelings, but we had a connection that I can't explain. When I left, I promised to return and I feel that regardless, I need to fulfill that promise. Do you understand that at all?"

I sighed, "I think so. I'm here for you father and I don't want you to think I am angry, just surprised, that's all. But I am on this adventure with you and whatever it is you need to do, I'm willing. Just one question," I paused. "Does mother know anything?"

"Heavens no, I could never hurt her that way, she is a wonderful woman," said father. At once I realized that nothing was as it seemed. I saw my father for the first time as an individual and an imperfect person that was looking for acceptance and encouragement. He was not evil, he was not perfect, he was simply a human being.

"You old dog," I said with a smile, as I headed up the stairs to the open deck. I'm sure he knew then that the secret of his mission was safe with me.

Alabama in the summertime was sweltering. I was glad that we didn't stay long, besides I was quickly running short on body parts for the mosquitos to attack. We finally made our way to Montgomery and to the grave of Sarah Gayle. I stayed in the carriage at the cemetery to allow him to fulfill his promise and pay his respects in private. He took a folded paper and a small bouquet of wildflowers. I watched as he walked off to say his goodbye. I could almost have forgotten for a moment that he was my father. I empathized with his feelings as a man who had also lost someone special. It gave me time to think about what other things I may not know. I made a mental note to use the journey home to find out.

The trip home was long and mostly boring but at least it was warm. I spent plenty of time on the deck relaxing and enjoying the fresh air. When father joined me one morning, I proceeded with the questionnaire I had been silently compiling in my head. I asked about my grandfather and grandmother's marriage but as far as he knew there was nothing more there to tell. I asked for details about the death of my two brothers several years ago. First Daniel had died in a duel not far from our home in Washington and the details were sparse. It was a shock to my family, and we had dared not press for information and risk upsetting our parents further. So, my siblings and I were left with more questions than answers. I wanted to know if the altercation had to do with a woman? I was beginning to understand just how deeply that seemed to cut a man. It wasn't just me. I wasn't odd for how I felt about Virginia. It seemed to be the source of many aching hearts.

John, my other brother had died suddenly and painfully of an illness that was never officially diagnosed. He left behind two children and a pregnant wife. My father and John were particularly close, and I knew this was a touchy subject. I'd always wondered why after losing my brother, his wife Ginny, delivered the baby and sent the infant to live with my parents? We'd had my nephew at our home since the day after he was born. The answer he gave was that it had already been decided that this baby, if a boy, would be named after my brother John. Ginny had been unwilling to go back on that decision. But her broken heart and the sight of my brother's same square face when she looked at the baby boy, rendered her unable to care for him. "She sent him away because grief does terrible things to a soul," was his final remark on the upsetting situation and I left it at that.

The second most shocking revelation of the voyage was to learn about my brother Frankie. I thought I knew everything there was to know about Frankie but apparently, even heroes have secrets. I don't know if it was because we were already sharing but father came right out and told me that Frankie had been charged once with rape. I had been only twelve at the time and no one had felt it was appropriate for me to know, especially considering our close relationship. So, ten years later, and for the second time in two weeks, I felt as though I'd been dealt a blow to the stomach.

"Frankie would never do that," I jumped to my feet, ready to fight anyone who said otherwise. When I calmed down father explained that no Frankie wouldn't, and he didn't. He had however made a shameful decision to get involved with another woman while already married to Elizabeth, who was with child at the time. This other woman heard Frankie's family name and had taken advantage of the chance to either become famous or rich and accused him of abducting and raping her in Annapolis. Frankie had fled to Washington in fear and left poor Elizabeth to discover the story from the law officers who showed up at her door looking for him. Fortunately, he was able to prove his side of the story and the accuser became inconsistent in hers. The charges against Frankie were dismissed. That didn't change the fact that he'd had an affair and had to face Elizabeth which must have been worse than any judges sentence. I was angry with Frankie for a minute. In my eyes, Elizabeth was the perfect wife to him and had always been so good to me. I couldn't believe that Frankie had been stupid enough to do something like that. As I thought it through, I realized that it was also the second time in two weeks that I was going to have to accept that people are not perfect and that if Elizabeth had found a way to forgive him, then I would do the same.

I remembered back to Frankie asking me what name I was going to use in the pub that night and now it was all making sense. I was disappointed, or disillusioned rather, that the two men I looked up to most both had succumbed to some form of indiscretion with the opposite sex. I wasn't sure what to think but I do know the fantasy and sanctity of marriage died a little for me on that trip.

Chapter 4

Ellen Swan

Our law office was thriving, and the capital was growing larger every day. Slavery was the main topic of discussion in most circles and the debate, at least in Maryland, wasn't so much if slavery should continue, but more of what should be done about ending it. Some believed in outright abolition and others like father felt that simply turning slaves free offered them nothing but a one-way ticket to poverty with no means to support themselves or their families. He saw it as a punishment crueler than kind at its roots. Our family had owned slaves my entire life and some like Uncle Clem and Eliza were so much like family that I don't know that I ever took notice of the color of their skin until society forced it on me. I stopped short of supporting the beliefs of the African Colonization Society, of which father had been a long-time member. I believe that the ACS was coming from a place of good intentions in creating a colony in Africa to which freed slaves could return but it was difficult to imagine Clem or Eliza leaving our family at all, let alone to be sent off on a ship to Africa. In my mind, it was not the solution, nor did I have any ideas on a permanent solution myself.

Father had provided legal help to many colored people who found themselves in trouble and were unable to pay for a decent defense. Most were friends or family of the slaves we owned, and it was done out of father's strong sense of justice. But it was a very complicated issue and each time he acted as their legal defense, he faced the backlash from his friends and colleagues, who believed he was placing himself and his family in a dangerous position and that he was being a hypocrite. They didn't agree with his decisions and it was a difficult predicament for him to be in, being a slave owner and arguing their freedoms.

Father struggled for some time with the situation until he reached a breaking point. While we'd been enjoying the tranquility and relaxation at Terra Rubra father startled everyone by abruptly asking for a carriage to be prepared and for Uncle Clem to be placed in it. He would not say what he was going to do or where they were going, but along with two of my older brothers, they disappeared down the driveway leaving the rest of us staring after in disbelief. This was not typical behavior for father, and we were filled with dread wondering if he had somehow lost his mind.

Moments later, a newspaper was discovered on the kitchen table where he had left his coffee and his breakfast still hot. The newspaper featured a scathing story ridiculing the ACS and mentioned Francis Scott Key as a fraud who campaigned for colonization only because he wanted to discard the slaves, and it called him a racist slave owner. Apparently, that had been his motivation for the sudden departure and he was on his way to somewhere to do something about it.

Later we learned that he was so furious at being called a fraud and a racist, that he decided to make a point, if not for the critics, for his own family and friends. They had traveled the twenty or so miles to cross the Pennsylvania state line to Gettysburg. In the free state, they had appeared before the justice of the peace. A fee was paid, and papers were signed, setting Clem Johnson free. Uncle Clem had been confused and terrified and wept thinking that father was going to sell or leave him behind after all these years together. Clem stated he did not care to end his service to the Key family and asked father to please keep him on, to which father immediately agreed and offered him a position as farm foreman. The whole thing had cost several hours, and many tears shed amongst the worried family members on all sides, but when it was said and done the entire group was back at Terra Rubra by supper, and that night we all, family and servants dined together. When Uncle Clem asked to say the grace, he thanked God for the entire Key family by name, one by one, and I understood then that father would never have left Uncle Clem behind in Pennsylvania. It had been a statement to both his critics and to the slaves themselves that he was not their heartless keeper, but we were a family, and this family chose to stay together.

After our trip West, things continued to be interesting in Washington. It was great fun entertaining nearly all the single ladies of upper-class Washington. Many times, my mother cross-examined me as though she were the expert lawyer in the family. When would I "settle down" and "start a family?" She was beginning to worry that all the attention had gone to my head and that I was developing a reputation as somewhat of a philanderer. "Your good looks will only get you so far Philip," she often said. "You still have to be a good person."

I wasn't worried about that, only being in my twenties, I had plenty of time to sample the milk and buy the cow. That's how I looked at it, and the milk in Washington was exceptional. Everyone was well connected in this town. Most of the girls I saw were daughters of a congressman or a state's attorney. This was both thrilling and daunting at the same time. Seeing the daughter of anyone who was in the Washington elite always had the potential to further or hinder my career, and so I was careful to tread lightly with those ones. I never threw around my name or my father's position as U.S. attorney or the fact that he had written the famous "Star-Spangled

Banner" for personal gain, or for mischievous purposes, except just this once...

President Van Buren reappointed my father as U.S. attorney during his administration at Andrew Jackson's recommendation. The three were very well acquainted and shared a similar political opinion. It was the position my father valued most of all his accomplishments and he was very good at doing it. He was his happiest during the years that he held the prestigious post. It gave him peace and purpose and the ability to help people and that is what he loved to do.

Unfortunately, the 1840 election brought about a change of administration and a change of employment for Father. William Henry Harrison was elected, inaugurated, and promptly died of pneumonia. The Vice President, John Tyler took his place and rumors immediately spread and headlines blared "Francis Scott Key to be replaced!" It was no secret that the two shared no common ground. Father had supported the campaign against him in the recent election and things had gotten heated between the two. Immediately upon returning from our trip west, it was official. Father was relieved of his duties and Tyler's choice, from back home in Virginia, was in place. It was expected, and everyone knew that this had nothing to do with ability or the benefit of the people. This was pure politics. All political motivations were selfish and though I was learning this game well, it infuriated me, and I couldn't help contemplating a bit of revenge on this new President who'd fired my old man.

President Tyler had a lot of children, some girls, some my age. Liz Tyler was eighteen and I was twenty-three when I asked a friend to introduce us at an upcoming reception being held at the capitol building. I knew exactly who she was though I feigned surprise at the introduction. I intended to get to know her much better by the end of the night. She was fair but not beautiful and nice but not sweet and although I considered feeling guilty about it for a moment, I pushed it down and proceeded with my plan. As we were introduced,

I turned on some of my father's famous charm and it went exactly as I hoped. I captivated her with stories of my childhood and dropped names left and right of the people I had come to meet through my father. I recited the first verse of the Star-Spangled Banner for her. Even for the daughter of a President, she was as star-struck as most by my "fame." She was giggling and glassy-eyed within an hour and I had captured her affections by midnight. She was young, gullible, and easy to work. I refreshed her glass of wine several times, and half listened as she went on and on about who knows what. She was no different than any of the other Washington girls whom I'd seen and had no interest whatsoever in seeing again. It wasn't difficult to convince her to sneak off with me for a late-night stroll.

Then, I lied, through my teeth. I asked if she believed in love at first sight, told her she was beautiful, that I'd never met anyone like her, that I wanted her to meet my family, all the things that she could have wanted to hear. I steered her to a secluded area of the grounds in a grove of red oaks and made my move. I kissed her intensely and let my hands wander over her curves and up under her gown. I lowered her to the ground, and she didn't stop me, so I took full advantage of the moment. It was even easier than I thought it would be. The wine had properly clouded her better judgment. She was obviously a virgin, it took some time and effort to finally be able to thrust deep inside her and I covered her mouth with my hand as she cried out in both pleasure and pain. I pulled out in time to avoid finishing inside her and there was blood mixed in with the mess that now stained the petticoat under her gown. I held her a moment and kissed her as we both caught our breath. We headed back towards the building and I promised to see her again soon. The guests were beginning to retire for the evening. I kissed her hand and said goodbye knowing full well that I never, ever, intended to lay eyes on her again. I knew it was wrong and it wasn't even her fault, but it's what I needed to placate myself, and even the score, for what her rat of a father had done to mine.

I never told father about the act of revenge, he would not have approved. He was a forgiving man, unlike myself, and so it remained my secret. Together we visited an ailing family friend who'd been like a second father to me and I briefly considered confiding in him knowing that he was too weak to lecture me on the injustice of my deed, but he passed in the night before I had come to a final decision. I took it as a sign that this was a secret best kept to myself. Not even the dead wanted to know what I had done.

Father took the passing of his old friend especially hard, perhaps he saw his own mortality in watching him take his last breath. Perhaps he sensed that his own time was not far off. He wrote notes to all of us children and to mother and a poem to his sister Ann, reminiscing about their childhood home and sweet memories they shared there. I was in Washington working at our law office when suddenly I became alarmed by the smell of something burning. I ran up and down the stairs and hallways searching for the source and found nothing amiss. Puzzled I returned to my desk and dismissed the incident without further thought. Shortly after, a message was delivered from my sister Elizabeth in Baltimore notifying me that our father was ill, and I departed at once.

I blamed the cold weather, President Tyler, and the city of Baltimore itself when my father died there on January 11, 1843. He'd lost both a good friend from childhood and his esteemed career in such a short time span, perhaps he simply lost the will to fight. Winter fever overtook him after traveling through harsh conditions to see mother who was visiting my sister and her family. He arrived frozen to the bone on their doorstep, and they were never able to warm him again. He shook with chills, and struggled to breathe, for three days before the man I worshipped, the pulse of our family, the author of the Star-Spangled Banner, was gone forever.

I wallowed in self-pity for the rest of the winter, sleeping until mid-day and refusing to return to the law office. Nearly everyone had stopped trying to offer consolation to me, as my severe mood chased them off one by one. I barely ate and lost weight from my already slender frame. I let my facial hair become disheveled, and my eyes had taken on a dull sunken look. My younger brother and sisters persisted the longest, but I'd convinced myself that they too would soon die, and leave me alone as well, so I rejected their efforts. Only Alicia, six years younger than me, refused to give up. Alice, our family name for her, barged into my bedroom each day and stood next to my bed, pestering me until I would finally give in and open my eyes. At only seventeen and less than a hundred pounds, she used every bit of strength she could muster to try and pull the covers from my bed. She opened my windows and let the cold air in until I was so chilled that I had no choice but to finally rise and close them myself. She brought me tea every day, though I wouldn't touch it. She read to me from the newspapers and ignored my grumbling. She sketched cheerful pictures and placed them by my bedside. She was a lovely young lady with deep brown eyes and a wide smile that brought light to any room. Eventually, I began to look forward to her torturous presence.

One day she placed a drawing beside my bed, and I was startled to see she'd drawn a dark, ghostly figure, with its skeleton protruding from under saggy skin, and two dark pools for eyes. "Alice, what is that?" I asked her in alarm. "You," she said forcefully. I shrugged as she turned on her heels and left my room without another word, only to return one moment later. She had fetched her looking glass from the vanity in her room and she held it up to my face. I was shocked to see the resemblance to the frightening portrait she'd sketched. I sat up straight on the edge of my bed and kissed her cheek. "I'll get up," I said. My sister had made me realize that wasting away in my bed was doing nothing to honor my father's memory. What I needed to do was pull myself together and return to the law office and continue his good work.

Frankie and Elizabeth had big plans for me when I arrived for a visit in the spring. Annapolis was gorgeous as always and it proved difficult to stay in a foul mood there. Especially considering the current house guest of my brother and sister-in-law. Ellen Swan was the beautiful, blond, daughter of an associate at the bank where Frankie worked. She'd come to Annapolis for a few weeks with her father and was staying with my family during her trip. They had known she was coming at the same time I was arriving but didn't mention it to me in any of our recent correspondence. The pieces began to fit together when we discovered that we were both born the same year, 1818 and that we had many common interests. When we mysteriously found ourselves alone on the first occasion, I realized we were being set up. She was certainly attractive, with angelic, soft features, and a sweet voice. Nervous, but trying not to be rude or awkward, I engaged her in conversation, and we talked for hours. We shared stories of time spent in New York City. We both enjoyed theater and could quote Shakespeare endlessly. We also found we shared a fondness for Frankie and Elizabeth's children. Call it romantic, or simply a product of the environment, but very early on in the visit, I could envision this woman as the mother of my children.

After father died, I spent some time soul-searching and it registered to me that I did want to be a father myself. I had learned from the best and wanted to experience a family life of my own creation. So, by the time I met Ellen, I was looking for more than a casual relationship and she fit the part perfectly. She was sweet and thoughtful and very pretty. She reminded me in many ways of Elizabeth, whom I'd always adored. For the first time since my separation from Virginia Timberlake years before, I made a conscious decision to open my heart and take a chance again on love.

Frankie and Elizabeth could not have been more delighted. They were very parental in trying to make sure that we were taking the appropriate time to become fully acquainted, but they were as excited as us to make it public. Elizabeth threw a fine dinner party for Frankie's colleagues and I was strategically placed near Mr. Swan, Ellen's father. Fortunately, we hit it off immediately. He was aware of my interest in his daughter and we had a grand first introduction.

Ellen's mother had passed away, but her father assured me that she would have been pleased to meet me. The weeks flashed by and before I knew it, I had far overstayed my visit and needed to return to the Washington law office. First, I paid Ellen's father a visit at the bank and was given his blessing to ask his daughter to be my wife. On pins and needles I waited for the children to go to bed for the evening, and in front of Frankie and Elizabeth, and a fine evening fire, I proposed to Ellen and she cried happy tears and said, "yes, of course!"

Our November wedding was a splendid affair at Terra Rubra. Guests came from Washington, Baltimore, and New York, filling the inns and taverns around Fredericktown. We were blessed with a sunny, clear autumn day and I was glad for the slight chill in the air since I couldn't seem to stop sweating. I restlessly combed at my mustache with my fingers and my stomach was suddenly feeling queasy. I had downed several shots of whiskey by 11 a.m. to calm my nerves. I stood in front of crowded courtrooms every day of my life, why was I so nervous about standing before this crowd today? The faint whinny of visiting horses could be heard to the rear of the house where the parade of guest's carriages had been parked. The only person I wished could have been in attendance, who was not, was father. I knew that he would be pleased with our decision to marry at his beloved Pipe Creek.

One hundred folding wooden chairs had been borrowed from three different churches for the event and were set up in long rows on either side of the aisle. Deep autumns shades of red and yellow ribbons were draped along the chair backs adding color to the sea of brown wooden slats. Rectangular flower boxes planted with seasonal mums, and six black wrought iron floor-standing candelabras, each burning five candles, lined the walkway for the wedding procession. When high noon arrived, Frankie's daughter, Lizzie, in her lovely cream-colored gown caused a collective sigh of adoration as she arrived first to lead the way, throwing rose petals from the little basket she carried, onto the ground. The bride's attendants followed, and just as Ellen reached the end of the aisle near my side, a small gust of wind swept through and blew out several of the candle flames. The attendants quickly relit the wicks, but I had caught the scent in the wind, and the smell of the extinguished flame reminded me that my father was there in spirit. A warm comfort that the whiskey had failed to provide overtook my body.

Ellen was stunning on her father's arm. The white lace gown perfectly outlined her delicate figure and her long blond curls escaped from under the pearl lined veil. Her deep blue eyes appeared even more exquisite with the reflection of the blue skies above. Gazing at my bride, and the manor house that meant so much to my family looming behind her in the distance, I was filled with emotion and gratitude. Frankie, my best man, pretended to have lost the wedding bands for a moment during the ceremony, to my mother's obvious horror, but, if it weren't for my brother and his comic relief, I may have cried like a baby while promising to cherish my new wife always.

Being married to Ellen was easy, fun even. She was so practical and positive, that I always felt that I was doing alright in her eyes. It wasn't a romance for the ages necessarily, but it was a good fit and partnership. I loved our new life together. We were thrilled when we discovered that we were going to have our first baby. I passed out cigars to everyone I knew the night that our daughter Elizabeth was born. Never had I been so overwhelmed with pure joy as I was the first time I held the tiny bundle in my shaking hands. I would have moved mountains for her, and when she wrapped her tiny hand around my finger, I knew that everything was right in my world. I was exactly where I was meant to be.

My mother had moved to Baltimore with my eldest sister, and my growing family moved into her home on C Street just as my first and only son, James joined his two sisters. The birth had been a difficult one this time and we discussed that having three children was a nice size for a family. It had deeply frightened us when complications arose during his birth, but we both tried to be strong for each other. Neither wanting to alarm the other; that's how we loved. Now things were really busy in the new Key household. Caring for the thriving law office and three young children required an enormous amount of attention and effort, and although we fell into bed exhausted at the end of every day, we were thankful. We had servants of our own but preferred to be as involved as possible with caring for our small family.

The children enjoyed Terra Rubra as much as I had as a child. I showed them the sandy creek beds where we played and learned to fish. They climbed the same giant oak tree in the front yard that I scaled hundreds of times myself. We explored the barns and played chase in the wide open spaces. The farm hadn't changed a bit and it was comforting to have that stability to rely on. Having children was a bit like reliving childhood yourself only with more power and control over your circumstances. I understood why my parents had brought us here so often. Your mind was free at Pipe Creek. The beauty of the countryside and sunsets over the mountains were things that did not require decision making or effort. They were simply there, to be enjoyed, and it was the purest form of rest to just relax and listen to the sounds of nature and the happy squeals of a new generation of baby cousins now toddling around the farm without a care in the world.

We accidentally conceived Alice at Terra Rubra when James was three years old. Part of us, God's plan perhaps, had forgotten the fear we felt during James' birth. We were lulled into a sense of security with the passage of time. Apparently, we were not tracking the days correctly and we messed it up because sure enough, Ellen's belly swelled with baby number four as we returned to Washington after a long vacation. The pregnancy went well enough, and we had convinced ourselves that everything was going to be fine.

"The baby is coming," was the brief message I received at my office. I was working as the District Attorney as my father had done, thanks to the help of a fellow I had met years ago and become reacquainted with in Washington. It was the man my father had disliked immediately, Dan Sickles, and I recognized him from the brief encounter at the Astor House in New York City. He remembered me as well. Our previously discovered similarities still existed and we became friends, although our political backgrounds somewhat clashed. He had friends in the current administration of President Franklin Pierce, and because of his close relationship with James Buchanan, who it seemed inevitable would become the next commander-in-chief, he was able to call in a favor on my behalf and the post was eventually mine. I was most grateful, and I enjoyed the position and his friendship very much.

I rushed home immediately to find a flurry of activity happening. My sister, Alicia, was entertaining the children in the backyard and came forward to let me know that Ellen was in labor and that the midwife had been alarmed by the amount of blood present in the amniotic fluid and had sent for the doctor, who had only just arrived. I rushed inside needing to hear no more. I ran to the birth room and my stomach turned violently when I saw for myself the amount of blood that was present. The mattress and bedding Ellen was lying on was red, as though dyed. There were bloody towels and rags everywhere and the metallic smell of blood filled the entire room. "Ellen!" I cried out in shock and panic as I ran to her bedside. In typical fashion, she faintly assured me that she was doing fine and that the doctor had managed to slow the bleeding. "Stay with me Philip," she whispered, and I felt my chest tighten immediately. I hadn't been present in the actual room during any of the births and although there was no chance I was leaving her side, I was terrified of the scene unfolding in front of me.

"I need you to push hard and strong Ellen," said the doctor. "You are going to bleed when you do, but we've got to get this baby out right now."

His calm demeanor eased my nerves slightly and I held my breath and my wife's hand as she pushed with all her might. She was so powerful and determined, I nearly winced from her grip on my hand. The baby's head appeared and within a matter of seconds I heard the cries of the newborn and watched the doctor hand her off to the midwife. He turned his attention back to Ellen and the now troubled look on his face penetrated my bones like a bolt of lightning.

"Is she okay? Is she okay?" I asked over and over, as if in a trance. I watched Ellen use her last breath to expel a bloody river containing something that looked like a mound of organs onto the bed between her open legs. I tried to open her eyes with my fingers and I called her name repeatedly, but it was useless, she was gone. I exploded with emotion, mainly focusing my outburst on the doctor who was examining the afterbirth and ignored me. When he turned my way, he held a smaller version of the infant that he had handed off to the midwife, a second baby, a twin who hadn't survived.

"Placental Abruption, one live birth, one stillborn, time of death of mother and baby 11:33 a.m.," he stated for the record as his nurse recorded the information in his log book. "I'm so very sorry for your loss," said the doctor.

I looked from him to the new baby being cradled in the midwife's arms, to my wife's lifeless body and it was more than I could bear. I tore from the room still covered in blood myself, ran out the front door of our home, and into the street where I let out a scream of grief that was probably heard at the far ends of the city. I remember nothing of the remainder of the day, I may have been given a sedative by the doctor, I don't know. I barely recall the days that followed, my clearest memory was Ellen being laid to rest in her family plot in Baltimore.

Just as she had in the weeks after our father's death, my sister Alicia, (Alice) stayed with me, caring for my three older children, the new baby, the household, and for me. Without her, I may have given up completely, but she refused to let me slip away into that dark place. She forced me to rise each morning and interact with my children, who were grieving their mother and needed me desperately. Although she was my younger sister, I realized that Alice had become my savior, my guardian angel. I was eventually asked what I would like the baby to be called, and I conjured up a moment's worth of clear thought and responded, "Alice, call her Alice."

PART TWO

TERESA BAGIOLI SICKLES

CHAPTER 5

THE SEDUCTION

There was never a time that I didn't know Dan. We lived together for a while when I was just a baby in a most unusual household. Dan and my parents shared a mutual friend in New York City. Mr. Da Ponte was the owner of the home. He was a quirky old man who had collaborated with a gentleman named Mozart on several opera pieces, and caused scandal after scandal in Italy, before he settled quietly in America. My mother, Eliza, or as she preferred to be called, Maria, showed up on his doorstep at the age of fourteen. She was orphaned and penniless and carried only a letter that directed her to Mr. Da Ponte who was named in the letter as her grandfather. Knowing his sons and their illicit history with women, he did not bother to doubt, nor was he surprised that a day like this had come. He already harbored several houseguests with varying degrees of personal tragedy so what was one more. He invited the pitiful girl inside and there she stayed.

My father, Antonio Bagioli, had been a gran maestro traveling the world with an Italian Opera Troupe. He befriended the elderly Mr. Da Ponte while boarding at his home during his New York performances and he too decided to stay. It may have had something to do with a young lady that he encountered there because within a short period of time he was married to my mother and I was born.

Lozenzo Da Ponte Jr., the owner's youngest son, also lived amongst the varied tenants and happened to be a friend of the Sickles family. Dan's parents were at their wit's end with this rebellious and volatile son of theirs. Lozenzo who was a college professor seemed to have a good influence on the young man and helped them convince Dan to return to his studies under the condition that Dan would be allowed to live with the Da Pontes in the city.

So, another member was added to the bizarre collection of boarders. Among such a gifted group, beautiful music was made, languages intermingled, and a new family was born from the ashes. Dan was eighteen years old when I was born. Having no experience with infants whatsoever he had been slow to warm to the idea of interacting with such a frail and tiny creature but as I grew into a little girl, he bounced me on his knee, tickled my toes and entertained me with riddles. I called him Uncle Dan and he was one of the many adults who influenced my childhood.

After the old man died, the house belonged to Lorenzo Jr. and everyone remained there and carried on with their lives. After several years, Lorenzo Jr. became very ill and passed away as well. Dan had not taken the news of his mentor's death well and although there was no hurry for us to move out of the home, my parents chose to leave quickly. Dan's behavior at the funeral and in the days after made them nervous and being unsure of his mental state they quietly moved our belongings into a home of our own on Broome Street.

It was an eventuality that we would have our own home at some point, but Dan saw it as an abandonment in his time of need and he was devastated. He dropped out of school and looked for a job in a New York law office while studying for the bar. He came to our home often and although he was a little older in years than my parents, they treated him like a lost son and spent many hours giving him advice on the future of his career and helping him with the decisions that weighed on him at the time. My mother and Dan were especially close. She often soothed him through the fits of rage he was prone to, and she seemed to be the one person who could bring him back under control. His volatile temperament didn't trouble me since I had grown up witnessing it firsthand, but I suspected my father was never entirely comfortable with Dan being around me.

He found a room about a block away from our home and moved closer. He was a regular at our family meals for years and finally reported one evening that in a stroke of luck he had been hired by a lawyer named Benjamin Butler who had very impressive political connections. He began his new job and to my parent's relief I am sure, they were released of his clingy dependency on them and he began to visit us at more reasonable intervals.

By now Dan had seen me grow from an infant to a child and into a young lady but it didn't seem he had changed much at all. He was slowly working his way up in the world, possibly by unscrupulous means, as he often found himself facing accusations and suspicions that portrayed him in an unfavorable light. I understood almost nothing of this as a child. He often mentioned a woman named Fanny whom he claimed to have a relationship with, but he never brought her around. My father hinted that she must be a figment of his imagination. I knew nothing more of Fanny than her name back then, but he insisted she was real, my mother had asked once if she was also for hire. I had no idea what that meant but I always assumed my mother wanted to know if she could have Fanny help us with the housekeeping.

Boarding school in Manhattan was where I blossomed most. I was nearing my fifteenth birthday and becoming a young woman.

I had my father's Italian complexion, dark brown hair and wide brown eyes. Compared to the other girls my age, I seemed to have a more exotic look and was once likened to Queen Cleopatra, which I quite enjoyed. I often received compliments on my appearance which encouraged me to experiment with cosmetics and the latest hairstyles while with my new friends. My mother nearly disowned me when she arrived at school for an awards ceremony and I was wearing a bit of rouge.

Due to my unusual start in life, I found it very easy to understand new tongues. I excelled at speaking foreign languages and hearing Italian since birth, I focused my studies on it. I became a girl capable of holding my own in the school of distinguished young ladies with whom I attended. I returned only on holidays and breaks to my parent's home at the other end of the city.

One such evening I was at home alone when Dan let himself in as he often did. He wandered into the parlor where I was lounging with my feet up ready to open my copy of the brand new novel, "Uncle Tom's Cabin" that everyone was talking about. Unprepared for visitors, I was caught off guard and somewhat indecent in my appearance. On this hot and humid night, I wore only my thin silk shift. I tried to cover myself as he entered the room and I nervously blurted out, "They aren't here, they've gone for the evening." My parents had been invited to a tribute performance of an opera written by Mozart and Mr. Da Ponte. They'd left for the theater an hour before he arrived. I wondered to myself why he wasn't invited and attending the performance himself.

"Then I suppose I shall have to watch over you in their absence," he stated with a wry smile.

"I'm fifteen years old Uncle Dan. I hardly require watching over," I replied. "Could you please excuse me so I can go to my room and put something more on?"

"I don't think you should do that at all Teresa, and don't you think it's time you stop calling me Uncle. We aren't actually kin and it's a bit of a childish term of endearment don't you think," he said.

"What shall I call you then…Dan?" I teased. It felt strange even saying that out loud, but he was right, we weren't related. I was becoming interested in the opposite sex and working on having confidence with boys. When I heard myself testing out my flirtatious voice in my reply, it surprised even me.

He walked quickly to the chair where I had been relaxing with my feet dangling over the armrest. He had a mischievous look in his eyes. Reaching down he grabbed my foot and began tickling my toes. I shrieked and tried to wiggle my foot free of his grip. He was enjoying his moment of dominance, but he finally let go and said, "Do you remember when you were small and I would do that to you? You have always been so ticklish…and beautiful," he added with a tone of voice I found unfamiliar. "I used to tuck you in at night sometimes and tell you stories and you'd close your little eyes and drift off to sleep to the sound of my voice. Do you remember?" He reached down and cupped my chin in his hand and I looked up at him squinting my eyes, pretending not to remember. His hand felt good on my skin and a warm feeling surged through my insides. He was far older than me but looked much younger than his age. He was tall, handsome and fit with blue eyes that sparkled when he spoke. His teeth were dazzlingly white and perfectly in line. He looked twenty-two in my opinion, instead of thirty-two but he was not.

"What am I doing?!?" I thought to myself. It was as if I were outside my own body watching a scene play out. This was Uncle Dan. I couldn't be having these kinds of feelings. It was inappropriate, to say the least, and yet here I was letting him touch me. Out of curiosity, mostly, of what would happen next in a scenario like this one, I played along.

"Do you want me to remind you," he asked kneeling down on his knees so that he was looking at me directly and something in his voice made me whisper "yes." He slid his arms underneath me and in one motion he stood and lifted me from the chair holding me like a new bride going over the threshold. He carried me slowly to my bedroom. He knew our home well. I didn't need to direct him to my bed. He placed me down gently with my head on my feather pillow. He crossed my hands placing them over my stomach and smoothed the sheets beside me so that I felt like I was lying in a coffin for a moment. He kneeled beside me and brushed my hair back from my forehead. "A story?" he suggested. I nodded and closed my eyes feeling both the urge to spring from my bed and run, and the urge to be kissed by a man at the same time.

"Once upon a time," he began. His voice was low and seductive, and I waited impatiently for each sentence. "There was a beautiful young lady named Teresa. She became more beautiful with each passing day. As a baby, she was adorable, as a child lovely, and as a young woman she was breathtaking." I felt his fingertips on my wrists and he began to slide them slowly up my arms to my shoulders. I shivered at his touch and he whispered "Shhhhhh." He continued. "The lady was so beautiful that all of the young men in the kingdom wanted her for their own. They brought her sweets and flowers and wrote her love poems every day, but none touched her heart and she was not interested in any of them. An older farmer who lived near the girl had watched her grow up and he had admired her from afar. He'd never married or fallen in love, because he knew in his heart, that even though she was but a child that she would grow into a woman and that she was his true love. So instead of wasting time and money on frivolous things and courting uselessly, he minded his crops, built his farm, saved his money, and perfected his farmhouse. When the girl was old enough, he declared his love for her and unlike the silly young boys who vied for her affections with trinkets, he had the best to offer her in life. He had loved her enough to be patient and built her a life that she never even knew was being prepared just for her."

"And were his efforts rewarded," I questioned? I opened my eyes and his face was in front of mine.

"You tell me," he responded. I sighed and closed my eyes inviting him to move in for a kiss. It was more thrilling than I had imagined. Of course, I hadn't imagined it being with a man twice my age or a man who I'd known my entire life. It felt right, though I knew it was wrong, but caught up in the moment I dismissed my logical thoughts and let my body decide the next moments. He pulled me to his chest in a sitting position and lifted my shift over my head. I was bare in front of him and I could feel that this was going to be it. My first time, my virginity, my innocence, all these thoughts crossed my mind, but my body did not want to resist. I submitted to his touch and experienced all the sensations that my young body had never felt before. He was gentle and loving and I forgot the fact that he was a grown man and me practically a child and I allowed it all to happen. When it was done, he held me close and we laid together there in the small bed I slept in my whole life and he promised to always take care of me. He was entirely serious and I realized that my life had just shifted direction completely. I was only fifteen, not old enough to marry but this man intended to have me as his wife and like the farmer, he'd saved everything he had, and he was offering it to me.

My parents would be furious, beyond furious. Our relationship had to be kept secret, at least until we figured out what to do. We continued to see each other when possible, and in a daring move, he picked me up once from boarding school in a carriage under the premise of being sent by my parents and I spent the entire day shut in his bedroom making love and letting him worship my body.

I suddenly felt too old for school; too mature for the juvenile behavior of the girls my age. I had graduated into a new phase of life and I was ready to leave my childhood behind and become an adult. As the months of our secret relationship wore on, I became restless and moody. I was tired of sneaking around and lying to my parents. Making excuses for my whereabouts was becoming exhausting. On top of that, I wasn't feeling well. I was queasy and achy and always felt that I needed a nap. The day after my sixteenth birthday, I realized that I had not had my monthly and I acknowledged to myself and to Dan what I had been subconsciously suspecting. I was pregnant with his child. Dan was both ecstatic and troubled. This meant that we were out of time for keeping our involvement secret. Soon the truth would be impossible to hide.

Two days later we arrived at the office of the mayor of New York City and were married in the eyes of the law. The only thing that remained to do was to break the news to our families.

Dan called a meeting after hours at his office asking both his parents and mine to come. They hadn't a clue about the relationship and were completely blindsided by the news that we not only were having a secret affair but that we were now officially married. I listened from the next room but couldn't bear to face my parents just yet. It was a dreadful scene. My mother sobbed uncontrollably, and my father had lunged at Dan and was being restrained by Dan's father, George. Shouts rang out of "disgusting" and "cradle robber" and "scoundrel." Threats pierced the air and my heart stung knowing how disappointed my parents were going to be when they heard the rest of the story. Dan's mother provided the voice of reason and the foursome quieted long enough for Dan to continue that he and I were also expecting a baby. With this piece of information in place, there was silence. The silence was almost worse than the shouting and sobbing as each realized that not only were they on the brink of a vicious scandal if not handled carefully but that each of them was to become a grandparent. "It is done then," was the final remark from my father who then escorted my mother out of the office, and I, frozen to a chair in the next room never revealed myself to them.

Dan's parents sounded less angry but were more nervous about the social consequences. When they departed, and the lock turned I burst into tears and cried as Dan helplessly held me and I sobbed until I had nothing left. We decided it best to continue damage control in the morning and returned to his place where I fell fast asleep, his tear-soaked handkerchief in my hand.

The morning brought new light to the situation and my parents greeted us when we arrived at their home and asked to have a discussion. We'd had months to absorb the particulars of our relationship, but it had only been hours for them. Emotions were raw but all remained calm. They had many questions and some accusations, but Dan delivered each response with composure and I was thankful that he was doing all the talking. I felt very young again, here in my parent's house, at the table we dined at every day, discussing my condition as if I were not even in the room. I resisted the urge to run to my room and pull the covers over my head like a scared child. My parents insisted that we marry again in a religious ceremony, and Dan immediately agreed. It was then discussed that it was no business of anyone else to know the date on which we had married in relation to the expected birth date of the baby. It would be hard enough to discredit rumors when I did begin to show my pregnancy but to confirm it would mean outright scandal and none of us wanted that. The final stipulation that my parents presented before giving their blessing was that during the pregnancy and for as long as possible after the birth that we would live with them. It was hard for them to reconcile that their own little girl was becoming a mother and felt that I needed the support and stability that they could provide if we were under their roof. It made sense anyway because Dan's career was thriving and opportunities were presenting for him to climb considerably in the ranks. He would most likely be called away often. So, the new reality of life was accepted and there was nothing to do but move forward. Once again, just like when I was an infant, the four of us lived together in an unconventional family unit and made the best of a strange situation.

Baby Laura arrived on a hot summer day in 1853 and from the moment she was born I was fascinated by every tiny finger and toe, every sound she made, and by the way I could see her pulse in the soft spot atop her head. I counted her toes over and over and could stare at her for hours. I loved dressing her up in the tiny baby clothes that seemed so small before she arrived but were still just a smidge too big after. She was a sweet and docile infant and with the guidance of my mother, I was learning to be a mother myself at age sixteen.

Dan's current position with Mr. Butler involved hosting the out of state politicians and businessmen who were visiting New York City either for work or pleasure. He referred to it as "making connections." My parents were good-natured about allowing him the use of our home. They had always enjoyed meeting new people and were adept at making conversation. Father had begun teaching music classes in the city and was making connections himself. He taught members of some of the city's most influential families. This type of social mingling helped promote his business as well and it secured his reputation as a well-known and talented musical instructor for high society.

Two of the first guests we entertained were a man from Illinois named Abraham and his wife Mary. They arrived in a carriage too lovely for the awkward, unpleasant man inside it. Abraham was a lawyer and lobbyist in town conducting business for the railroad industry. He was a bit full of himself in my opinion, but I enjoyed Mary immediately. She was jolly and unpretentious and had a way of making you feel that you were bosom friends instead of new acquaintances. She had brought a gift for the baby and presented it to her as if she were young royalty. An elegant linked ribbon of gold held an exquisite coral pendant on a necklace that seemed an extravagant gift for a new baby, but Mary had thoughtfully had it inscribed exclusively for Laura.

"See here," she said to the baby and for me to hear. "M.L. is me, Mary Lincoln, to L.B.S. which is you little one!" My daughter cooed and grinned at her cheerful expression and Mary was instantly charmed by the child and I was charmed by Mary in return. She was the mother of only boys and it delighted her to know a little girl to spoil. She doted over Laura almost as an auntie would do for years to come.

CHAPTER 6

TO WASHINGTON

By the time Laura was three years old, Dan had been to England twice and missed most of her first's. I and my parents delighted at her first tooth, first word, and first steps while he was off to London with his new friend James Buchanan. James had been appointed to act as an American representative in England and was so taken with my husband upon introduction that he insisted Dan accompany him there as an assistant. With his charming personality and impeccable manners, this was often the case and mere strangers were often attempting to gain his companionship.

I was unhappy with the arrangement since it meant a large cut in pay, and we were supposed to be saving for a home of our own. My pouting did nothing to change his mind. He insisted that this kind of promotion was going to pay off for us in the long run and so I was left behind as a new bride and new mother as he made his "connections" abroad. During his second assignment, I received a most curious letter from the English Court addressed to myself and stating that they were sorely disappointed that I could not accompany my husband to London again and that my presence would be missed. "Again," I thought aloud? I assumed it was some sort of clerical error and tossed the letter into the trash thinking nothing more of it. I had barely been out of New York City, let alone to England!

When Dan finally did return home for good, we bought our first home in the area of Bloomingdale, New York. A lovely riverfront house where we had plenty of space and plenty of help. I had my parents nearby, a nursemaid to attend to Laura and servants to do the housekeeping. Like every proper family, we added a family pet to mix as well. An adorable greyhound puppy with a sweet boxy face and the longest, skinniest legs you've ever seen. We named him Dandy and his antics provided a much-needed distraction for me. I'd never owned pets growing up and it surprised me daily that I could feel such affection and love for an animal. I preferred Dandy's company to any other and spent a good deal of my time training him or relaxing with him as my pillow and sunning ourselves down by the riverbank. There was nothing more for me to do than spend money on shopping ventures and socialize independently, but even that had become tiresome. I was trying to become accustomed to being lonely. Dan was so preoccupied with his mission to convert the swamps and rocky terrain behind our new home into a central city park. He might as well have been in England still. I began to realize that some of his means and associates were suspicious in their integrity. The one time I'd dared to question his business practices, I'd received a back-hand across the mouth and a bloody lip. I didn't ask again. To his credit, the plans for his "Central Park" moved forward and in its completion, was a charming pleasure grounds for all the residents of New York City to enjoy.

When James returned from England, we held a grand welcome-home party, and I very much enjoyed the preparations for his arrival. I reveled in the planning and execution of the festivities, it gave me a sense of purpose I had not felt before. Even Dan complimented me on the magnificent details of the celebration. The Marine band played the Star-Spangled Banner as he descended the ship's gangway. Champagne and wine flowed freely amongst the gatherers at the dockyard. Banners announced, "James Buchanan for President." Much to Dan's delight two sailors then unfurled a banner over the rail of the ship stating, "Dan Sickles for Congress." Dan was at the front of the crowd to welcome his friend back to America and to New York, and I'm almost certain his excitement to see James surpassed the enthusiasm he had displayed when returning to me.

In November 1856, the same guests from the dockyard gathered again, but now the guest list had grown tenfold. The Astor House Hotel on Broadway Street hosted the election night party. James paced nervously, wringing his hands and mingling with guests. The returns were coming in from all over the country and James refused to hear the updates, only wanting to know the final result. I was pleased to finally meet his niece, Harriet. I'd heard so much about her from James and Dan, and she was just as adorable and lively as they had described. She talked excitedly about the prospect of moving into the White House with her uncle. James had never married, and Harriet was the closest thing he had to a daughter. It seemed he intended on taking her along as the first lady if the election went in his favor. At least I would know one person in the city if we ended up there as well. Dan was the only one who didn't seem a bit nervous. He drank brandy and smoked cigars in the drawing room as though it were any other night. The waiters, in elegant, black-ties, served hors d'oeuvres and drinks throughout the evening. The orchestra, directed by my father, played splendidly to provide entertainment long into the night. By the wee hours of the next morning, the votes had been tallied and the big announcement was seconds away. Everyone gathered together, breathless with anticipation, as the results were read. I gripped Dan's hand tight and squeezed my eyes shut, waiting.

It was good news all around! Dan won his seat in the House of Representatives and James Buchanan was elected as fifteenth

President of the United States. He shook his hand free of my grip and I expected to be swept off my feet by my husband, to celebrate this momentous occasion, but when I opened my eyes, he was gone. I saw only the back of his head as he fought through the cheering crowd, heading for James. Embarrassed, I slinked quietly into the background and signaled the waiter for another glass of wine. I watched Dan hugging James around the shoulders and kissing Harriet's hand. My mother was next in line for his attention, receiving the warm embrace that I had been expecting. My father shook his hand heartily and congratulated him on the win, pulling a long cigar from his jacket pocket and presenting it to Dan. I half-heartedly raised the glass of wine the waiter had just placed in my hand. "Cheers, to our life in Washington," I said, to no one in particular, tipping the glass and finishing it in one swallow.

Dan departed for Washington first and stayed with his friend, Jonah Hoover, while finding a home for us to move into. He wrote about a fellow named Philip he'd met once in New York, who was a mutual friend of Jonah's family. He said they'd become acquainted at the Astor House many years ago when Philip was traveling through with his father Francis Scott Key. Dan had never mentioned to me before that he'd met the author of the Star-Spangled Banner or his son, but of course, there were many things I didn't know about Dan.

Moving to Washington was an overwhelming experience and Laura and I took some time to adjust to the new surroundings. Boredom was a word that became not only foreign but welcome. The expectations of a Congressman's wife both suited and inspired me and the best way to describe our new life was demanding. We moved into a lovely home along the west edge of Lafayette Square near the President's house, which we could just see from our front window. We were, of course, good friends. A second level entrance was reached by a curved set of stairs and an iron balustrade. Some evenings Laura, Dandy, and I sat outside on those steps and watched through the gaps in the railing the comings and goings of people strolling in the park or watching for any sign of "Papa" returning home. Dan worked day and night on behalf of the state of New York, James Buchanan, and his own interests all at once. We rarely saw him but regardless I found my place easily and delightfully among the other elite political families.

Laura was tended by her new nanny Bridget, who also served as my lady's maid, and I was distracted doing what I was expected to be doing; socializing. Gatherings, called receptions were held daily at the homes of notable families and our chance occurred each Tuesday morning. In my quest to become the ultimate Washington hostess I challenged myself weekly to throw the most spectacular event in town worthy of note. I shopped the market myself to ensure just the right selections to impress our guests. Entertaining came naturally and Washington was brimming with folks eager to be entertained and indulged. Most Tuesdays Dan was too busy working to attend the function at our home and so the quest of schmoozing the already privileged fell to me and I handled myself well in my opinion. Soon my Tuesday reception was the most sought after invite in the city and I was making so many friends I could barely keep the names straight. I was expected to attend the receptions of others in return on my free days. It was exhausting running to and fro trying to remember faces, names, and schedules. I spent very little time at home during the day. When his schedule allowed, Dan and I held Thursday evening dinner parties which were attended by his associates and their wives. It obviously didn't hurt our reputation that President Buchanan himself was a regular attendee. His notable followers were never far behind.

Of all the new friends though, I was most pleased to become reacquainted with Mary Lincoln. I'd thought so fondly of her and she was one of the first to welcome us to the city. She and Abraham were in Washington visiting from Illinois. There was a good deal of discontent developing in the nation and Abraham was revisiting the idea of making a run for Congress. He'd served from 1847-1849 and Mary knew the city well from their time spent here. Rumor had it he was capturing the attention of many prominent Washington politicians who were encouraging him to throw his hat back into the Congressional ring. I cared little for the matters of politics, and I saw even James as more of a friend than President. I was mostly pleased because it meant that my friend Mary would possibly be staying in the city and I was more than happy to have her companionship.

Mary and I had so much fun together and I was most happy in her presence. Mary was short and a bit round with the most unusual wispy hair that seemed unwilling to stay put under her bonnet. It was such a contrast to Abraham's tall slender build that it was amusing to observe them standing together. We chatted for hours about our children and husbands. She continued to dote on Laura now four years old, and the child loved "Aunt" Mary dearly. It seemed as though in a city full of forced acquaintances and cordiality I had found a real friend who I enjoyed spending my time with and so I nurtured our friendship to the best of my ability. We were on the topic one afternoon of departed loved ones gone to heaven and I discovered that Mary thought herself to be somewhat connected to the other side. We joked about holding a séance to conjure up the spirits of previous first ladies who could give us advice on surviving in Washington. We often walked the avenue and visited our favorite sweet shop, Gautier's, where Mary insisted on treating us to sweets and goodies much to Laura's enjoyment. Dan and Abe also were becoming acquainted as husbands will do under influence of their wives chosen friendships. Our families got on marvelously and Mary was the closest friend I'd ever had. I became more confident than ever in this new lifestyle we'd been thrust into.

The inauguration ball hosted for James Buchanan on March 4, 1857, was where I first laid eyes on Dan's friend, Philip Barton Key. Philip had been widowed and left to raise four small children alone. It seemed tragedy excluded no family, no matter how prestigious the last name. In the following weeks, Mary and I saw it as our personal mission to involve Philip and his children in our outings. Besides the fact that he was easy on the eyes, he was kind and courteous and had a great sense of humor. Underneath the confident exterior, you could feel a sadness in the man, yet he refused to express it openly. We enjoyed his company so much that soon, we wouldn't have thought of not including him. He was similar to Dan in some ways, same height and build, same sandy-brown hair, perfect teeth, very good looking, but he wasn't a workhorse like Dan, he enjoyed spending time with his children and having his free time. Philip's duties as district attorney rarely held his attention long.

He had been born near Washington and knew every nook and cranny in the city. It was like having our very own city guide, and many afternoons we strolled about with him in the lead. He and Dan were both lawyers of course and had developed a friendship of their own. When it came time for new appointments in the district attorney's office, Dan asked James to consider keeping Philip in the position. "It would be a patriotic gesture to the poor widow," he insisted. Because of course, Philip's father had once held the same position. Favors were flying at the onset of the Buchanan administration, and James did enjoy Philip personally, so the request was granted.

I'd met an overwhelming number of people and I enjoyed the wide range of social events to which I had access, but over time a few people like Mary and Abe, then Jonah Hoover and his wife Angelica, and Philip and his sister Alicia became my favorites. Alicia was Philip's youngest sister and adored her brother greatly. She had married a Congressman from Ohio named George Pendleton and lived for a while in Cincinnati. During a visit home, she'd been witness to the horrible tragedy of Philip's wife dying in childbirth. He'd clung desperately to Alicia in the following weeks and she never could leave his side again and so the entire Pendleton family returned to Washington for good. Alicia's and Philip's children were raised together and shared a nursery and a nanny. For all intents and purposes, Alicia was their mother now. Our children were playmates to each other. Philip's daughter Alice, Alicia's daughter, Mary, and my Laura were very close in age and not a day went by that they weren't begging for the company of one another. Mary's boy Tad was a bit more reserved but had taken a liking to Laura and so the two of them played often as well, usually with Mary hovering nearby listening for the slightest sniffle. She worried a bit too much in my opinion, Tad seemed a strong and healthy boy to me.

The first indication that my husband was a liar and a cheat came in the form of a rumor that I had captured the attention of the Royals while in London. Apparently, I had made a striking impression because my name had been mentioned in a London newspaper that had come home with Jonah from one of his trips abroad, as packing material in his luggage. Angelica had been cleaning out his old hat box and browsing the crumpled headlines when she spotted my name. She was always fascinated with the Royal family and so to her, discovering my alleged association seemed the next best thing. She arrived at my door the next morning excitedly gushing over the news article when I stopped her. "There has been a misprint, Angelica, I've never been to London."

"No, it says here that you were most delightful, and the queen found that you to be…"

"Angelica, I said, I've never been, do you hear my words?" I didn't mean to be sharp with her, but I was annoyed and sure that she had read it improperly and I momentarily lost my patience. "I apologize, but if I had been to London, I'm certain I'd remember it and I assure you I have not. May I read the article for myself?"

"Of course." She held out the paper and in something between an apologetic and disappointed sigh she handed me the London Post and turned to walk away. "I'll call on you later Teresa," she said as she descended the front stairs, hands on hips and her brown curls bouncing with each step. I had to giggle inwardly at the thought of her imagining me mingling with her beloved Royal family. It was a bit flattering.

Sure enough, the article stated that I'd been presented to the Queen by the American minister to London, Mr. Buchanan. It went on to describe my gown, my hair-do, and my charming American accent. It seems my appearance made such an impression that my gown was in high demand to be duplicated for the ladies of London. "What in God's name?" I questioned aloud. I continued reading and discovered it was with great regret that "I departed to attend to matters back home" and that my presence as the hostess was replaced by Miss Harriet Lane, the minister's niece. Of course, those characters were now Mr. President and his niece as First Lady.

It was odd. I wasn't sure what the inaccuracy implied besides that an incompetent journalist existed in London, but it stirred an uneasy feeling in the pit of my stomach. I decided to pay a visit to Harriet and show her the article. Perhaps she'd be able to offer some sort of explanation or could relay to me her experience when she arrived there. I walked the half block through LaFayette Park to her front door.

Harriet welcomed me warmly at the President's house and I followed her through the wide winding corridors to her inner chambers. We were served cheese, fruit, and cider. The fire was stoked, and the room brightened considerably. Harriet was always dressed so elegantly. I wondered if she had an occasion to attend or if she dressed this way first off every morning. Her uncle was an incurable bachelor and while residing at the White House in Washington had indeed brought his only niece along to provide a woman's touch to the accommodations and to have an ornament to decorate his arm at public functions.

I presented the newspaper to Harriet and when she finished reading, she stared at me puzzled by my obvious anticipation. "I don't understand Teresa. An old newspaper from London that mentions both of our names. Am I missing something?"

"Missing something? I have no idea what that article is referring to. It says I was presented to the queen prior to your arrival. Were you in London? Is this making any sense to you?" I was becoming more frustrated by the moment. "I have never in my life been to London Harriet!"

"Weren't you?" She said, looking as confused as I felt. "When I arrived, you'd already gone. I was there, yes, and I heard you spoken of frequently. We weren't acquainted at the time and so I didn't give it much more thought. I figured you'd come and gone and that I'd meet you eventually since my uncle and your husband had become dear friends and here we are! I don't understand Teresa, if you've never been to London, then who was it we all presumed to be you?"

Suddenly, my blood ran cold and I felt as though I might faint. I attempted to stand and instead my knees went weak and I sunk again into the sofa that I'd been sitting on. Instantaneously, I calculated the time frame and my whereabouts, and a name flashed through my mind. "Fanny," I thought. We were still in New York. I had just given birth to Laura, I would have been in no condition to travel with a newborn. Nor was I able to provide for my husband's fleshly needs. A feeling in my gut told me that I had been replaced and impersonated by a woman I knew very little of except her name, Fanny. It was the only female name I'd ever heard Dan speak as a child. He'd never introduced her to my family, and for good reason as he eventually admitted to me that she was a prostitute with whom he had a certain relationship. "Are you alright Teresa? Should I call for the doctor?" Harriet was kneeling beside me and I focused my eyes on her concerned face.

"No, no I'm fine. Just stood too fast is all. I'm sure there is a perfectly reasonable explanation for this silly misunderstanding." I resisted the urge to run from the room and instead I composed myself and announced that I needed to return home to check on Laura. I faked my way through saying "good day" and "see you soon" with a smile on my face but as I turned the corner of the hall leading to the entryway, I felt the hot tears pooling in my eyes and then escaping down my cheeks. I ducked into an empty room and bent over hardly able to breathe when I let the sobs escape my tightened throat. Instantly, I knew everything. I didn't need a confession or an admission of details. In my heart, I knew everything I needed to know. Fanny, his whore, had gone to England with my husband posing as me, as his wife. She'd spent months with him being indulged by the Royal family pretending to be Teresa Sickles, being introduced to the queen as so.

Worse yet, James knew, he was there the entire time and unlike Harriet, was aware of who I was. There was no mistaking, he'd known all along. How did he look me in the face for all these years? I'd considered him a friend. I realized he'd only ever been a friend to Dan. She'd taken my place in his bed and preoccupied his thoughts while I was back in America completely unaware, naively trusting him, missing him and nursing his newborn daughter. I saw the entire scene play out in my mind. The only thing I could not picture was her face, I'd never seen it and now I never wanted to. Dan was an unfaithful bastard and I was a stupid stupid girl.

If Dan had taught me anything, it was to lie. The earliest days of our relationship trained me to deceive my parents with a straight face and to act calm and casual outwardly, regardless of what was going on inside. I planned to use this to my advantage. I collected myself on the short walk home and began thinking of what I wanted to do with this information. I certainly wasn't going to explode on him with accusations and anger only to have him deny everything and lie directly to my face. His fits of rage were terrifying, and now that Laura was getting older, I avoided antagonizing him at all costs. Hurting me, shaking me, and pushing me around was one thing, but if he were to hurt Laura, that would be more than I could bear. What good could possibly come of that? I was the mother of his child and his wife. I was trapped. Instead, I decided my most viable option was to stay put and get an enlightened view on who he really was. Without the shroud of success, who was this man? Did I even know him at all?

I told no one about my discovery. I played the part of the dutiful wife and did what I knew was expected of me. What had changed was that I had turned off my emotions, like a valve. Never once did I lose my composure and in fact, I became so mechanical in my thoughts and actions that I almost convinced even myself that everything was fine.

"Perhaps I'm crazy, it's probably nothing. I don't have any actual proof."

These thoughts tried their best to claim the space in my mind, but my heart could never forget that it knew the truth. I began to see Dan as nothing more than a roof over our heads, a provider, and a bank. I no longer felt guilty about spending whatever I wanted on new clothes for Laura or myself, and in some way, this was my secret revenge. I began to slowly demand all the finer things in life that I had never felt entitled to before. A brand new carriage, jewelry, a French perfume that I never intended to wear, the latest of each type of household appliance for which I had no use.

I taunted him, to my great satisfaction by suggesting that we take a trip overseas to London so that he could show me where he stayed during his time there and introduce me to the royal family and to his English friends. Never would I have gone through with planning such a trip, but seeing him squirm, his mind racing with possible explanations upon presenting his *real* wife, and the look of panic on his face each time I mentioned it was well worth the effort.

He attributed my new found love of material possessions to becoming a true Washington wife and he scolded me on my careless spending and my lack of appreciation, but he never withdrew my privileges, and so it went on like this for many months. I was empty inside and I was drowning in jewels as fast as I was drowning in misery.

CHAPTER 7

FALSELY ACCUSED

Philip, Mary, and I took our children to the park together for a spring outing. It had been such a cold and miserable February in 1858 and everyone was delighted to be spending time outside again. Laura and Alice giggled and played happily while Tad watched some construction going on across the street. He was fascinated by the workers digging and placing stone blocks one on top of another developing the landscaping around a new building called the Smithsonian Institution. I'd prepared a picnic but hadn't thought to bring a sweater. It was still early spring in Washington and though the sun was shining, it was chilly. The children didn't seem to mind much but Mary, who fussed incessantly over Tad, her youngest child, decided that he'd catch a cold for sure in the weather and decided to take him home. Philip and I stayed a while longer with the girls. "Are you too cold," he'd asked me, as he peeled off his overcoat and placed it over my shoulders. It was warm from his body heat and it smelled like him. I dismissed a momentary feeling that there was something wrong with wearing his jacket, but I was cold, and it felt comfortable to be cuddled up inside of it. "I do believe it looks even better on you Mrs. Sickles," Philip playfully stated.

Laura and Alice were spinning like little tops in the grass when suddenly Laura lost her balance and toppled over sideways on to the ground. She let out a cry that only a four-year-old who's fun had just been entirely ruined can do. I began for her, but Philip was quicker. He was to her in a flash, lifting her off the ground and placing her into my lap. He addressed the scuffs on her legs with a dab of water and his handkerchief while I dried her tears. He was so gentle, so kind, and it filled me with a sense of warmth that I'd never felt in the presence of my daughter and my own husband. He was a father of four I supposed, and so he had much more experience in dealing with children, but something else stirred in me. It was a form of adoration not only at the way he tended to her but just that he was there. He was at the park with his daughter and with us, doing nothing particularly special, and yet seemed to be having a wonderful day. His presence was calming to me, and for a second, I wondered if this was how it was supposed to be all the time. Dan worked and worked and any request on his time seemed a burden. A wonderful day to Dan would be forcing a vote to go his way, closing a big deal, or perhaps a visit to his mistress Fanny in her New York brothel, but not picnicking in the park with his daughter and wife.

Philip's little daughter Alice watched, terrified that her best friend had been hurt, and Philip, not missing a beat scooped up one girl in each arm, held them both together, and announced that he would be their horse to carry them home. This made the girls giggle, and as I gathered the rest of our belongings in the grass, I watched from the corner of my eye while he played and laughed with them and I remember thinking that it was a most beautiful scene, one I wished I could capture to keep forever.

After that day, I confess I began looking for reasons to be near Philip. There was something comforting that felt right when he was present, and I craved his company. I began to feel alive again.

I thought it might be only my imagination, but it seemed he also was making an effort to appear more often near me. He became a regular attendee at my Tuesday morning reception, and we began to cross paths at most of the receptions I regularly attended when I'd never seen him there before. One such place was at the home of his sister Alicia. Her Monday morning "at-home," as it was sometimes called, was one of the most sought after invitations in the city. Monday mornings were quickly becoming my favorite part of the week. I adored Alicia with her amusing laugh, quick wit, and her natural beauty. She had a rare personality that was either extremely enlightened or extremely outlandish, I never decided which, but she spoke her mind and I admired her for it. We understood each other, both being the young wives of ambitious congressman. She more than anyone seemed to sense my loneliness in a city full of people and had been kind enough to assure me I was making all the right acquaintances. She'd given me fair warning of those to avoid as well, and so far, she had always been right.

Apparently, good looks run in the Key family. Philip was handsome for sure, possibly the most handsome man I'd ever seen, but I hadn't noticed before the way he smiled with his eyes or how he held his arms just right when talking with other guests. He seemed at ease, strong and confident no matter the situation and I felt safe when he was around. Of course, I was married, and he and Dan were friends, so I was satisfied with enjoying his public company, for a while.

Within our social realm, it was not unusual to be appointed a male escort who accompanied a lady both for safety and social reasons when her husband was unable to attend events. Silly young things that had ambitions in the political arena were always more than happy to volunteer their services when Dan was unavailable. Usually, I'd find myself in the company of some brown-nosed aid or clerk who wanted to rattle on about his resume to me in hopes I'd put in a good word with Dan. I found it so desperate and exhausting that when Philip offered to Dan to fill the position for an upcoming ball, I could hardly conceal my excitement. "I suppose that will do," was my casual response to Dan when asked if this was agreeable to me. But inside I was tingling with excitement.

Nervousness set in early the day of the ball, and I couldn't eat a thing. I hoped not to get sick on Philip's feet. "A fine moment that would be," I thought. "Does momma look nice?" I asked Laura as she watched me put the finishing touches on my hair and makeup before leaving for the evening. "Momma looks pretty," she replied, and I kissed her on the top of her head then descended the stairs to be on my way. I paused and affectionately patted Dandy who was looking very disappointed by my departure. His tail swished quickly back and forth for a moment as though he thought I might change my mind. I told him to go see Laura, who had become his new best friend and he obeyed starting reluctantly up the wooden staircase.

The carriage was waiting outside, and it was a gorgeous fall evening. The leaves were almost completely turned, and they boasted their warm colors like a painting hung upon a mantle. The evening sun was setting, and the air was cool and crisp. No need for a shawl of course, perhaps I'd need someone to offer his jacket again if the evening grew too chilly.

Philip was stunning in his blue and gold uniform. He was the leader of the Washington militia's Montgomery Guard and he looked utterly magnificent as he waited at the door to the carriage for me to descend the stairs. "Good evening madam, you look beautiful," he said as he kissed my hand and helped me enter the carriage. He was entirely attentive and appropriate as a chaperone. Dancing with Philip was a wonderful surprise, one of many talents I did not yet know he possessed. His grace and elegance was not a surprise to most guests who had obviously observed him before, but to me; I felt that I was seeing him for the first time. The evening ended all too soon and I was delivered back to my stately prison. We bid farewell and with a final glance over my shoulder we locked eyes for a brief second and then he was gone.

Sammy, one of my usual escorts was not so pleased with the arrangement and he had openly glared at me from across the ballroom the entire evening. I knew he had a fondness for me, he had told me so himself, but he was Dan's clerk and knew that our friendship was merely a professional courtesy. But something in his demeanor that evening told me that I should request other arrangements in the future. Sammy had always been too blunt in our conversations in my opinion and he did seem to enjoy any bit of gossip, but I had always thought of him as harmless.

I had underestimated his malice. In a jealous state, he'd apparently spent the evening after the ball sulking, drinking, and purposely or not, devising his revenge. No impropriety had occurred between Philip and me, although I did find it interesting that never before had observing me with another male escort conjured up such animosity in Sammy. Was it something in the way Philip and I interacted? We'd both been very proper at all times that evening, completely aware of being subject to public scrutiny. If Philip's feelings for me were anywhere near as strong as my true feelings of adoration for him then perhaps it had been impossible to mask, but I'd used restraint to the greatest of my ability. A small piece of me, despite the coming controversy, was tantalized by the thought of Philip possibly returning my affections.

In typical Dan style, he'd calculated his every move before I even knew that anything was happening. I returned home from my trip to the market to find my mother in the parlor. She stared at me coolly and didn't rise from her seat to greet me. On the other side of the room stood Sammy. He shifted his weight from left foot to right and back continuously while staring at the floor. His trembling knees shook his whole thin, bony frame, and his long stringy brown hair fell over his eyes and forehead as though he was trying to hide behind them like a curtain. "What is going on here"? I demanded.

Dan entered the room. "Your mother was just about to tell us. Sit Teresa." In shock, I obeyed instinctively and sat across from my mother, dropping my market bag to the floor without any regard for the fragile items inside. My own mother was here, looking scornful, and not invited by me, so I knew that she and Dan had conspired behind my back for this moment, though I did not yet know the subject matter. That was just like Dan to use my own family against me. To put me in the most vulnerable position possible before an attack. I braced myself.

"Today in his office Dan received a most unpleasant report," she began. "It seems Mr. Beekman," she accusingly pointed toward Sammy," has expressed concern to a friend that my daughter has had inappropriate conduct with Mr. Philip Key, who accompanied her a few evenings ago to a party here in the city. Mr. Beekman's confidant has told another who told another and so on until the message was finally repeated to Dan."

Dan was doing his best impression of the forlorn husband, for my mother's sake, and he added sadly, "this is why I have brought us together."

Sammy and I both began voicing our protests at the same moment and so I held back my words to hear exactly what he was saying first. His claim was to have been heavily intoxicated on the evening in question, and he admitted saying several unpleasant things about women in general, but that they were not directed at me or meant to imply any wrongdoing on my part. He looked terrified as he continued objecting and apologized for having spread any unintentional rumors. He insisted on my innocence on my behalf and apologized directly to me for having caused such troubles.

I almost felt sorry for Sammy except that I was the target of this fabrication, and I remembered the look in his eyes the evening of the ball. I knew he probably hadn't intended for things to go this far, but he'd been jealous, angry even, and I was only somewhat surprised to learn that he had behaved in such a way. He was, however, pleading my case for me so I was willing to let him finish.

Dan spoke sternly, "You are a young man not yet married but one day you will realize the gravity of the situation you have created.

A man's wife is a testament to his character and an attack on her integrity is also an insult to her husband. Do you understand?"

"Yes sir, I do. Please accept my deepest apologies," Sammy begged of him.

"You may go then. Be aware that Mr. Key is sure to confront you on the matter as well. Prepare yourself since his honor is challenged," stated Dan as he practically pushed Sammy to the door of the parlor towards the entryway.

I stared at my mother in disbelief, "how could you be so willing to accuse me when you never even asked for my side of the story?" I broke down in tears as she lowered her eyes and moved closer to my side putting her hand on mine. She said nothing but I knew that she had been swayed. It still angered me, mostly toward him but at her as well. She always sided with Dan. Yes, she had known him long before I was even born, but I was her daughter! This was exactly how Dan controlled a situation. He had come to her as the wounded victim, exaggerating the scenario, so that in the event the gossip had been true, she would have been sympathetic to him leaving me nowhere to turn, and that was exactly how Dan Sickles operated. To add insult to injury he never apologized for my embarrassment or for involving my mother, and that evening he did not come to bed.

From what I understood Philip was furious upon learning of the situation. His immediate reaction was to threaten to challenge Sammy to a duel. He realized in a calmer moment that he was dealing with a boy young enough to be his son, and so instead he exercised leniency and collected written statements from all the young men involved including Sammy. He requested letters from witnesses who had observed nothing but the most proper behavior the night of the ball until the lawyer in him was satisfied that he'd substantially proved his case. He'd employed Jonah to deliver the letters to Dan who was appreciative of his efforts and stated to Jonah, "Well enough, I like Key."

Philip and I seemed to have a silent understanding after the incident to avoid each other hoping to negate any possibility of questionable behavior between the two of us. We greeted each other in public as always but were careful not to find ourselves alone under any circumstance. I missed him dearly though and now my sadness was compounding. I thought about him every day and wondered if he was missing me as well.

Mary and I were regularly having our tea together in the morning. Being the mother of all boys, I think escaping to my home with just one quiet little girl was a welcome retreat. We had a spacious home in a pleasing location and she and Abe were still staying in a small part of a boarding house in town. She complained of the conditions of living with Abe and the three boys in a single room. I imagine she needed some space and welcomed her anytime.

I inquired one day if she had heard the gossip regarding Philip and me. I was curious how far the rumor had traveled in the city. She had heard, and she'd also heard that Sammy had since resigned his post and returned to his home state of New York in shame. I had a brief moment of satisfaction at this development, but I did not state it aloud. I couldn't help but blame Sammy that Philip could no longer be a part of my daily life. I was struggling with the loss still. I tried my best to put on a happy façade, but I was downright miserable.

Mary seemed to notice my melancholy sigh. She, Laura, and I worked a picture puzzle at the dining room table. She looked at Laura at said, "Don't ever grow up little one. It's no fun." Laura giggled and replied that she would try her best.

"Although I admit I may not have blamed you if it were all true, he's a handsome one. I miss following his backside through town," laughed Mary playfully.

"Mary!" I exclaimed, hoping that Laura wasn't following the conversation closely. She asked constantly about playing with Alice and it broke my heart to keep them apart. I was trying not to do anything to provoke Dan and that meant acting as though the incident was no matter to me. Laura had seen Dan's erratic behavior many times already at five years old, and I knew that she craved far more attention from him than he offered, but he was her papa and I had no intention to sour her opinion of him. A childish innocence was a good quality to have, in fact, I sometimes envied it and wished that I could have made mine last.

CHAPTER 8

IN A MARYLAND MINUTE

Toward the end of summer, Alicia sent an invitation for Laura and me to come to her family home outside Washington. They were vacationing there and asked if we'd like to spend a week at a place she called Terra Rubra. She described its tranquil streams and fresh mountain air and promised that our children would have the most delightful time together in the Maryland countryside. It seemed an offer too good to refuse and so I accepted.

August was the month that killed the most people in Washington. Between the mosquitos, the heat, and stagnant air it was downright unbearable, and I was excited to escape it. Alicia soon had a carriage sent for us. With Dan away in New York, as usual, I saw no reason to ask his permission. He barely noticed we existed, and I had my suspicions that more than business was keeping him gone so long. I'd write to him when we arrived there. I packed our things into just one trunk and fussed over Laura's hair, weaving it into a long braid while we waited for the carriage to be loaded.

The ride was long but scenic. The coachman pointed out all the most interesting landmarks along the route including Sugarloaf Mountain and a lovely cottage where George Washington had regularly stopped for a rest in his travels. By midafternoon we passed Fredericktown and arrived at the Key family plantation. It was even more beautiful than I'd imagined. The sunlight reflected in such a way that the entire manor house seemed to be aglow and the long shady lane leading up to it looked to be a pathway to paradise.

Laura and I were warmly welcomed by a whole troupe of Key family members. We had scarcely stepped foot on the grass when Laura was whisked away by the other children who were anxious to show her the animals, the farm, and Pipe Creek. Alicia made the proper introductions and though I'd never remember all their names, each person greeted me kindly. I wondered if this was what it was like to be part of a large loving family. It was no wonder Alicia and Philip were such wonderful people. I'd been an only child and even on holidays our gatherings with distant relatives were small and lacked the jolly nature of a celebration.

"This is my mother Polly," stated Alicia as she escorted me toward the most darling little old woman who was just coming out of the house and down the few front steps.

"Most honored to meet you, Mrs. Key. Thank you for having us," I managed to say. I was struck by how small she was, hadn't Alicia told me that she was one of eleven siblings? I couldn't imagine how this frail creature had endured eleven births until she spoke up.

"Welcome to Terra Rubra my dear, she bellowed! I have heard so much about you and I'm glad that we will have a chance to get to know each other a bit," Polly continued on, "You are going to just love it here. I've got your room all made up. Cook is preparing us a wonderful supper and so you just make yourself right at home!"

I could only smile in return. I hadn't expected such an energetic greeting upon first sight of the woman, but I quickly realized that she was as lively as they come, and I couldn't wait to get to know her better.

After unpacking, Alicia and I settled down on the wooden swing hanging from the front porch with a glass of freshly made mint tea. "This is a family favorite," said Alicia referring to the glass of tea. "Mother's friend Anne who lived at Rose Hill made the best mint tea and she took a couple of her mint plants from there and gave them to mother. Over the years, those two tiny plants have become a mint forest!" She pointed to the horizon and I couldn't see exactly where she was looking but it certainly was green and lush, and I was willing to take her word for it.

"This is so different than being in the city," I said, stating the obvious. "I think my friend Mary would like it here as well. You know Mary Lincoln, right?"

A dark scowl came across her face. I don't believe I'd ever seen her frown before. "Mary is no friend of mine and you'd be smart to keep your distance too." As Alicia said this about Mary I wondered if we were talking about the same person. Mary was so nice!

Alicia went on, "Let's just say our families are not compatible. Don't you pay attention at all to matters in Washington Teresa? My Aunt Anne, who you met earlier, is married to Roger Taney, the Supreme Court Chief Justice. He recently delivered a decision of the court in a case regarding slavery. They call it the "Dred Scott" decision in the papers and even though it wasn't his ruling alone, he was the spokesperson and the backlash seems to be coming back on him. I think it's very unfair. Uncle Roger is a really good man and he is just doing his job. This whole country is at odds now, the states in the south are saying they are going to start a new government, no one knows what to do, it's a disaster."

She looked as though she might cry. Puzzled I asked, "but what does that have to do with Mary?"

"I guess you know that Abe Lincoln, Mary's husband, is running for Senate. He is making Uncle Roger out to be a monster and trying to make everyone hate him. It's just not right. Besides that, she gives me the creeps always talking about mystical things, I don't care for her one bit."

Apparently, I hadn't been paying attention in Washington. If I spoke about politics at all and didn't make a fool of myself in public, then to me it was a good day. Maybe I should pay attention, if for no other reason than to know not to mention certain friends to others. I thought maybe Alicia was overreacting to the situation, but I wasn't about to tell her that. Not everyone gets along, I understood that much. Mary had always been kind to me and Laura and the politics weren't really our business. In an effort to lighten the mood, I asked her to tell me more about her family and about the beautiful property sprawled out in every direction. Within seconds she was back to her cheerful self and chatting about the adventures they'd enjoyed here as children. I managed to slip in a question about Philip and she nonchalantly added, "didn't I mention, he's coming here, tomorrow."

My heart skipped a beat at this bit of news. Philip was coming here? I shouldn't have been so surprised. This was his family's estate after all. I had convinced myself that my feelings for Philip were childish and unbecoming of a wife and mother so why was I feeling so queasy? I excused myself as soon as possible and said I'd like to take a stroll around the property. I needed time alone to think. Things were worse than ever with Dan. He constantly berated me for the smallest mistakes, called me spoiled and bratty and spent more and more time back in New York. It was lonely with him or without him, it barely mattered where he was at any given time. It was always on the tip of my tongue to divulge everything I knew of him to anyone who'd care to listen. I stopped short of shouting accusations at him during our arguments where he had the audacity to challenge my faithfulness. It would do no good to confront him without absolute proof. I'd spent so much time in self-induced denial that I often became conflicted within myself. Was I right about him? What if I had it all wrong and he really was a hardworking devoted husband and father doing the best he could for his family. I'd feel foolish and wasn't sure he'd ever forgive me if I wrongly accused him. I wanted another child but since he rarely shared my bed anymore, that was unlikely. He often stayed all night in his study when he was at home. He claimed to be overrun with work and then spent most of his free time during the day napping. I wondered what else might have been keeping him up in the wee hours of the night after Laura and I had long been asleep. Dark, late nights were conducive to the wicked behaviors I knew men to be capable of, and it was not beyond my imagination that Dan would partake in them.

I walked along the edge of the large pond that was located at the eastern edge of the plantation and admired the beautiful water lilies floating so peacefully and decorating the surface like icing flowers on top of a frosted cake. The water was crystal clear, and you could see to the bottom for some distance. I stopped walking, focused in on the waterline and for just a moment wondered if it would be so bad to drown. What if I just walked in and didn't stop until the water sealed over the top of my head. Would my natural instincts take over and make me fight for my life or could I control the urge to struggle and simply allow the water to fill me up and overtake me? It wasn't so much that I wanted to die, but that I wanted an escape route. I saw no way that my life could possibly be different or better. If I complained, no one would understand. On the surface, my life was perfect. I had money, freedom, and a handsome looking husband but the truth was I had married the wrong man. I cursed myself for being such a stupid impatient girl and I blamed him for robbing me of my youth and happiness. A trap is a trap regardless of its form and I felt my situation was sucking the air out of me as sure as the water in the pond would do. I thought of Laura and her sweet innocent face flashed in my mind along with the treasured images of her and Alice being held tight by Philip in the park that day. It snapped me back to reality and I realized that I didn't want to die. What I wanted was for someone to rescue me and to hold on to me tightly.

Philip arrived the next morning looking as dashing as ever with his riding coat and long boots. I wasn't accustomed to seeing him look so informal, but it suited him well. He greeted his way through the family and finally he and I came face to face. "I didn't know you were coming," I said softly enough to not be overheard.

"I knew that you were," Philip said quietly as he leaned in to kiss my cheek.

Maybe it was being away from home or maybe being surrounded by so much love and warmth amidst the Key family but as he said this my defenses dropped and any ice wall that I had managed to build around my heart to prevent this very feeling melted away. I knew immediately I had no chance of maintaining a standoffish relationship with him. He kissed and hugged Laura and swung her happily around in circles while she giggled and squealed. She loved him too, I could feel it. Dan was so detached and distant, and this man smiled and played and so openly showed affection, how could she resist? How could I?

We dined that afternoon in the outside garden at a table set for eighteen. It was one of the most amazing meals I had ever experienced. The food was beyond compare. The cook at Terra Rubra was certainly an expert. Bacon wrapped chicken breasts served with a creamy crab sauce, oysters on the half shell, sausages and sauerkraut, warm biscuits with fresh butter, several types of vegetable dishes, deviled eggs, apple turnovers and even ice cream for dessert, which made Laura's entire day. The adults were served coffee and of course, mint tea for everyone. The satisfying event took nearly two hours to complete and, in that time, I thoroughly enjoyed the family stories that were told and the laughs that were shared. Who knew that Francis Scott Key had grown little gardens in the shape of each child's name when they were born or that he almost became a minister? What a kind-hearted man he must have been. I wished I'd had the opportunity to meet him. Philip seemed to have inherited most of his best qualities and Alicia had certainly inherited the Key charm. I felt blessed to be sitting among them enjoying this beautiful day.

Gradually the table cleared. The children ran off to play. Others went to take naps or walk off the large meal. I stayed, and Philip stayed until we were the only two left. Inherently I knew that he wanted me to wait until the crowd was gone so that we could visit alone. From the very beginning, Philip and I had a way of communicating that required no speaking. It was as though our minds were linked and I cannot explain it fully, but we were connected in some indescribable way that one would have to experience to understand. It was a comfort to feel so in tune with another person. When we were free to speak, we both started to speak at the same time. We laughed and argued a moment over who should go first when he blurted out, "I'm in love with you Teresa." I was momentarily stunned. That wasn't the first sentence I'd imagined, but I was feeling it as well and I replied, "I'm in love with you too." We stared into each other's eyes trying to comprehend what the other had made known aloud.

"Well now that's a fine mess we've got then isn't it," he chuckled and sat back in his chair never taking his eyes from mine. If it had been anyone else, it may have felt awkward but there alone in the garden it was anything but. It was peaceful and sweet and such a relief to confess what I'd been holding onto for many months. It was also a relief to know that he shared my feelings. It wasn't imaginary or a figment of my imagination, it was real, he was real, and he was sitting in front of me telling me so.

The revelation didn't change the fact that I was married, and he was friends with my husband. "What do we do?" I asked. I knew that no answer was a good one. If we acted on our feelings, that would be wrong and dangerous. If we didn't, my heart would shatter into a million pieces. It was the first of many times that I considered that we'd have been better off keeping our feelings to ourselves. It wasn't as though either of us had done anything to attract the other, it just happened, somehow, and now it was out in the open between us.

"Meet me out by the carriage house early tomorrow before anyone else wakes up, before dawn. I have a place I want to show you." With that statement, he stood and offered his arm for me to walk with him to the house where we were back in open view.

The rest of the evening was a blur as I went through the motions of socializing and caring for Laura before putting her to bed for the night. I tucked her in tightly next to Alice in a small trundle bed on the second floor of the farmhouse and the girls held tightly to each other's hands as they drifted off to sleep.

My mind was preoccupied with so many conflicting thoughts that I worried I'd give myself a headache. On one hand, I was feeling guilty for wanting to meet him as requested but on the other, I was euphoric at the thought of spending time with him alone. I did not sleep a single wink and by 4:30 in the morning I gave in to the latter and decided to climb out of bed and find my shoes. I told myself all kinds of things while walking through the dewy grass to the carriage house. "Dan was doing the same thing. I wasn't being unfaithful. Nobody would know. I deserved a little happiness." All of which were true and yet poor excuses at the same time, but I had made a decision and I was going to see it through.

Philip was waiting for me with his horse, Lucifer, ready to go. He took my hand and lifted me up into the saddle, and with my back pressed tight against his chest, we set off. I didn't ask, and he didn't say, where we were going. A few minutes into our journey I could feel his hot breath on the side of my neck and I instinctively reached for his hand, laced my fingers through his, and pulled his left arm tight around my waist. Nothing else mattered at that moment, not Dan or my parents, or even Laura. We were in a world of our very own, and the sadness and pain that I'd been feeling for so long disappeared and I was finally happy, truly happy, even if it was complicated.

Lucifer trotted along the grassy bank of a mountain stream. The sun was beginning to rise, and the beauty of our surroundings took my breath away. Crystal clear water flowed over the rocky creek bed. Philip pointed out schools of long, thin, silverfish, swimming haphazardly between each of the miniature waterfalls, created by the water rushing over the rocks. We stopped at the bottom of a steep incline that blocked our ability to continue forward on horseback. Philip lowered me to the ground with his strong muscular arms and hopped down himself, and then tied Lucifer to a tree. "Are you up for an adventure?" He asked, flashing me a sly grin. Nothing could have kept me from his side at that moment. We walked a short way around the base of the rocks and came to a point where the hill began to ascend in a stair-like formation. "Here we go," he said, and we began climbing the stony staircase, hiking higher and higher until a plateau appeared, and he announced that we had reached our destination. "This is McAfee Falls, in all its glory," he said leading me toward the edge of a wondrous cascading waterfall that crashed into an inviting swimming hole below.

"Philip, it's astounding," I managed to say. "Do you bring all the ladies here?"

"No," he replied, "I've only brought one other person here, and that was a very long time ago. We sat at the flat top of the rocks just above the waterfall and I laid back in his arms and we kissed. It was a kiss that felt like a dream and it took me a few seconds after it ended to reopen my eyes and remember that I was awake. He was stroking my face and looking at me with the most intense and engaging smile on his face, and we said to each other over and over "I love you, I love you." It was as if time on earth was soon to expire and we had to fit this declaration in as many times as possible before our final breath. We kissed again and again, and he held me tight as I'd always wished. I could have died that morning and been the happiest girl in heaven.

We reluctantly returned to the house just as the rest of the family was beginning to rise. I took a seat in the kitchen and pretended to be the first one awake, as one by one the others wandered in looking for a morning cup of coffee. "Good morning!" I greeted each one, and a good morning it was.

Frankie and Elizabeth arrived at Terra Rubra later that balmy summer day with their children and Philip was bursting with pride as he introduced them to me. Frankie was Philip's older brother, and best friend and the bond between the two of them was obvious. Frankie had a gentle manner and reminded me of the descriptions

I'd heard of their father. Tall and handsome of course, he was a Key. Elizabeth was just as sweet. She made her way through the family members greeting and hugging. She was treated the same as any blood relative. I wouldn't have known she was by marriage from the warm interactions. This family was unreal to me, had they no faults? Frankie had a seat in the parlor to relax a bit and I had the thought to fetch him some of the mint tea. It seemed to be a popular beverage here and they'd traveled all morning.

I offered Frankie the glass of tea and noticed the look of bemusement when I handed him the glass. "Well aren't you most thoughtful," he declared. He patted the chair next to his and I took a seat. I wasn't sure if he knew who I was right away but as we talked he alluded to the antics in Washington and I realized that Philip had spoken of me for sure. "So, you are from New York and have been transplanted into Washington. How do you find it?"

I don't know why, but this struck me as absolutely hysterical and surprising myself even, I burst into laughter!

"Well… enough said. I completely understand," Frankie said laughing along with me. We talked at length about the joys of living outside of Washington. He had heard of my father as a composer and claimed to tolerate the opera on occasion when forced to do so by Elizabeth who enjoyed the theater very much. We talked about their home in Annapolis and he insisted that I visit as soon as possible. Frankie adored Philip, it was clear. He went on and on about the childhood they had shared in Washington and how he was so very proud of his brother following in their father's footsteps. Everyone in this family was so supportive of each other, not to mention kind and interesting. We conversed so easily and merrily that I found myself again, as always, enamored, with yet another member of the Key family.

CHAPTER 9

THE FORTUNE TELLER

Returning to Washington was depressing after experiencing the beautiful countryside and warmth of Terra Rubra. I busied myself as much as possible, but my mind was occupied by Philip. "What were we going to do? Was there anything we could do?" I tried reasoning with myself. It seemed like an impossible situation, but I had fallen in love with him and I was helpless against the power of my own thoughts. I hadn't seen him for a few weeks, he'd gone to Annapolis with Frankie and Elizabeth straight from Fredericktown and he promised to let me know as soon as he was back in Washington.

I was forlorn and irritable during those interim weeks. I cared little about attending the receptions I had once enjoyed. I only felt like sitting, sometimes lying down, and thinking. Thinking about everything that had transpired and what it all meant. Playing it over and over in my head. I couldn't understand how being in love could be making me so miserable. My emotions were scattered. In one moment, I pictured Philip and I living together happily ever after and in the next I convinced myself that he was probably just toying with me and had no intentions of pursuing me. I had heard the rumors of his flirtatious tendencies. I wrote letter after letter telling him all those things and then burning each one in the fireplace in my bedroom.

The only company I could tolerate was that of Dandy. He was comforting in his silence with an occasional exaggerated sigh that matched my mood as he took up his position at the foot of my bed. Laura seemed to be especially cranky as well, and I often left Bridget to deal with her because my patience was so frail. Dan had returned from New York and stayed only four days before going back to New York. He was trying to squeeze in a business trip with his father before the fall session of Congress began when life would be even more hectic. I hardly noticed his arrival or departure.

I halfheartedly attempted to keep up appearances and if I wasn't being my usual self only Mary noticed. We'd assumed our morning ritual of taking tea in the parlor now that she and Abe had returned from Illinois. Mary was going on and on about the boys and the troubles they gave her on the visit back home when I heard, "Teresa! Hello!" I had drifted from listening properly to staring blankly into space and now she was calling my name. "Where did you just go, Missy? You looked to be a hundred miles away. What is wrong with you?"

"I'm so sorry Mary, I was listening, I was just…thinking." I looked away feeling ashamed of my rudeness and Mary not being one to settle for vague answers said, "Well if you talk about it, you'll feel better." I remembered Alicia's unexpected warning regarding Mary, but this was my friend. Alicia must have misjudged her. Mary was one of the kindest friends I'd ever had. Sure, she was a bit different, but she was absolutely harmless. Still, I didn't share the real reason for my distraction and instead blamed missing Dan and feeling lonely for my gloomy mood. I hinted slightly that I questioned his loyalty to me but she didn't pick up on it and so I let it go.

"I know exactly what you need," said Mary suddenly. "A reading! It always makes me feel better when I'm down. Sometimes the promise of better things in the future is all you need to lift your spirits."

I knew Mary believed wholeheartedly in the spiritual realm and I hesitated to discourage her passion, but I wasn't as comfortable with the idea. "I don't know Mary, it's really not for me."

"But you've never been", she said rising to her feet. "All you have to do is sit there, it'll be my treat this time. I know an excellent clairvoyant named Diane over in Georgetown. If you don't like what you hear then you can just forget all about it. But you never know, you might become a believer." She pulled me up from the chaise and started decisively toward the parlor door and into the front foyer where she collected her shawl and waited for me to follow. Apparently, we were going, and we were going now.

We arrived at the doorstep of the fortune teller and I marveled at the tiny cottage tucked carefully away behind a large hedge, hiding the entrance from street view. I supposed clairvoyants knew you were coming and didn't need to be able to see to the street. The creaky wooden door had a sign saying "enter" and had the posted fee of fifty cents near the bottom right corner. Inside the tiny two-room shack, we found burning candles of all shapes and sizes as well as a round wooden table near the door with two seats across from each other. Strange objects and statues were scattered throughout the room every which way. The smell was odd, and I couldn't put my finger on what it was, but it was floral and pungent, and I was sure that's how we'd smell as well by the time this was finished. Diane emerged from the back room and immediately recognized Mary and came rushing to embrace her warmly. "Mary, my dear, dear Mary! I knew you were coming soon but I wasn't seeing when, so this is a surprise, and you've brought a friend. That's wonderful," she said hugging me too.

Such a warm greeting put me at ease a bit and I looked around the room as the two women chatted a minute more. I imagined we'd be sitting at the round table and I wondered which chair was to be for me when I heard, "Sit, sit." Diane finally nudged me into the chair closest to the door and sat directly across from me at the table. "Now my dear, this is your first reading, yes? It can tend to get a bit personal and so would you like Mary to step into the other room while we talk?"

Half because I wasn't sure I wanted to be alone in this strange situation and half because I didn't have much faith in the process, I declined the offer and said that Mary could stay. She began with a small prayer and then reached across the table and briefly examined and then squeezed each of my hands. "You are at a crossroads, my dear," she began. "You are on the verge of a major decision that will affect the lives of many people. The outcome hasn't been set in stone yet but by the last week in October, it will be. A decision will be made, and you will move forward with it. Life is going to be very interesting for you. You have one child, a girl yes?"

"Yes," I confirmed feeling more nervous than before. "Her name is Laura."

"And you are married of course. However, I can see that you will have two loves in this lifetime. I am not implying that anything is going to happen to your husband dear, it could be many years down the road, but I do believe you will love again. All you need to do in the meantime is care for your child and for yourself. I don't have a great feeling about the marriage now, it feels a bit, I don't know, empty. Your capacity to love is there, it's temporarily stifled but don't fret. Focus that love on Laura and on yourself. Be careful with your health as well, you are not fragile, but you are sensitive. Your circumstances will determine your physical health and so you must exercise daily. I see you walking through a garden or a park and it appears you have a lovely home where you can open the windows and let the fresh air in and you need that every day."

"Alright," I mumbled, not wanting her to think I wasn't listening.

"Shhhh," she scolded. "It's important to know that you are going to have an improvement in your energy soon. You will feel alive and vibrant but be cautious. You don't want to get carried away by that. You must keep your feet on the ground, you have someone who depends on you and you must consider them carefully. I don't know if you are from a well-known family, but I get that sense around you like you mingle in the lives of the rich and famous and that is good. I do not see money troubles for you and who wants that?! Not me!"

I noticed she peered out the corner of her eye at Mary, who was doing her best to appear not to be listening. "Be careful with your secrets as well, hold them close to your heart. Things can get very complicated when we are too loose in the tongue. I'm not saying you have anything to hide but if you are keeping something to yourself know that it's alright, we all do it. You also have wonderful friends around you," she continued, steering away from the path of the warning. "Treasure them because we all need friendship and I think that's important to your health also to choose wonderful friends who can support you. I do not see more children for you. I don't want you to be sad about that, it's for the best. One more thing, I want you to go home and write to your mother, she thinks of you often and you should invite her to visit soon."

She moved quickly into saying another brief prayer in conclusion and then it was over. As we stood Mary rushed forth gushing, "that was just wonderful, thank you so much, Diane!" She paid her the fifty cents and promised to be in again soon for her own reading. My head was spinning but I managed to say thank you and goodbye as we headed back out the door and into the bright sunshine.

"No more children," I whined as soon as we were on our way in the carriage. I wasn't sure if I believed it or not, but she had been exactly right on several things. Enough that I was now putting some degree of merit into her words as I went over them in my head. Mary was delighted that I wasn't completely disenchanted by the reading and that I seemed to be considering it seriously. I think she felt as though she had done her duty by introducing me to her beloved spiritual world.

"So, do you have secrets Teresa," she asked as we came upon my home? "Of course not, I am an open book," I said slyly as I climbed carefully from the carriage. I winked at her and darted up the front stairs before she could respond. I waved and the carriage continued on to deliver Mary home as well.

The following week, after our visit to Diane, Abe's run for U.S. Senate ended in defeat to a Mr. Stephen Douglas. Mary had to begin packing since they were returning to Illinois for a while. Mary was so unhappy with the outcome, but Abe seemed anxious to return to his home and to his law career. They promised to travel to Washington as often as possible to visit. I was losing my best friend and felt very much alone.

I figured that I could at least take the advice to write to my mother and so I spent an afternoon preparing a letter to send off in the morning post. I didn't completely forgive her for jumping to Dan's side against me, but I didn't say that. Even at twenty-one years old, I still craved her approval. Instead, I relayed how well we were and that I had ceased many of my social activities so as to repair my reputation. "I haven't been to a single ball since," I reported proudly, thinking she would be satisfied with that development. I was wrong.

She arrived a few days later, letter in hand and livid that I was "neglecting" my social responsibilities and acting like a petulant child. How did I expect to support Dan's political career and build relationships for my daughter's future if I was going to hide in the house as though I'd been guilty of the rumors? Did I think that pouting was going to repair my reputation? Was Dan aware of how I was behaving?

"Well mother, Dan doesn't know much about anything because he is never here and even when he is, he pays little attention to me," I replied, fighting back the tears threatening to come through any second.

"And you blame him for that," she raged on. He is providing for his family and working hard, and instead of appreciating that and doing your part, you complain about him. What have you become Teresa? You are a spoiled, unpleasant wife and that is why he pays no attention to you. The sooner you realize it the better. Now, when is the next noteworthy ball? You will be going, and I will be staying here to see that you do."

Defeated and ashamed I had replied bleakly, "a costume ball next month."

I decided on Little Red Riding Hood for the masquerade ball and Dan was supposed to go as the woodcutter. My mother had sewn the costumes herself made from carefully selected materials she'd purchased from New York and had sent to Washington. She was determined to send me to this ball looking my best on Dan's arm as his loyal wife. She had been staying at our home for weeks and when Dan finally returned from his trip, she informed him that she was staying on to re-train me into being a proper wife. They'd had a good laugh at my expense, but I found nothing funny about it whatsoever. I wanted this ball to be over so she would return home to New York and I could breathe again.

The night of the ball, Dan came down with a terrible stomachache and was unable to attend. I briefly hoped that meant I wouldn't have to go either, but my mother would not hear of it. She insisted that going alone was better than not going at all and sent me off in the carriage with instructions for the coachman, John Thompson to look after my safety. I was determined not to have a good time and that may have gone according to plan except that as I entered the grand hall to join the other guests a tall handsome English huntsman caught my eye. Crisp white trousers and a red velvet jacket and a smile that I knew anywhere made my heart beat faster.

Philip was here at the ball. I didn't know he'd returned from Annapolis and yet there he was. He escorted Alicia who was cleverly dressed in a costume meant to depict her fathers "Star-Spangled Banner." She looked exquisite in a floor-length, white, satin gown.

A red, white, and blue sash was draped over her shoulder bearing the words *E Pluribus Unum,* our nation's motto. A tiara with 13 shiny stars atop her head and an eagle broach made of gold, complimented the costume perfectly. She and Philip were the most wonderful sight. I controlled the urge to run to them from across the room and instead offered the proper greetings to each friend I passed by on my way. It took an eternity, but I finally made my way to them and practically breathless I found myself again whispering to Philp that I hadn't known he was coming. With a wry smile, he again answered, "I knew that you were."

What I had dreaded for weeks became one of the best and most memorable nights of my life. I shuddered to think that I almost hadn't gone. Although if I hadn't things may or may not have ended differently, who is to say? Dancing and merriment filled the hall and the drinks were flowing freely. After several hours, most guests were at least somewhat inebriated, and Philip and I finally took the opportunity to slip out the double doors that led to the patio unseen. As soon as we were alone, he pulled me in for a long sweet kiss. I had been waiting so long for this, it didn't seem real. I almost couldn't grasp for the first few minutes that he was here kissing me again. Kissing him was so nice, effortless and romantic. I knew it wasn't right, but it felt so right and when I was with him nothing else mattered to me.

"When did you come back? Why didn't you tell me," I asked looking up at him with a pouty lip as he held me tight standing in the cool autumn air? "I just got here yesterday," he replied "and Alicia told me that you were attending tonight, and I wanted to surprise you. Is that bad? Maybe you don't like surprises."

"No, it's not that, at all. I just missed you so much the last weeks and my unhappiness may have been easier to endure if I had known to look forward to seeing you here." I tried not to sound displeased, but he could tell that I was feeling very emotional. He kissed my forehead gently and said "I'm sorry sweetheart. I never meant to hurt you. No more surprises I promise."

"Can we please go somewhere else," I asked?

"Wherever you want," he said. We left through the back gate and walked around to the front of the mansion where the carriages were waiting. "Won't Alicia wonder where you've gone? Should you find her first?"

"I told her not to wait up for me," he winked. "She can take the carriage home when she's ready."

I wondered what exactly Alicia knew about her brother and me. Not that it mattered to me now, and I trusted Philip's judgment. If he chose to tell her our secret, then I knew that I could trust her too. "We'll take Mr. Key to the National Hotel John," I announced to the coachman, and we were soon on our way. It was the furthest point away I could think of within reason. Hidden away and alone inside the carriage we kissed again and again, and I allowed him to touch my body for the first time. He ran his hands down my bodice and up my thigh. He smelled so good. I could have breathed in the scent of his collar and neck all night and never be satisfied. His hands were magical on my body and I was filled with a kind of passion that makes a person do just about anything. We gazed at each other in disbelief. "This is crazy," we'd pause to say and then be right back to each other's lips a few seconds later. There was no getting around it now. We were having an affair. I was being unfaithful to my husband. A line was being crossed which could not be undone and for the moment neither of us wanted it undone. When the carriage stopped in front of the hotel, we collected ourselves and tried to keep a straight face.

"When will I see you next," I asked?

"Come to Alicia's reception on Monday morning," he said. "I will be there and by then I will try to figure something out for us. I want us to have as much time together as possible."

I hated for him to go and I wondered how he would get home since we were on the other side of town now. He didn't seem concerned and I was so giddy that I didn't think to ask him just then. He kissed me once more. "Two days," he stated. "We can make it for two more days, right?" I must have looked doubtful because he assured me that we could, and with that, he stepped out of the carriage and into the night. I smiled the entire ride home, breathing in his lingering scent. This is what happiness feels like I thought. This is what I have been dreaming of since the day I met Philip Key.

CHAPTER 10

AFFAIR IN MOTION

I wanted to look perfect when Monday morning arrived, and I was preparing to attend Alicia's morning reception. I fussed over my hair and changed clothes three times before finally settling on a blue wool dress with a white fur collar and cuffs. It was a chilly November day and I wanted to be warm in case I happened to find myself on a stroll out of doors. Laura didn't want me to leave and she and Dandy pouted on the floor of my bedroom near my feet while I was trying to dress. I became frustrated and ordered them out when I had nearly tripped over them several times. Laura began to cry, "I want you to stay with me, mommy." Pangs of guilt tore through me and I paused to pick her up and held her close. I breathed in the sweet scent of her for a moment and considered doing just that. "I love you so much," I assured her. "I won't be gone very long. I promise."

Alicia's reception was crowded as usual, but I had no problem spotting Philip immediately. I pretended to be uninterested in his presence as I greeted the hostess and her other guests. Alicia boasted the most delectable spreads of food and drink and always a violinist or cello player to provide background music. Her guests were some of the merriest and pleasant. I had a few squares of cheese and a glass of wine as I mingled amongst the crowd. I wasn't hungry in the least, but I didn't want to appear out of the ordinary. I found my way toward the formal dining room which was far less occupied than the parlor. Philip immediately appeared at my side. The sight of him sent tingles through my spine and my stomach flip-flopped as his fingers brushed against mine when he traded my empty glass for a full one. It was nothing short of thrilling to be near him again and I struggled to contain my emotions.

The way he was looking at me made it hard to breathe. I had missed him more over the last two days than I had ever missed anything in my life. Even though we couldn't touch, couldn't act on our true feelings here, I was content to be in his presence and was at peace with the moment. He'd made a clear point of slowly pressing his hand against my fingers when he'd replaced my glass and just that slight touch was enough to set fire to my desire to be closer to him.

What were we thinking I wondered? This was clearly a terrible idea to be this close to him in public, we'd caused scandal before even when we had been only friends. This was sure to draw unwanted attention. So why was I standing here hoping for another moment of "accidental" touch? He turned and walked toward the family area of his sister's home, a place where reception guests were not meant to go, and he motioned for me to follow. Once we were alone in the back hallway, he gathered me in his arms and stared directly into my eyes for a moment before we engaged in a most magical passionate kiss. At that moment, I would have done anything he wanted, anything to keep him kissing me. Even if he had done so in the parlor in a room full of people I don't know if I could have stopped him. I melted at his touch.

Just as we were pulling apart footsteps could be heard coming in our direction and we quickly looked around for an escape route.

There wasn't one and I had quickly started going through excuses in my head of what I was doing back here alone with him. I stood frozen in fear as he stepped in front of me partially blocking me from the view of whoever was approaching. The first dose of reality struck me just then as I instantly realized the ramifications of being caught together. My life would be ruined, Dan was so hot-tempered and unpredictable that I wondered what exactly he might do to Philip. Laura could be taken away from me; would Dan do that? I wasn't sure but terror suddenly gripped my insides. Just then I heard Alicia's startled voice. "Philip!" she'd exclaimed.

A second that felt like a minute of silence ensued and if she had realized I was there she made no indication of it. Instead, she turned around and retreated in the direction she had come. I breathed a sigh of relief as Philip turned to face me. "Go first, I'll follow soon after," he whispered as he nodded to the front of the house. He didn't seem worried and I tried to calm my shaking nerves as I obeyed and returned to the reception. I was too shaken to continue socializing, and so I decided to go. I didn't say goodbye, I wasn't sure exactly what had just happened with Alicia and my state of mind was not stable enough to face it at that moment. Philip would have to figure this out on his own I thought as I descended the front stairs and motioned for my driver to bring the carriage forward.

I was gone within seconds and when I was finally alone, I burst into tears. The tears were of both relief and guilt. I may have managed to escape this time but if I continued down this path my luck would surely run out at some point. The mental image of Laura being ripped crying and screaming from my arms terrorized my mind. I couldn't do this to her. I shouldn't do this to Dan. Mostly, I worried for Philip, the thought of anything happening to him because of me was almost too much to bear and I felt vomit rising in my throat. I knocked on the roof of the carriage for the driver to stop. We were several blocks from home and I wanted to walk the rest of the way. I needed the air and I needed time to pull myself together before returning home.

Dan arrived unusually early from work. The session had ended on time for once and he had come straight home. I was playing a game of checkers with Laura in the parlor when he arrived surprising us both. "Papa," she'd happily cried jumping into his arms. Dandy had been resting his head on my knee dozing and he too rose to join in the greeting. "My little family," Dan stated flatly. Laura hadn't noticed his unenthusiastic remark, but it was not lost on me. I supposed I probably deserved it, not that he knew that. I was a wicked wife and didn't deserve the adoration of a husband.

"Abe and Mary will be joining us for dinner," he said aloud as he was putting away his gloves and coat. "And Tad too," he said playfully tapping Laura on the end of her nose.

"Yay," she shouted, her little hands clapping excitedly. She turned and began for the stairs. I knew she was headed to the nursery to prepare for the arrival of her friend. Poor Tad was doomed to be having a tea party this evening. My heart smiled imagining them drinking the pretend tea upstairs while we were having the real thing downstairs. It was good for her to have other children to play with, she spent much of her time alone nowadays and Tad was such a sweet boy.

Mary and Abe are here in Washington?! What's the occasion," I inquired? Not that I needed a reason to be glad to see them, but they had been back in Illinois for weeks and Mary and I usually arranged these things and I hadn't heard from her.

"Bloody Kansas," he muttered. When I looked at him in confusion. He explained that the President asked him to arrange the meeting. The country was falling apart over the issue of slavery and there was talk of states threatening secession from the union altogether. James took it very personally and worried that his legacy would be as the divider of the nation. It wasn't looking good for him to be in the running for a second term.

Senator Stephen Douglas of Illinois was a thorn in the side of the President and the two were interlocked in a bitter dispute over the issue of admitting Kansas to the union as a free or slave state. James decided to enlist the help of the one man who had faced down Douglas already, although he'd lost, Abraham Lincoln.

At half past eight, I heard the whinny of horses and the wheels of a carriage crunch to a stop in front of the house and I excitedly rushed to the front door to greet my dear friend Mary and her family. Our home was aglow with warm candlelight and the servants were setting the finest china and silver for the occasion. The cool December air wafted inside as I opened the door to welcome our guests. Mary was as exuberant as ever and she pulled me into a tight embrace as soon as she entered. How I had missed her in the short time they'd been gone. She stood back and looked me up and down. "You look marvelous Teresa, happy and marvelous," she said with a wide grin.

Laura bounded down the stairs screeching "Taddy!" The two friends had missed each other as well, Laura making it quite clear by wrapping her small arms around Tad's not much bigger frame and squeezing him tight. She let go of him and turned to Mary with her chin proudly in the air showing off the necklace she wore especially for the evening. "You gave me this when I was a baby Aunt Mary, I'm big enough to wear it now!" Laura beamed with pride as Mary gushed over her and the beautiful gold and coral pendant that hung around her tiny neck.

"I remember like it was yesterday sweet girl," Mary replied scooping her up and hugging her tight. "We were at your grandmother's house in New York and you were such a beautiful little baby. Our initials are right here on the back you know," she said turning the necklace backward against her hand and admiring the inscription.

Laura reveled in the attention and flattery of one of her favorite people and Bridget had to practically peel her from Mary and lead her and Tad off to the nursery.

Abe removed his customary stovepipe hat and hung his belongings on the coat rack in the foyer. Dan came forward and greeted him with a hearty handshake and welcomed him back to Washington. "Thank you for coming Abraham. President Buchanan certainly thanks you as well. He should be arriving very shortly," Dan explained while leading Abraham to the parlor for a before dinner drink while Mary and I checked with the servants on preparations.

James and Harriet arrived moments later, and we all joined together in the dining room where proper introductions were made between the President and Mr. and Mrs. Lincoln. "Very honored to meet you, Mr. President," gushed Mary, "Isn't that right Mr. Lincoln?"

I giggled to myself at the way she referred to her own husband so formally, I couldn't imagine calling Dan, Mr. Sickles. We took our places at the long oval table so exquisitely set for six and Dan proposed a toast, "to new friendships." The crystal stemware clinked together as the guests repeated the toast and sipped the fine bubbly champagne filling their glasses. Mary and I talked with Harriet about the new place settings she selected for the White House and about the new gardens that she was planning for the grounds as soon as spring arrived. Then the men moved on to the topic of the evening and I inwardly cringed. Politics was so uninteresting to me but Mary and Harriet seemed engrossed in the conversation and so I sat silently and tried to follow.

"I understand you have returned to your law offices in Illinois Mr. Lincoln. I was sorry to see Mr. Douglas win the Senate seat last month," the President said to Abraham. "Douglas certainly has made it his mission to drag my name through the mud and I think you are the one living person who can relate to that. I followed your debates with him in the papers and I don't know how you showed as much grace as you managed. The man is a weasel. He's destroyed my presidency and it's no secret that I despise him, fellow Democrat or not." James folded his napkin and dabbed at his forehead beginning to shimmer with perspiration.

Not that James was faring well to begin with as President, I thought to myself. Dan fretted constantly for his friend over the difficulties that arose during the years he had been in office.

Mary spoke ill to me of Stephen Douglas for months while Abe fought ruthlessly with him for the Illinois Senate seat, and James had triumphed over Douglas after his own brutal campaign for the Democratic nomination in the 1856 Presidential election. I could only surmise that this dinner had something to do with the fact that James Buchanan and Abe Lincoln shared a distaste for Douglas.

James continued, "I asked Dan personally to arrange our meeting tonight. You and I, Mr. Lincoln, may be of opposing political parties, but we share a common opponent. I don't believe I will be given a second term in office and my wish is that *anyone but* Stephen Douglas takes my place if it comes to that. The next election isn't too far off, and it seems that you and Douglas are being considered as potential candidates. Those stirring debates during the campaign have sparked interest in the two of you nationwide, brilliant if I may say."

I could tell by the look in Abe's eyes that James had his full attention, but Mary was the first to respond, "Are you saying that you want to help my husband become the next President of the United States?"

"Precisely," replied James, "and with my support and Dan's help, I believe we can make that happen. I'd rather see the opposing party in power than to have this country run by a scoundrel of my own political affiliation."

Abraham looked from Mary to James and then to Dan, and replied, "where do we begin?" James nodded in satisfaction and Dan replied, "Welcome back to Washington Abe."

Harriet was feeling tired and after dinner returned home to rest. The male trio talked strategy long into the night. Dan was to get in touch with Democratic newspaper editors willing to publish a glowing autobiographical sketch on the Republican, Lincoln in upcoming editions, and encourage opposition support. Abe was to begin immediately on the narrative and have it ready for Dan by the time he and Mary boarded the train back to Illinois on Friday.

Dan was never one to miss an opportunity to make connections especially when he saw that it could benefit him personally. Being useful in any way to the next potential president could be of vast benefit. So, though he'd never taken interest in Lincoln's political aspirations before, suddenly, Abe was of immense interest to Dan.

Mary and I observed from our position in the armchairs near the fire, and Mary stated, "He will be President, I know it, and it's all thanks to our friendship with you and Dan! You and I are going to redecorate that drab house over there," she said happily pointing out the window in the direction of the White House. "New china, drapes, furnishings, you name it! Teresa and Mary rule Washington!" she declared in her most dignified voice. I pondered that for a moment and hoped that I hadn't just found myself in the middle of a dire predicament.

I thought of Alicia and Philip and the troubles Alicia had mentioned at Terra Rubra between their family and the Lincolns, but surely that had all been ironed out by now. I noted to myself to remember to ask her about it sometime. Besides, politics was for the men to worry about. Why should I concern myself in such matters?

I had resigned myself to stay away from Philip for a while if for nothing more than his own protection. Several times I thought I would catch a glimpse of him passing by or walking in the park and I determined that my mind must be playing tricks on me. For nearly a week, I had managed to evade him. I held my usual Tuesday reception in the second week of December. The holiday season was in full swing and the receptions were even more elegant and festive than usual. The temperature was unseasonably mild and that brought folks out as well.

Amid a conversation with Angelica Hoover, I gasped aloud, and my knees began to buckle beneath me when Philip appeared at the entryway of my home. He stood there, patting Dandy and looking as handsome as I constantly imagined him. My heart was fluttering too fast and my words were all running together trying to maintain small talk with Angelica. I watched as he poured himself a drink from the decanter on the bar and made his way around the room greeting and making his own small talk amongst my guests. He admired the Christmas decorations that had been carefully set in place just days before and I overheard his comment to his sister Alicia that I was a most tasteful designer. His words sent quivers through my body and I knew that I was back at his mercy and had little control over my decisions when it came to him. I knew that he wasn't leaving until the last guest had gone and we'd had a moment alone together. I was both helpless and eager at the same time, fighting to maintain my composure.

He pretended to prepare to depart as well when my last guest was leaving but as soon as Angelica was inside her carriage, he whipped his winter shawl back off and closed the door to the study where we now stood alone. He picked me up off my feet as I shrieked in surprise and he put his lips to mine. I gave in immediately as we came together once again like a hand in a glove.

"Why have you been avoiding me, darling," he frowned? "I thought maybe you had a change of heart, so I came here today to find out for myself once and for all. Even if it was bad news, I had to know, and to kiss you one last time."

"Oh Philip, it's not that at all," I explained on the verge of tears. "After the other week at your sister's house, I got scared. We almost got caught together. I don't understand what happened. Why did she just walk away? Does Alicia know about us?"

"She does," he confessed. "I told her some time ago that I was in love with you. She can be trusted, you don't need to worry about her. She adores you and she wants so badly for me to be happy. She would never tell a soul, I promise."

Well, at least it made sense now why she had not said anything upon discovering us in the back hall. She had seen me, I was sure, but her loyalty to her older brother was fierce. If he was sure that she could be trusted, then I had full faith in his judgment. I explained to him the recurring scene in my head of Laura being ripped away from me if we were discovered. I told him that I feared for his safety most of all. By the time I finished letting out all the feelings I'd been keeping in for weeks I was in full blown tears. He used his white handkerchief to dab my cheeks and he patiently waited for me to finish, never taking his eyes off me.

"I've got you, darling," he said pulling me close to his chest and hugging me so tight that the whoosh of his heartbeat was all I could hear. He looked back into my eyes, "I've only loved one other woman in my entire life the way I love you and if that means being at risk of bodily harm to have you, then I am prepared for that possibility. I let her go and it nearly destroyed me and I'm not making that mistake again unless you say you won't have me."

"Your wife?" I assumed he was talking about Ellen and I began to say that it wasn't his choice that she had died when he cut me off. "Not Ellen," he went on. "I loved her, she was a wonderful woman but not this way."

"It was when I was very young, she was even younger. Her name was Virginia and she had to move away. We were too young to make it work on our own and I have always regretted letting her leave. I thought she was the only one who could ever make me feel this way until I met you. I'd forgotten how good it felt to be completely and totally in love with another person. If it's the last thing I do, I want to feel this again, to experience it one more time with you."

I was speechless and could think of no way to respond. No one had ever said anything like that to me in my entire life. Never had I felt so loved, so adored, and so cherished. It didn't matter to me anymore that I was married or that I had a child just upstairs. My heart had just married his, here alone in the study, and the only thing left to do was to consummate the marriage and there in my home that day we did just that.

For the following week, not a few days went by that we didn't find some way to at least see each other, if not spend time alone together. I was no longer lonely or sad, but for this, I had traded my peace of mind. Life had adopted a whole new meaning, a new reason for looking forward to the mornings, all of which revolved around Philip and the next chance to spend time with him, balanced with the terror of being caught. We were in our own world and I can't recall anyone paying particular attention to our interactions and to be honest I just didn't care. Part of me imagined that one day Philip and I would take Laura and leave Washington forever, but that was a silly childish wish. He had four children at home still who needed their father and a career as the district attorney for Washington.

"Dan is a scoundrel," he would say. "How could he have earned the heart of a sweet woman like you, Teresa?"

"I thought you and he were friends," I half-jokingly asked. "Besides he didn't earn it, he stole it and I was too naïve to protest."

"Hmm," said Philip, thoughtfully stroking his soft, dark mustache. "We were friends for a while but the more he opened his mouth; the things he says about women; about you; he is definitely a scoundrel, let's just leave it at that. I want to take care of you. I want to make you happy. We will find a way, Teresa. To hell with Dan Sickles."

We began to meet daily and as we did the days seemed to slip by faster and faster. I lost track of what day it was and barely took notice that Christmas was less than a week away. All that mattered was finding my way to him and feeling his love and his body next to mine.

We developed an unsophisticated code of signs and signals that we could use to communicate with each other in public. We arranged to arrive at predetermined locations on the same day and time. He would come to my home whenever possible. His signal to me was his white handkerchief. To get my attention he would stroll about Lafayette Square Park in front of my home with it in hand, either pretending to be dabbing himself or simply casually swinging it in one hand while walking along. I found myself constantly at the front window hoping to see that he was there waiting for me. If it was safe for him to visit, I'd fling open the window of the extra bedroom as my signal back to him and he'd arrive shortly after.

Dan was still away from home consistently and so having time together was without difficulty. Philip came to my weekly reception and stayed until everyone had gone when we could lock ourselves in the study to be alone. We also met, uncoincidentally, at the receptions of many of our friend's homes. We would leave in the carriage together under the pretense of giving him a ride to our next destination and if anyone had noticed and found it unusual, not much was said, at least to us. Philip's friend, Albert had once commented to him that he had noticed a "certain conduct" and was concerned by his attentiveness to me. Philip was prepared with a defense of having paternal feelings toward me, being so much older, and that he was simply looking out for the welfare of his dear friend Dan's wife in his absence.

If Albert was unsatisfied with his answer, he made no comment. The coachman John and my lady's maid Bridget pretended not to notice our behavior and even if they did, an accusation against the lady of the house by a servant could surely lead to a lack of future employment not only in our home, but in our entire city. So, we continued meeting day after day while trying our best to be discreet in all possible ways. Our desire to be together far outweighed any fears of discovery. We had discussed the consequences of our actions so many times that the possible scenarios had become diluted in intensity in our minds over time. I confided in him about Dan hitting me and the countless times he pushed me against walls, his hand on my throat, threatening my life, during his angry outbursts. If Philip had felt any guilt about deceiving Dan, it had now turned to hatred and he fought to control the urge to rip Dan to shreds himself.

Philip was far too recognizable in the city to meet very often in public. The congressional cemetery was our clandestine location often times. Who would think to suspect us there, paying respect to congressmen who'd served before my husband? It was isolated and just large enough that we could disappear from view of the carriage. There was a lovely memorial garden with a stone bench that we would frequent. Sometimes for just a chat or for a quick embrace and sometimes for more, mostly depending on the chill of the air. As long as I was setting eyes on my love each day, I was satisfied with even a brief encounter.

CHAPTER 11

THE STRANGE HOUSE

Going to New York for the holidays was a time I was dreading. I'd be away from Philip for more than two weeks. Dan had been re-elected to Congress in November and he wanted to have some time in New York before the new session, which in translation, meant he'd be working. The only saving grace was that Mary, Abe and their boys joined us at our home in Bloomingdale, and I was thrilled to be spending Christmas with my dearest friend. We decorated and made cookies with the children and shopped in the city for the finest gifts' money could buy for under our Christmas Tree. We drank hot spiced wine around the fire in the evening and enjoyed our tea in the sunroom in the morning. Besides missing my love, I was decently happy during the weeks in New York. My parents invited all of us to Christmas dinner, and we joyfully recalled the time we initially met the Lincolns at this very home years before on their first visit to the city.

My mother was especially cheerful at Christmas dinner. The cook had prepared a bountiful feast and the blessing was said by my father who kindly mentioned by name each of the Lincoln children and of course Laura in his giving thanks. The ambiance and the food were wonderful, and it was lovely to be in the company of my dearest friend and my parents, who I realized that I had not seen much since our move to Washington. Gifts were exchanged and the children played happily on the floor with their new toys. Laura had been given a dollhouse by her grandparents and Mary, who had been in on the secret, had purchased some furnishings, including a miniature tea set to go inside. The boys took turns trying to swing a ball into a cup attached to it by a string and were having no luck with the toy at all, except that no one had yet been injured.

The men retired to the parlor to enjoy a cigar and Mary and I kept watch on the children while mother supervised the cleanup in the dining room and kitchen. Mary and I chatted quietly about our usual list of topics. When I mentioned being anxious to return to Washington, Mary had been shocked.

"What on earth for," she replied. "I thought you would be in all your glory here. Your family is here, Dan is here for once, though I will say he seems to enjoy the company of your parents more than their daughter, but that's not my business. At least you are together for Christmas. There is no one worth missing back in the capital."

My eyes grew wide and I fought the sudden urge to cry. Mary looked at me completely puzzled and I knew that she wasn't going to be satisfied with anything but the truth, so I said, "Let's go for a stroll and have some fresh air."

As we walked along the city sidewalk bundled tightly against the sting of the cold air, I thought about how to choose my words. "Mary, I need you to swear to complete secrecy. You are my dearest friend and I want so badly to share something with you, but you must promise that you will tell no one, ever until the day that you die."

"Of course, I promise you, Teresa," she began. "You are my dearest friend also and I would never share your secrets with another. You and Laura are like family to me."

I reminded her of the troubles we often discussed regarding Dan and me, only this time I told her about the London news article and my theory of what transpired there. I expanded on my longtime suspicions about his infidelity and his angry outbursts and his physical abuse. I confided my misery over the emptiness of our married life.

"I've found someone else," I finally blurted out. Before she could respond I continued. "You know him, quite well actually, and we have been seeing each other for a few months and I know what you are going to say Mary, and I know it's wrong, but he makes me so very happy."

"Alright, I'm not your judge first off, that's his job, not mine," she said pointing up to the direction of the sky. "Now, who are we talking about? Philip Key?"

Now it was my turn to be astonished. "How did you know that Mary? What made you say that!"

"I've known you long enough now Teresa. I've seen the way he's looked at you and to tell you the truth I'm not a bit surprised. He is a handsome one not to mention funny, attentive, and unattached. Even when the three of us were spending time together I could tell that you felt a certain way about him. I wasn't thinking that you were acting on it, but I certainly noticed the spark."

I was stunned. I wasn't expecting the conversation to turn this way, but it had certainly made things a bit easier to explain. "Are you mad at me Mary? Am I a terrible person? Do you think I am a fool?"

"Honestly Teresa," she began. "Yes, I do think you are a fool, but only because I care about you, and Philip as well, and if anything were to happen, I can't stomach the thought of what might become of my two good friends. It's very dangerous territory and I just hope that you have not taken that lightly. Now, do I think you are a bad person? Of course not. You are one of the sweetest, most kind women I know, and everyone deserves a little happiness in their life. I hate seeing you so unhappy all the time."

I threw my arms around her neck and kissed both of her cheeks. "Oh Mary, thank you for understanding. You don't know what a terrible burden this has been to bear alone."

I had been so afraid to tell anyone, and now that I had, I felt lighter than I had in a very long time. As we walked back that night to my parent's home, I felt that my feet barely touched the ground.

Dan made a point of introducing Abraham to as many of his New York associates as possible during the week. They were making all the connections that Abe would need if he really was being considered as a presidential candidate. They visited the governor's mansion for breakfast and met Dan's powerful Tammany Hall associates for drinks at night. We toured Dan's Central Park and attended several dinner parties and before I knew it the second week had passed, and it was finally time to go back to Washington. Abraham was most grateful to Dan for taking him under his wing, so to speak, and I was happy to spend Christmas with Mary. I couldn't have been more excited for the return to Washington, though I worked hard to mask my enthusiasm.

Monday morning, I was up before the sun and counting the minutes until I could dress and depart for Alicia's reception. I knew that he would be there, waiting for me. Philip didn't disappoint and as I arrived, I could see that only one guest had arrived earlier than me and that was of course Philip. He wrapped me in his arms and smothered my neck and forehead with sweet kisses, right in front of his sister. She smiled and was not surprised in the least, so I hoped that when she excused herself that it wasn't because she found our behavior repulsive. Before another guest could arrive, he slipped a carefully wrapped tiny box out of his coat pocket and placed it in my hand.

"What is this Philip?" I said in surprise. "I haven't gotten you anything." I quickly unwrapped the small box and there inside was a brass key and nothing else." I was confused.

"I've got someplace to show you," he said as he led me out the servant's entrance and into the back alley, then through the streets of Washington.

"Where are we going," I asked, winded from both cold and anticipation.

"I've found us a safe place where we can be together, alone. It's walking distance to your home, but no one will recognize us here," he explained as he pulled me toward the corner of K and Fifteenth Street. It wasn't long before we came to an unremarkable neighborhood several blocks away from my home and the President's house. It was a place I'd never been, and I probably would have been frightened to go if it weren't for Philip beside me holding my hand. I wasn't understanding what was happening yet.

We stopped at a doorway and Philip looked to me to produce the brass key that apparently unlocked the door to this mysterious home. The heavy door creaked and gave way. The air was cold and stale inside and I wondered if this was the home of a friend of his or possibly even a dead person. There were hardly any furnishings and it was in need of a good wash. He took my hand and turned the key from the inside now locking us in as he pulled me in close. He kissed me then, more passionately than ever and I turned to mush in his arms. I was his alone, at his mercy, and there was nothing that would have stopped me from being with him at that moment. We kissed and stumbled our way to the stairs, and he carried me up to the second-floor landing. I barely noticed the broken banister and dusty floorboards. What I focused on was Philip, the look in his eyes was so intense. I followed him down the hall and into one of the rooms. There was nothing but a bed and at that moment that was all I wanted to see anyways. Before we reached the doorway, he was already pulling loose his tie from his collar. When we crossed the threshold, I finally grasped that we were totally and completely alone for the first time. One of the best experiences of my life was about to happen.

We made it to the bed that was covered with nothing but a plain sheet and one measly pillow but at that moment it didn't matter. I would have made love to him on the bare floor. He sat and pulled me down on top of him. I straddled his lap as he took my lips with his and I sighed with the pleasure of feeling him so close. We kissed until I could no longer contain the exhilaration of feeling him growing hard underneath me. I moaned in anticipation as he shifted me from his lap to the bed and began to undo the buttons of my dress. It sent shivers down my body feeling his hands running along my skin and I was breathless as he untied my corset. He removed his own shirt and unbuttoned his pants while kneeling over me and I could do nothing but stare at his beautiful body. Finally, the moment arrived that his naked body was touching mine and I felt that I was floating in the clouds. His lips on my neck, his tongue on my skin, his hands on my breasts. I arched my back in pleasure and waited for the moment that I would feel him entering me. It wasn't our first time, but it was the first time that we were completely free to do as we wished. Not having the stress of someone possibly approaching any minute to discover us made all the difference. We removed every stitch of clothing from each other including my wedding band which he tossed to the floor. We were able to take our time, fully enjoying each other's body for the first time with no rush. With Philip kissing and nibbling every inch of me I was beyond euphoric and there was nothing else in the world at that moment but him, and this strange little house where we were making love.

His slow and steady movements lulled me into a trance, and I became overly aware of every movement, every breath, and every heartbeat. The sensations were overwhelming. I was feeling his touch, his kiss, him thrusting into me, and his immense love all at the same time and I never wanted to be away from this man, ever again. When it was still, I returned from my daze and he was kissing my forehead, my hair, my face and I was hearing "I love you, I love you." And I loved him too. More than I had ever loved anything before.

"I'm going to save you from him, Teresa," he whispered beside me. "I'll find a way, I will not allow him to continue to mistreat you. He is a crook, an unscrupulous, despicable excuse for a man. He may have his connections, but I am a lawyer too, and I will find you a way out if you want that. I can take care of you, and Laura, you deserve so much better than him."

"Yes, please," I whispered back, and he held me tightly.

We exited the little house on the K Street side in broad daylight and I wondered how he planned to keep this a secret but after what we had just experienced it barely mattered to me. I felt so content. For the first time in a very long time, my body and soul had everything I'd ever desired. We took our time walking back to Alicia's where my carriage was still waiting and as I departed, I was already hungry for the next time I could see him and feel his touch.

Nearly every day through January and into February we met at our house. I often wore a shawl or a hood to be sure I wasn't recognized coming or going, but it didn't seem as if anyone was paying attention anyway.

On my second visit to the strange house, Philip had a surprise ready for me. He met me at the door and covered my eyes with his hands and led me the rest of the way in. When he removed them, I was delighted to see that he had really cleaned the place up. There still wasn't any more furniture on the first floor than before, but he had been busy. The railing was repaired and the floors swept and he'd even had firewood delivered. "There is more to see up there," he pointed towards the stairs.

I was sure that there was, and I hoped that included him and me in a moment. I followed him up to the same room where we'd made love before and it melted my heart to see that he'd brought proper bedding including several plush pillows, a bedside table with candles already aglow, and even a curtain to place over the window for privacy. The was a fire smoldering in the hearth and the room was warm and cozy.

"This is all very sweet of you," I said tenderly. He was behind me and wrapped his arms around my waist. We had both been aching for a repeat of the prior happenings in this space and now the mood had been set with his thoughtful preparations. I soaked up his scent and his voice and the feel of his touch. I wanted to remember every second of my time with Philip. I couldn't get enough of him. Never had I been so loved, so wanted and so adored.

CHAPTER 12

THE BETRAYAL

A Wednesday in February, the twenty-third, of 1859, to be exact was the last day of bliss before I first knew something was terribly wrong. It was like any day and my spirits were high as they had been for nearly two months. I had seen Philip every day and we'd made love dozens of times at our secret house on Fifteenth Street.

Philip wanted me to attend the reception of Senator Douglas's wife with him that morning. This was an unusual and questionable call for me to make. Senator Douglas was the man our President, and friend, James' had sworn as his enemy. The one Dan was working tirelessly to discredit. The same Senator Douglas who'd claimed victory over Abraham in the campaign where Abe had made those detrimental comments against Philip's Uncle Roger and upset Alicia so very much. Dan would disapprove of my visiting their home for sure. It would be disloyal to Mary and Abe. James and Harriet would be appalled and yet for reasons I couldn't explain I wanted to go. I wanted Philip and Alicia to know that my loyalties were changing, and so even though I was responsible for Laura that morning on my own, the nursemaid Bridget had gone to see her family, I agreed to let him make the arrangements. I could not take Laura along of course. Children were not typically invited guests to these events and even if she were able to come, she was old enough to remember names and faces and could possibly share with Dan where we'd spent our morning.

Philip arranged for her to visit the home of the Hoovers for a few hours. I was thankful for the way he cared for her welfare as a father figure. He wanted only the best for her and I both. It warmed my heart that he'd given it thought and felt she would be happy and cared for playing with Jonah and Angelica's children. He arrived in the square that morning, white handkerchief in hand and several moments later we started off together with Laura between us holding our hands and skipping merrily along.

I was a bit nervous about being questioned by the Hoovers and so when we reached the corner, he and Laura continued on to the Hoover's while I started on my way toward the Douglas home. It was cold and I could see my breath as I walked along Pennsylvania Avenue. Had I made the wrong decision in agreeing to this. My desire to be with Philip overwhelmed my sense of reason and I told myself that we were being careful, everything was fine. I wasn't sure if this was true, but it's what I told myself most days.

We stayed only twenty minutes at the reception, Philip introduced me and if anyone found it odd that I was in attendance, they hid it well. We had a bite to eat and made small talk with Mrs. Douglas. Without notice, we departed separately to meet back up at the strange house. He entered through the front door and then came to greet me at the back. It was cold in there that day and we didn't have much time before we had to fetch Laura from the Hoover's. We made love in our clothes on the first story, never even making it to the upstairs bedroom. It wasn't lost on me the paradox of being dressed in my finest black silks with an elegant velvet shawl and my fancy feather bonnet while laying with Philip on his own grey shawl on the bare floor of this unfurnished and shabby house in the dead of winter. But inside I was warm and full and maybe it was a strange house, but it was ours, and stranger things were about to happen.

I didn't know about the encounter since I'd exited through the back door and was on my way to Laura. When Philip had locked up the house and left through the front door, he'd been approached by a man bundled in a winter hood pulled so tightly that his face was unrecognizable. He'd mumbled a few indiscernible words to Philip before handing him a small yellow envelope and hurrying away. Philip, not wanting to draw attention had tucked the letter into his pocket and saved it for later.

The day had gone quickly after that. Laura had spent a wonderful afternoon with her playmates and chattered on incessantly about it as we walked the short distance home. Looking back, I later wished that I had taken more pleasure in her childish joy and perhaps listened with a bit more interest and held her a bit closer. It was to be the last time that my sweet girl would enjoy the innocence of a carefree day with her playmates worrying about nothing more than dolls and teapots.

Octavia Ridgeley was becoming more of a regular presence in our home. She was a tolerable enough girl, only eighteen years old, and adored fiercely by Laura. She and her widowed mother were neighbors of ours, only a block away, but Octavia seemed to prefer spending her time with us when possible. Dan had known the late Mr. Ridgeley and he'd encouraged a gloomy Octavia to call on us as often as she'd like when her father died. It was meant to cheer the girl and provide me company. This only irritated me, however, because it often meant Philip could not come into my home even if Dan was away. Regardless, she was helpful with Laura and I had grown accustomed to having her around. Though only a few years older than her, I never felt that we were contemporaries, but more like an older and younger sister. She was waiting when we arrived home and Laura squealed with delight when she saw Octavia in the front window looking out for us. Dandy was with her and by the time we climbed the front stairs they greeted us together at the front door.

"Hello Octavia," we greeted her in unison. Dandy wagged and pranced around our feet waiting for his greeting as well and Laura hugged him tightly around the neck. We all laughed as he licked her cold pink nose seeming to try to warm her up.

"Mr. Sickles asked my mother to have me come this evening.," began Octavia. "He said you were going to the theater and that Bridget wouldn't be home until morning. He asked for me to watch over Laura," she explained.

"Yes," I said, suddenly remembering our evening plans. "Did Mr. Sickles say when he planned to arrive home? I want to be sure I am ready when he gets here."

"I'm sorry, I don't know. But if you like I can help you get ready or I can at least keep this little one busy," she said playfully sticking her tongue out at Laura who grabbed her hand and began dragging her toward the library where I'm sure she was headed for her favorite book of fairy tales that Octavia enthusiastically read to her often.

We had four seats for the evening show, but I could not remember for the life of me who was accompanying us. I had been focused on little else besides Philip for the last few months and if Dan had mentioned it at all, I wasn't paying attention. At half-past seven a carriage arrived and through the upstairs window, I saw our friend Henry hop out and climb the stairs to the front door. That was a pleasant surprise, I enjoyed Henry immensely. He traveled the world frequently and had the most amusing stories to share when he was in the city visiting, which wasn't often. I wondered who he escorted for the evening as I made my way down to the front hall. He was dressed finely as usual with his customary top hat which he removed to bow in greeting as I reached the landing.

"Henry, it's wonderful to see you! When did you arrive in Washington," I asked as I donned my winter shawl, hat, and warmest gloves? We chatted as we made our way to the carriage. He mentioned that he'd come from France and visiting the royal Bonaparte family with whom I knew he was well acquainted. I looked forward to hearing more about them as the evening progressed. The door to the carriage was opened as we approached, and my astonishment was impossible to hide when appearing inside were Mary and Philip!

I had expected to see any number of young ladies we knew, as well as Dan inside and I couldn't have been more surprised to find the two people I cherished most sitting across from each other on the red velvet seats of the fine carriage that sat in front of my home. Thoughts were mounting rapidly in my mind as I tried to piece the scenario together that must have led to this astounding moment.

"Good evening Madam," stated Philip with a wink as I climbed into the seat beside him. Mary and I reached across and squeezed each other's hands and squealed a little in the excitement to be seeing each other and spending the evening together. Many questions raced through my mind at once. I had shared with her about Philip, I wondered how she felt now being witness to us together in person. Did he know that she knew? Had she made any indication that he could have recognized? Why was he here? Why was she? I didn't know whether to be nervous or overjoyed. Was this an enormous stroke of luck or was something sinister happening here that I was not yet privy to?

As casually as possible I stated, "Isn't this a most remarkable convoy of friends off to the theater? It's so good to see each of you. How has this little ensemble formed and where is my husband?" On the brief ten minute ride to the show, I discovered that Abe and Mary were to join us originally. When Mary had gone earlier to the White House to fetch her husband for the evening, she'd found Abe, Dan, Philip, James, Henry and others engrossed in a flurry of investigation sorting through boxes of documents for some bit of information that had become imperative. Dan and Abe apparently considered themselves vital to the investigation and were not willing to cease working to attend the theater. Dan had suggested that Philip escort me for the evening and in turn, Philip had asked Henry to accompany him to complete the quartet. How fortunate, I thought to myself.

Philip had been feigning friendship with Dan for months, mostly in an effort to remain available to me, but also to keep a close eye on Dan. He didn't bother to pretend to like Abraham however, both men were well aware of the division between their families. It was difficult for him to contain himself and at times I worried he would act recklessly and explode on Dan and Abraham right there in the White House. But his determination to remain amicable until he figured out a way to free me from Dan helped him stay the course. He was determined to find proof against Dan that could send him to jail, where Philip believed he belonged, or at least enough reason for me to have our marriage annulled.

I was sure that Philip had feigned indifference to Dan's request while silently being overjoyed to do the favor asked of him. Henry was always willing to oblige when it came to a social function and so it was decided. Lucky for me it was a marvelous arrangement and what had begun as an evening obligated to the theater with Dan had quickly become a night of immense enjoyment with my best friend and my love.

I sat between Mary and Philip during the performance and hardly noticed the show because at every opportunity Philip was accidentally making physical contact with me somehow which sent jolts of desire through my body. He touched my arm, my hand, my back as I was seated, and each touch made me more and more desperate for the next one. This man was a compulsion to me. The urge to be touching him, seeing him and talking with him was an impulse over which I felt no control. I loved him more than I'd loved anyone or anything in my life and the passion between us was something both foreign but welcomed and could not be contained within the confines of reason.

The next day I asked to be driven to the market and Philip was waiting outside in the square where I pretended to be surprised to see him and offered for him to join me. Once alone in the carriage, Philip produced a small yellow envelope with no markings and removed its contents. He seemed different, jumpy even.

"This was given to me yesterday afternoon, by someone I did not know when we parted ways outside the house," He continued on, "It's a message that could mean almost anything, but see here." He handed me the page and one line of nonsensical letters were scrawled across the top.

It appeared to be written in some kind of code and Philip had deciphered it just below. "It is Known," I read quickly. "What is known, Philip? What does this mean? Do you know this handwriting?"

"No, I don't recognize it at all, and I can only guess that the meaning is referring to our relationship but it's quite vague," he replied hesitantly. "I wanted to show you last night at the theater, but we didn't have a single moment alone. What do you feel it means?"

"How should I know Philip," I replied. A sudden cold chill had run through my body and even as I tried to assure myself internally, a terrible feeling had overtaken me, and I was visibly shaking. "What things are you involved in that you would want unknown? Besides us of course. Is there something else this could be about?"

The carriage slowed as we arrived at the market. I jumped down without waiting for assistance from the footman and made my way quickly into the morning crowd of sellers and buyers. Philip followed close behind.

"Teresa, stop. We have to discuss this," he pleaded. I hadn't completely absorbed the brief contents and I needed a moment before I could have this conversation. Too harshly I turned and told him to leave me alone to think, and I could see in his eyes that this hurt him deeply. It also had attracted the attention of several passersby. I attempted to regain my composure and proceeded to the butcher stall to make my intended purchase while Philip followed behind.

"Let's just behave as if everything is completely normal for now," he said quietly behind me as the butcher handed me the brown paper package containing my cuts. "We don't even know if this is about us, so we shouldn't attract unnecessary attention until we learn more."

He was right of course. It was probably our own paranoia working against us and the worst thing would be to act guilty before being proven so. We agreed to go on with our day as planned and to discuss it again later at the Willard's Hotel where we were both invited to a late night gathering. Hopefully, by then the mysterious author would offer more information or disappear completely never to be heard from again. That may have been too much to hope for, but what other choice did we have? Philip got back in the carriage with me and we were nearing my home when he signaled for the coachman to stop and he readied himself to exit before we came into plain view in Lafayette Square

"It will be alright darling," whispered Philip. "Your eyes, they look bad," he said as he took one last look back at me before stepping down to the street. "Give me a smile. I will see you this evening. I love you." I did my best to smile and he was gone.

That evening after our usual Thursday dinner party had concluded, Octavia and I excused ourselves to freshen up for the rest of the night's festivities at the Willard Hotel. There'd been a sick feeling in my stomach all day and I hoped no one had noticed that I hadn't taken a single bite at dinner. I changed my clothing for the third time today and at this point, I couldn't even remember now what I'd worn first this morning. The anxiety was blocking out fluent thoughts and I was edgy and unfocused. I felt as though I were sitting on pins all day waiting for a dramatic revelation to take place any moment, but it hadn't happened. Perhaps I should have a brandy I thought as I put the finishing touches on my lips and rubbed stain into my pale cheeks. My nerves were going to have to be calmed if I sought to display ordinary behavior and if I were going to have any chance of speaking to Philip tonight, I needed to act ordinary. I asked Bridget to pour me a drink and when she returned,

I finished it in one swallow. Octavia giggled and commented on my early start to the evening and I laughed it off as naturally as possible. Laughing was not coming easily at the moment.

The carriage held only four and so Octavia, I, and two of our dinner guests left first for the Willard and Dan was to follow after with his friend Samuel Butterworth who was in town visiting from New York. We made our way into the party and the brandy had helped calm my nervousness enough that I found myself carrying on a normal conversation with other guests, although I couldn't say what we talked about. Philip made his way to my side as soon as he saw us enter the foyer and we exchanged a glance that made me think there was nothing to report. If this was good or bad news, I didn't know. He was uneasy as well, I could feel it. His normal high spirits were halved and the pained look on his face did nothing to alleviate my own fears. We needed a moment alone and it was only going to be a short time before the carriage returned with Dan. In haste, we took a chance that we wouldn't normally take and excused ourselves from the group to have a private conversation. Philip pulled me aside into a coatroom just outside the sitting area and he spoke quickly. "We should leave now. You and I should go. I have a very bad feeling Teresa and if it *is* known, then that puts you in danger and I won't have it. We can go to Frankie's in Annapolis until we figure out what to do next."

I struggled to keep up with his words and I almost would have thought he was kidding but for the way he held so tightly to my wrists that it began to hurt a little. "Philip, that's crazy, we can't just leave here with nothing. What about Laura, your children, my things? Did you receive another letter today?"

"No, nothing; it's just a bad feeling," he said flatly, letting my arms drop to my sides. We looked at each other deeply and I knew that he could feel what I felt, there was no need for any more words. We had always been connected mentally, capable of sensing each other more than any other form of communication. No need for wasted breath now. There was no proof that there was anything to even fret about. Running off was a bit rash until we knew more about this mysterious letter, nothing else had yet happened and there was a good chance we were panicking over nothing at all.

We ducked out of the little room not a moment too soon because Dan and Samuel had just arrived out front. I went forward to greet them and Philip headed in the opposite direction.

Unbeknownst to us at the time, another letter had in fact been delivered that evening. But this time it hadn't been delivered to Philip but to Dan. A young lad had brought it just as Dan and Samuel were stepping into the carriage to join us at the Willard's. The darkness would have made it hard to read and in the hurry to rejoin us he stuffed the message into his jacket pocket unopened.

Well after midnight we returned home completely exhausted, and while Octavia and I went immediately upstairs to prepare for bed, Dan had gone to his study to relax before joining me.

He must have remembered the letter as he removed his jacket and placed it over the back of the desk chair in his usual manner. I imagine him with a whiskey in one hand, as he opened a small yellow envelope and read the words, addressed to him, that would change many lives and the course of history forever.

Washington, February 24th, 1859

Hon. Daniel Sickles

Dear Sir with deep regret I enclose to your address the few lines but an indispensable duty compels me so to do seeing that you are greatly imposed upon. There is a fellow I may say for he is not a gentleman by any means by the of Phillip Barton Key & I believe the district attorney who rents a house of a negro man by the name of Jno. A. Gray situated on 15th Street btw'n K&L streets for no other purpose than to meet your wife Mrs.

Sickles. he hangs a string out of the window as a signal to her that he is in and leaves the door unfastened and she walks in and sir I do assure you he has as much the use of your wife as you have. With these few hints I leave the rest for you to imagine.

Most Respfly

Your friend R.P.G.

CHAPTER 13

FORCED CONFESSIONS

Waking on Friday morning I reached across my empty bed to find that I had spent the night alone. The bedsheets were cold and undisturbed on his side. Though that was not entirely uncommon, the sick feeling in the pit of my stomach returned instantly. It seemed colder than usual and I noticed that the fire had not been tended overnight. The day was dark and outside my window, I could hear the tapping sound of tiny ice pellets hitting the window. I reluctantly left the warmth of my covers and wrapping myself in the gray wool blanket from the bed I walked to the window to have a closer look at the weather outside. The entire neighborhood was coated lightly with a thin layer of ice and a light drizzle was falling on top of it. The window was frosted at the edges and using my fingernail, I scraped at the ice crystals forming inside the glass and watched as they fell like dust particles floating in a beam of sunlight. But there was no sun today, nothing but gray winter skies and freezing rain falling down. I called for Bridget wanting her to help me find something warm to wear. There was no response and in fact, it seemed strangely quiet overall. I padded to the door of my bedroom and could hear voices coming from the kitchen a floor below. Descending the stairs, I could make out the voice of my daughter with her high pitch and childish inflection while the other voices were low and mumbled. Laura, Octavia, and Bridget were seated at the small kitchen table having an egg and toast breakfast. It was an odd setting; one I'd never seen before. My daughter and young guest were sitting solemnly at the table used by the help and Bridget was eating with them as opposed to serving their meal. A tray of food had not been brought to my room, my fire was out, and my daughter was dining at the servant's table.

"What is the meaning of this Bridget?" Too harshly, surprising even myself, I shouted at the trio and found them staring back at me in just as much shock. I rattled off my list of displeasures as I paced the doorway of the kitchen still wrapped in my blanket. I felt as though I were dreaming and expected to wake at any moment warm in my bed upstairs.

"I'm sorry Ma'am," said Bridget quietly. "Mr. Sickles was in a way when he left the house today. He ordered that I was not to tend to you in any way, only to Laura. He also said I wasn't to allow you to be alone with Laura. He says he has someone watching the house."

When she said this, Laura began to cry, and I went to her and picked her up into my arms. She wrapped her arms and legs around me and nuzzled her little face into my neck holding tightly. I fought back my own tears as I looked in disbelief from Bridget to Octavia waiting for one of them to explain.

Octavia spoke, "I stayed this morning because Laura was so upset. Mr. Sickles was so angry, and she was frightened by it. She didn't want me to leave so we came in here as a distraction and tried to get her to have a bit of breakfast."

"I see." I stared frigidly at Bridget. "I can take care of my own child. Why wasn't she brought to me? You are still my lady's maid;

you owe me that respect at least. Did Dan say why he was so irate by any chance?"

"He said nothing more, just that the house would be watched," she explained with her voice breaking on the verge of tears. "Only because it was so cold in your bedroom ma'am. I didn't want her to catch a chill in there. The kitchen was already warm with the fire. I would never keep her from you of course. We were just waiting for you to wake."

I softened a bit toward her when I saw how frightened she herself was. Dan could be extremely intimidating, and I felt for her and Octavia both that they had witnessed that side of him. I wasn't entirely sure what had happened while I slept but I had a good idea that my world was about to crumble around me and that it had already begun. I sat with Laura at the servant's table encouraging her to finish her breakfast. I wanted her to know that I was not angry with her, or Bridget, or Octavia. I refused Bridget's offer for my own breakfast, though I appreciated the fact that she was willing to go against Dan's wishes in some small way to show me some kindness. Laura refused to eat another bite and so I carried her back upstairs to her nursery where the fire could be tended to and we stayed together for the morning hours there. Thankfully, Octavia did most of the talking and playing while I was lost in my own mind going over and over possible scenarios. I was anxious for Dan to come home but also scared to death of the inevitable confrontation. It felt strange being anxious to receive bad news, but I was desperate to know what was happening.

I needed to warn Philip that something was amiss. I hoped and prayed that he wasn't already being hunted down by Dan. For all I knew they could be at the dueling grounds in Bladensburg right this minute. I shuddered at the thought and forced it out of my mind. I conjured up possible alternate justifications that could explain why Dan was so angry with me. Perhaps he'd heard more rumors. I could possibly talk my way out of that. If there was no proof, then surely, he would have to calm down at some point and accept my word.

We'd been through that before. What could possibly have happened between midnight and 8 a.m. to cause this chaos? Perhaps it had nothing to do with Philip at all. Maybe this was just another of Dan's outbursts of jealousy and rage that I'd grown accustomed to over the years. In my heart of hearts, I knew that this was different and ominous but trying to convince myself otherwise was all I could do to get through the hours without falling apart completely.

Philip and I hadn't made any plans for the day yet. We usually figured it out once we'd arrived at the morning receptions or he would simply hop into my carriage just beyond the square and out of sight. Then we would have discussed if it were possible to meet at our rented house for an afternoon tryst. I wondered if me not showing up was enough of a disruption to our daily routine that he would realize that something was very wrong. Perhaps he'd go to Frankie's alone until I could get word to him that we were in the clear. I hoped but doubted it very much. If he thought it possible that I was in any peril, he'd never leave me alone to fend for myself.

I searched endlessly in the park across the street from the window, half expecting to see Philip trying to signal me, but the day passed and there was no trace of him. We'd not discussed a sign for danger. Waving a white cloth or string was our signal and opening the window showed that it was safe to proceed. Even if I saw him signaling, what could I do? If the house was, in fact, being watched, then I wouldn't want to signal him to come forward to the front door. If I didn't answer the signal would he come to the door anyways due to worry? Perhaps if I were to place a red cloth in the window, he'd see it and read into it to mean danger. I silently scolded myself for not having anticipated the need for a different kind of signal. I decided red would be too conspicuous and I didn't want to attract further attention and so I did nothing.

I lay awake next to Laura in her bed that evening for hours staring at the ceiling and waiting to hear the front door open and Dan's footsteps on the stairs. I must have dozed off eventually and I was awoken feeling Dan's hands shaking me gently awake. "Come to bed darling," he'd said and in a sleepy daze, I followed him to the bedroom where we'd climbed into bed together and gone to sleep as though the entire day had been a bad dream just as I'd earlier wished.

Dan was gone again before I woke, but this time a fire remained in our bedroom hearth and the warmth was comforting both physically and emotionally. For an hour or more I didn't dare budge for fear that I was stepping into some sort of trap meant to toy with me. I thought over the events of the previous day and felt completely baffled and confused. What had happened, or not happened that had changed the situation so drastically between morning and night? Finally, Bridget entered carrying a tray with tea and an assortment of pastries and placed it at the foot of my bed. I sat up and eyed her suspiciously waiting for her to say something. "I don't know, I really don't," was her only sympathetic comment. I wondered if Dan had specifically ordered her to feed me again or if she had inferred it on her own by seeing us asleep together in the morning. My thoughts were so disorganized that I could only nod in response.

Laura appeared noiselessly in my room and joined me on our bed. She laid her head in my lap and I smoothed the hair back from her forehead and kissed her tiny fingers. She smiled up at me and said, "I love you, momma." I wrapped her tightly in my arms and told her that I loved her also. We stayed that way for a few moments before she ran off to wake Octavia who had stayed again last night at Laura's request.

It was another cold day and snow covered the world outside our home. Being a Saturday, fewer folks than usual were passing through Lafayette Square, but this was Washington and the city never closed. Men in long overcoats and tall boots made their way steadily past our front steps on the way to the president's house. Laura enjoyed watching the trail of footprints fill in and become hidden by the newly fallen snow. Octavia had captured her imagination telling her that it was "magic." She clapped excitedly each time the footprints disappeared. The innocence of childhood was certainly appealing. I wondered if I had been so gullible and easily entertained as a small child. I made a mental note to ask my mother what I'd been like as a five-year-old girl.

While watching the magic show, Laura suddenly noticed Philip standing across the park talking with another man, and she squealed in delight, pointing and yelling his name as though he could hear her through the thick, wavy glass of the closed window. Dandy began barking enthusiastically at the commotion. My heart fell into my stomach and for a moment I thought I might get sick. I looked too and sure enough, he was there looking alive and well and for a moment I was overcome with happiness that my fears of the previous day had been unfounded. Philip was just fine. Laura began for the door and I stopped her and said, "now, now Mr. Key is busy working. We mustn't bother him." Looking disappointed but accepting my explanation, she returned to her post at the window, watching the snow.

I hurried upstairs to my bedroom window where I could see clearly into the square. Philip was talking with a man we both knew named Daniel. It seemed a casual conversation and after they bid each other farewell, I saw Philip turn in the direction of my home and my impulse was to hide. I stepped away from the glass quickly so that he would not see me looking at him. He stared a few moments as I peeked around the edge of the window frame and watched him walk off in the direction of Pennsylvania Avenue. Had he learned something speaking to Daniel or was he reading my thoughts from across the street saying "go, go, please just go." I breathed a sigh of relief as he walked away. Until I had spoken to Dan and figured out exactly what was happening, I wanted Philip nowhere near my home. Still unsettled from the day before, I worried that our house continued to be watched and I didn't want Philip so much as mentioned by any kind of spy reporting back to Dan.

Octavia and I had just sat down for dinner when Dan finally arrived back home. He walked toward us at the dining room table and fear gripped my heart as I could see immediately the wild look in his eyes and the stiffness in his manner. He sat across the table from me, never saying a word and not blinking. His icy stare was directed toward me. I swallowed hard trying to stay calm. The tension in the room was indescribable and no longer being able to stand it, I jumped up from the table and ran up the stairs two at a time to our bedroom and closed the door behind me. I leaned against the door hyperventilating and feeling like an animal trapped in a cage with no way to escape. I went to my bed and threw myself down covering my head with a pillow and wishing to suffocate and die quickly before he could make his way into the room.

He was only moments behind, and I felt the pillow being ripped from my hands leaving me exposed and staring into the angriest face I had ever seen in my life. He threw something at me, and I flinched before I could see that it was only a piece of paper. It was floating through the air in slow motion to the bed and when it finally fell beside me, he demanded, "Read it. Read it out loud Teresa."

He was practically spitting the words at me and suddenly I was very afraid for my life. With shaking hands, I picked up the letter and through blinding tears I attempted to read, "dear sir with deep regret…." I read through the entire letter and could barely breathe and only whispered when I came to the name "Philip Barton Key."

"Say it again Teresa, say his damned name," he shouted. I attempted again between sobs and he began screaming at me, "louder, say it louder. You had him in my bed right under my nose and now you can't even say his name? You will say it and you will say it a thousand times if I tell you to do so."

I collapsed then, sinking from the bed to the floor and wrapped my arms around my knees, attempting to hide my face in my arms. He yanked the back of my hair pulling my neck backward so that he could see my face. "Take off your ring. You are no longer my wife," he fumed. "Take It Off!"

He was becoming more irate by the moment and I dared not defy him now but as I removed the ring from my finger I begged, "please, please don't do this. I'm sorry Dan. I am so very sorry."

He laughed a maniacal sort of laugh that chilled me to the bone. "Oh, now she's sorry," he roared. "Were you sorry when you were taking off your clothes for him? Were you sorry when you invited him into my home while I was working to provide for my ungrateful wife? Were you sorry each time you entered the threshold of 383 Fifteenth Street? That's right darling, I know all about it. I've been to your dilapidated little shit shack where you were an indecent woman and he was a dishonorable man. I've talked to everyone in the neighborhood and they have been watching all your comings and goings. Did you know that Teresa? You and Mr. Key were the talk of the town over that way. You almost got away with it too. Last night before I returned home, I learned a bit of information that led me to believe that it was possible they were mistaken on the identity of Philip's whore. I almost felt bad for having investigated you. I was so relieved. Except then today," he paused, "today that tip was found to be an error on the part of a witness. It was, in fact, you all along darling, beyond a shadow of a doubt. It's funny though, they all knew who he was, but none could identify you by name. Do you know why Teresa?" He paused for a quick breath before continuing on. "Because you are nobody. You are nothing. An insignificant speck of dirt, and an unfaithful whore."

My eyes were fixed on the flame of the one candle that glowed on the desk of our bedroom as his words sunk in and cut deep. I had no defense, he knew everything. I didn't know how it was possible, but he had all his information correct and I could do nothing at this point to save myself or Philip. "What are you going to do," I asked quietly?

"It's what you are going to do Teresa," he replied. "You will write a full confession. You will answer any, and all questions asked of you. You will implicate Philip Key as the scoundrel who disgraced and destroyed this family. You are going to lure Key to your little shit shack and I am going to destroy him in front of your very eyes. If you choose not to cooperate then you will be taken immediately from this house and delivered to the asylum where you will stay for the rest of your miserable life. Do I make myself clear?"

He was not one to bluff and I had no doubt that between being a congressman and a personal friend of the President that he could easily follow through on his threat. He was cruel enough for sure, but would he take from his own daughter a mother that she loved and needed? It was not a gamble I was willing to make and so I nodded in agreement and hung my head in defeat knowing I was at his mercy and that I truly was an insignificant speck.

He prepared the writing desk in our bedroom and ordered me to sit there, pen in hand. "I'm going to ask you questions and you are going to answer each of them aloud and then you will write your responses as well, which will serve as your signed confession. Do you understand?" he asked in a most menacing growl. "Have you gone to the house on Fifteenth Street with Mr. Key? How many times?" Dan paced behind me and I stated that I had been there and that I didn't know how many times. "Write it down," he roared at me. I wrote with shaky fingers and cringed hearing him say Philip's name. "Who does the house belong to and when did you begin using it?" I tried to answer aloud, and he cut me off screaming, "just write it there and shut up."

It seemed he'd changed his mind on how this was going to work, and he was growing more unstable by the minute. I wrote my answers quickly as he began throwing questions at me faster than I could answer them. Some were reasonable inquiries and others were bizarre curiosities that must have been troubling his mind for whatever reason. He wanted to know when we'd been there last, and the details of that last Wednesday were much of the focus of his questioning. How did we arrange this meeting? Who arrived first? Where was Laura on this day? Did we have anything to eat or drink there? Was it warm in the house? Did he undress me or did I undress myself? What had I been wearing on this day? Which doors did I use?

When it seemed he'd exhausted his questioning regarding Wednesday's encounter, he started on a new line of questions. Had Philip been in our home without his knowledge? Had intimacies occurred? Where? Had Philip ridden in Dan's carriage? Had he drunk his brandy? Sat in his place at the table? The list went on and most things I managed to answer in writing, but he was firing questions so fast that I'm sure I must have missed a few. "You will add that I repeatedly requested that Mr. Key not be permitted in my home," he stated blankly. This wasn't actually true, but in any case, I saw no reason to argue the small point given the overall content. I wrote it as he asked and signed my name at the bottom. As I signed, he stipulated that I was to sign my maiden name as he no longer recognized me as Teresa Sickles.

He snatched the paper from the desk and began to read it over. His eyes flashed across the page left to right and looking ever more troubled he declared," you'll say I forced you to write it. You'll say that I threatened your life, won't you? You need to add more. I will tell you what you are going to write." He slammed the page back down on the desk in front of me, making me jump.

I listened and copied his words onto the page:

> *This is a true statement, written by myself, without any inducement held out by Mr. Sickles of forgiveness or reward, and without any menace from him. This I have written with my bedroom door open, and my maid and child in the adjoining room, at half past eight o'clock in the evening. Miss Ridgeley is in the house within call.*
>
> *Teresa Bagioli*
> *LaFayette Square, Washington D.C., Feb. 26, 1859.*

His erratic behavior was frightening enough to me, but I winced as he began yelling for Bridget and Octavia. I imagined how scared they must have been coming into our bedroom in what was obviously a hostile situation. He commanded them to sit and both girls sat together on the small sofa at the foot of the bed directly across from me at the writing desk. I tried to give them a reassuring look, but it was unconvincing even to me and both girls remained stone-faced and terrified.

"I've called you in here because as you may have overheard, Miss Bagioli has been a wretched wife and has carried on with Philip Key for quite some time now. She has served as a terrible example for you Octavia and I apologize for introducing you to her. I will need you both to sign as witnesses that she has not been coerced and has written this confession without physical force. You both were close enough to hear if she was being harmed and you will agree that she has not."

"Now sign," he demanded, thrusting the paper at the terrified girls who both shakily signed their names. He stopped and added as an afterthought, "Bridget, when is the last time that you saw Mr. Key here in this house?"

Nervously Bridget squeezed her hands together as she answered, "I believe it was the evening dinner party two weeks ago when Mr. Pendleton and his wife Alicia were guests. Mr. Key was here with his sister and brother in law if I remember correctly sir."

Dan seemed to ponder this for a moment before he turned back to me and demanded that I add yet another piece to the confession. He wanted me to explain and justify why Philip Key had been invited and was allowed into his home on that occasion. Of all the things to fret about, I supposed he didn't want to be known as a hypocrite and so I wrote it down just the same.

He excused the girls to prepare for bed and they were clearly relieved to be able to leave the room. I, however, was a prisoner there for several more hours. I watched as he paced the floor in front of our fireplace talking to himself and occasionally stopping to unleash some of his fury on me. He buried his face in his hands at times and was so distraught that I worried he'd snap and lunge for me, wrapping his fingers around my neck and squeezing until I was no longer alive.

Finally, near midnight, Laura, having been so disturbed by the events of the evening, had a nightmare and woke up screaming in the nursery. I rose to go to her and Dan immediately blocked my way and shoved me to the floor. You'll go to the guest room with Octavia now; you can sleep on the floor like a dog. I didn't want Laura to see me in this state or to have her witness his cruelty, and so while he went to comfort her, I crept quietly into the guest bedroom and sitting on the floor with my head resting on the seat of a chair, I cried myself to sleep.

CHAPTER 14

REVENGE

I woke the next morning on the Sabbath with swollen eyes and an aching back from sleeping against the chair in Octavia's room. My body was sore, but my mind was consumed by just one thought. I had to find a way to warn Philip and urge him to leave town. If he couldn't be found, then Dan could not force me to lure him into a trap. Who could help me? Bridget and Octavia were on the edge of a nervous breakdown as it was. They would be of no use. Could I slip out of the house without being seen? If I wrote a note and managed to hand it off to someone passing by with a bit of money for an incentive, could I count on it being delivered to Philip or would they turn the corner, toss the letter, and pocket the money, or worse yet, bring it to Dan.

Octavia was not in the room and I did not hear anyone else about. I stood cautiously using the window sill for support. The day was noticeably brighter, and the sunlight caused my eyes to squint as I peered through the glass and straightened out my back. The morning sun had melted away the snow of the day before and water dripped from the melting icicles that clung stubbornly to the branches and rooftops. There was no frost on the window, and I wondered if it would be a rare mild day at the end of February. Though momentarily distracted, my focus returned instantly as I caught a glimpse of a familiar brown overcoat moving across the grass. "NO, NO, NO," I uttered breathlessly. I froze as I recognized the figure walking across the square toward my house. It was Philip. He was carrying a white handkerchief and looking as handsome as ever. My heart pounded and my mind raced as I tried to decide what to do. I almost opened the window to yell to him but that would draw too much attention and Dan would see him for sure. I got the impression that he didn't realize the magnitude of the current situation and this worried me even more. He didn't know that he was in danger. He was parading in front of my house as though it was any ordinary day and Dan could be watching him right now from a downstairs window. Thinking quickly, I decided the most helpful thing I could do would be to go downstairs immediately and draw Dan away from the front of the house before he could spot Philip outside.

I headed toward the top of the stairs and seeing Dandy lying lazily across the top step, a quick thought flashed through my mind and I had an idea. I raced back into the bedroom to the writing desk and tore a piece of paper from the tablet I'd been forced to use the night before. What to say? What to say? I was beginning to write "Frankie's", but I feared that if discovered it could give away his safe haven, so instead in large letters I simply wrote, "GO." I returned to the top of the stairs and wrapped the strip of paper around Dandy's collar several times and whispered quietly in his ear, "do you want to go outside boy?" He perked up immediately and followed me down the stairs. I put my ear to the closed library door for a second but heard nothing, creeping to the front door as quietly as possible, I unlatched the lock and cracked the door open a bit at a time. When there was enough space for Dandy to fit through, I stepped aside and let him bolt through the opening, closing the door behind him.

My eyes darted left and right. I could feel the hairs standing up on the back of my neck. My breath caught in my throat and my chest heaved with panic. Nearly frozen with fear at the thought of being discovered, I backed away from the door slowly and tiptoed up the stairs and into the guest bedroom. I breathed a sigh of relief when all was quiet, and I moved quickly to the window to see if my plan had worked. Dandy knew Philip well and I was counting on the dog to detect him in the square and run to greet him. I hoped that Philip would notice the paper around Dandy's collar and would collect my message. It appeared that things were going as planned. I saw Dandy racing toward the park where he jumped and frolicked with Philip who was swatting his white handkerchief at him playfully. I couldn't see well enough to know if the paper was still wrapped around the collar, but I prayed that he'd seen and grabbed it.

Octavia and Laura were having breakfast in the dining room when I joined them. They looked tired and worn and I could only imagine how I appeared to them. A moment later, the front door burst open and in came Bridget with Dandy by her side.

"Look who I've found roaming free," she exclaimed. "How on earth did he get out of this house? It's a good thing I was on my way back from the morning service. He saw me before I saw him. Poor thing couldn't get back into the house."

"I don't know Bridget," Octavia spoke for all of us and looking perplexed stated, "Laura and I have been here having breakfast and Teresa has just now come down from upstairs."

I averted my eyes and let Octavia make the explanations while I petted the dog and quickly felt around his collar to find the paper, but it was gone. There was no way to know if the paper had made it into Philip's hands or if it had fallen to the ground, lost and useless, but at least there was a chance.

Just then the door to the library swung open into the foyer, and a disheveled looking Dan emerged, and without a word, he rubbed his eyes and as though gradually remembering the reality into which he'd woken, he turned on his heels and with a loud sob, he disappeared up the stairs. It was a dreadful thing to hear a grown man cry and the four of us in the dining room burst into tears as well.

What had I done? This was far worse than I'd ever imagined in my darkest dreams. I had destroyed everything, and the lives of so many people were going to be affected by my transgressions. Had I really believed that we would never be caught? What was going to happen to Philip? If he were harmed, I couldn't stand it, the guilt would be unbearable. What was going to happen to me? Would I end up locked in the asylum never seeing my daughter grow up? Was Dan going to kill me himself in a fit of rage? This was a complete catastrophe and it was all my fault.

I nearly jumped out of my skin when there was a loud knock at the front door. Bridget answered the door and George Woolridge, Dan's clerk and friend hobbled in. George used crutches to walk, he'd been crippled as a child, but his mind was as sharp as a blade. He announced that he'd been summoned by Dan, and Bridget showed him to the library and went to let Dan know that his guest had arrived. They could be heard in the library soon after. Dan was sobbing loudly, and George's calm steady voice could be faintly detected trying to console his friend. Dan would occasionally withdraw to the upstairs bedroom and return to the library when he'd pulled himself together slightly. During one of his episodes his friend Sam Butterworth had arrived and without invitation bounded up the stairs drawn by the sound of Dan's groans coming from the upper floor.

Laura was becoming more and more distraught as the tension in the house escalated and it finally dawned on me to have her taken to a calmer place where she wasn't being exposed to this horrific scene. "Octavia, will you take Laura to see your mother," I half asked, half ordered. "She can take her favorite toys along; Bridget will help you carry your belongings." Laura looked at me with wide eyes and began to wail. "Please don't cry my sweet girl," my heart was shattering into a thousand pieces hearing her pain. I hugged her tightly. "Octavia will take you to see Mrs. Ridgeley and all of the dogs, remember how many dogs she has at her house? They would love a visit from you I'm sure." She stopped her wailing at this recollection. Plagued now with hiccups she followed Octavia and Bridget up the back stairs and to the nursery to prepare for her visit. I caught the sobs in my throat watching her walking away and I forced the thought from my mind that it could be the last time I'd see her. I resolved that I would not allow that to happen, I would do anything asked of me to stay with my daughter.

When they'd gone, I crept up the stairs and into the guest bedroom where I sat catatonic on Octavia's unmade bed and stared blankly out the window into LaFayette Square where I'd seen Philip earlier this morning. Perhaps he'd read my message and had immediately gone home to gather his things and leave for Annapolis. Perhaps he was halfway there already and when tempers cooled, he could return to Washington to address the situation at hand.

Downstairs in the library, the men were speaking loudly, occasionally interrupted by Dan's moans of grief. Suddenly it fell silent and a shiver went up my spine. I looked again through the window and there, in the far distance, I saw Philip coming down Pennsylvania Avenue in our direction. They'd seen him as well, I knew it. All hell broke loose downstairs, the voices became frantic and I heard doors opening and closing and someone was coming quickly up the stairs and I held my breath thinking for sure that Dan was coming for me. Instead, he passed my door and entered our bedroom and I heard rummaging and items being tossed around as though he was looking for something. Clearly, he'd found what he wanted because just as quickly he was back downstairs and out the front door. I leaped to the window and could see Sam turning the corner of the avenue headed directly for Philip. He was alone, not with Dan and I was very confused. What was happening here? I watched carefully as Sam approached Philip at the corner of Madison Avenue across the street from the President's house. They appeared to be chatting casually and I got the distinct impression that Sam was stalling him there. "No Philip, don't fall for it," I thought aloud. Dread filled my body as my eyes scanned the entire square for any sign of Dan. As I feared, I spotted him marching purposefully down Madison Avenue directly across the square from our home. He was headed straight for the corner where Sam was stalling Philip.

I opened the window to scream out for Philip to run but my voice was unwilling to oblige. I was frozen in terror as the scene played out. I couldn't move. I couldn't breathe. I could only stare helplessly across the park watching the man I had married confront the man that I loved a block away from our home. I heard Dan shouting and Philip spun around to see him coming straight for him. A second later a gunshot rang out and screams from every direction pierced the air as people nearby ran in all directions not knowing where the shot had come from. Philip lunged at Dan and they wrestled in the street both struggling to stay on their feet. Dan pulled away for a moment and swung around to face Philip again gun in hand, pointing it directly at him. Philip began backing away and I heard part of what he yelled out, "murder." That was the last word I heard Philip say. Another shot rang out and I watched as Philip's body jolted and he stumbled sideways leaning for a second on the closest tree before crumpling to the ground. Dan came within three feet of his fallen body, said something that I was unable to hear and fired again into his chest. Philip lay lifeless on the sidewalk as one last time Dan held the gun to Philip's head. I cringed and squeezed my eyes shut, but no shot was fired. Perhaps he could see that he was dead already and so he stepped away and lowered the gun. I fell to my knees, silent tears streaming down the sides of my face and I repeated over and over, "no, no, no, no, no." I pounded the hardwood floor until my fists bled. I screamed the word no at the top of my lungs. I, myself crumpled on the floor like Philip had just done in the street and the devastation tore through me in waves of excruciating pain.

I must have blacked out or fainted because when I came to, I was still lying on the floor of the guest bedroom and there was an audible buzz of conversation and activity coming up from the floor under me. I listened trying to make sense of anything I could hear but it was distant and muffled. Suddenly, the door flung open and standing in the doorway looking like a madman, appeared Dan. I scurried backward away from him sure that he was here to shoot me next. He said one thing only, "I've killed him." And leaving the door open and the stench of gunpowder in the air he left me there and returned to the foyer where two police officers waited to take him to the Washington jail.

The rest of the day was a blur, and anyone I interacted with spoke to me harshly and looked at me with disgust. I certainly wouldn't be sleeping that evening, I thought. I wrote to my mother and father. I wrote to Mary asking her to come and see me, I was desperate to know if she hated me for the crisis I'd caused. I hoped that she was still willing to be my friend. I was going to need every friendship I could salvage especially since the newspapers were sure to already be tearing me to shreds. I was probably the most detested woman in all of Washington.

No one had sympathy for an adulteress who betrayed her husband, specifically one who was so well provided for and seemed to possess all of life's luxuries. Dan would have the sympathy of almost everyone we knew, and they'd turn a cold shoulder to me. Those who didn't hate me would pity me and I liked that feeling even less. "The poor girl taken advantage of by the evil Philip Key. How dumb and fragile she must have been to be so easily manipulated."

Nothing could be further from the truth. We'd fallen in love. I encouraged the relationship as much as he did. I was not stupid, and he was not evil. We had found ourselves in a complicated situation with neither one of us being sure how to best handle it. Our love for each other drove our offenses, not a desire to be cruel or to hurt anyone. Eventually, we would have been together, I had no doubt about that, he'd have found a way. But now he was gone, he'd been stolen from me right in front of my eyes and any chance I'd devised for happiness died with him.

If I were going to maintain my place in the life of my daughter, I was going to have to immediately pacify Dan's hatred for me and appeal to his fatherly emotions, if he had any. Though I despised him with every fiber of my being, my daughter was all I had left, and I would not let her go. A Reverend Haley had called at the door several times asking to speak with me. I had turned him down repeatedly but still, he returned, and I finally decided that perhaps I did need spiritual guidance as well as advice.

From his cell, Dan had ordered that no one was allowed into his home without permission with the exception of the clergy, and of course Bridget, Laura and me. He appointed his friend Henry to stand watch and to screen any visitor wishing to see me. I asked Henry to send the reverend in if he returned and within the hour, he was knocking at the door of the guest room where I had secluded myself. I'd not met him before, but he had a kind face and I believed right away that he was there with good intentions. First, he held my hands and said a prayer over me asking the Lord to forgive me of my sins. I nearly cried over the realization that maybe it was possible to be forgiven. This man had come with no judgment and I clung to his arrival as if he were the last person on earth.

I wept as I relayed the events of the last year or so that had led us to this place and he nodded with understanding and compassion as I spoke. I explained to him that Laura was my only child and my main concern was that we remained together. He agreed that the bond between mother and child was God's most precious bond and he was willing to speak to Dan on my behalf. I assumed that he meant he'd visit Dan in the morning but to my surprise, he meant to go there straight away. He asked if there was anything I'd like him to take to Dan. I hadn't had time to ponder this opportunity and short of sending Laura to him, which was absurd, I couldn't think of what else he valued in this house.

Suddenly the thought crossed my mind that perhaps he'd enjoy seeing Dandy. I was sure he was most frightened and uncomfortable in the jailhouse. I'd heard terrible rumors of the place being crowded with as many rats as prisoners and deplorable conditions. I truly felt for him though my anger at him for taking Philip's life took precedence. I asked the reverend if he minded taking Dandy there as a companion and he was more than happy to oblige my request. Perhaps he welcomed the company to travel at this late hour, so I leashed Dandy and sent him away with Reverend Haley.

The idea to send Dandy along had been a very good one. Dan had been comforted by a familiar presence and in sympathy for the dog, not the man, the jailer had moved him into his own cell which provided much more tolerable conditions. The reverend conveyed back to me that Dan was most grateful for this small improvement in his conditions and he asked if he might keep Dandy with him. I, of course, consented to the arrangement and he returned again to the jail to tell Dan. The good reverend was inspired and sensed an opportunity for reconciliation. He told Dan of my expression of remorse and asked Dan if he had anything he'd like to tell me in return. He'd produced a brass key from his pocket and told the reverend to see that I got it. I recognized it immediately as the key that Philip had presented to me that unlocked our strange little house. Had he stolen it from his dead body? I felt ill just considering it. Dan was cruel. He couldn't help himself. He never missed an opportunity to inflict pain.

Seeing the key deepened my anger and by sheer willpower, I managed to smile and thanked the reverend for his efforts and asked him to excuse me until the following morning. Henry was snoozing on the sofa in the parlor when I showed Reverend Haley to the door. I leaned against the wall and pondered how very quiet this house was without its residents. Laura and Bridget were staying at Octavia's mothers' home overnight. Dan would have Dandy of course, and then the coachman would be delivering the reverend home.

I wandered absentmindedly into the library. Seeing a dish of coins on the desk, I realized that I currently had no money whatsoever. I wondered if Dan had a stash in his desk somewhere that I could locate and use as provisions for the time being. His desk was cluttered, and the room had obviously been left in a hurry this morning. Chairs were carelessly askew, and half-empty glasses of brandy or whiskey littered the room. Atop the miscellaneous paperwork on the desk, I spotted a newspaper with a certain ad circled with several rings and it caught my eye. The date on the paper was Saturday, February 26, 1859, yesterday. The unsigned ad read:

"R.P.G., who recently addressed a letter to a gentleman in this city, will confer a great favor upon the gentleman to whom the letter was addressed by granting him an early immediate confidential interview."

R.P.G.? Why was that familiar? I remembered suddenly; that was how the devastating letter Dan had thrown at me the night before had been signed. I gasped putting together that Dan himself had placed this ad. He had no idea who R.P.G. was. I hadn't thought of that yet myself. I was astounded. The letter had been anonymous. He had tried to find its author by placing a classified ad. Who would do such a thing? Who hated me so much? Had the author answered his ad? I searched the pile of papers under the newsprint looking for a response but there was nothing.

I refocused on the original task of searching for money in the desk. I opened and closed drawers, searched the file folders, and looked under the desk itself to see if anything was attached to the underside. I saw nothing of note except I noticed that one of the file drawers appeared to be deeper than what I'd observed when searching it. I reopened the drawer and removed all the contents. The bottom of the drawer appeared normal at first but on closer examination, there was a small cutout along the back edge just large enough to place a finger under and lift. When I did so the bottom easily rose and opened to expose a secret compartment that was hidden under the contents of the original drawer. Inside was exactly what I'd hoped, money. There was also a timepiece that I'd never seen before and an old cigar box. Curious, I lifted the lid of the cigar box and peeked inside. It appeared to be a stack of old letters. There was something familiar about the handwriting though I couldn't place it. I removed the stack of letters for a closer look. Each was addressed to Dan and each was sent to an address I recognized as a past or present place of employment of my husband.

I opened the letter at the bottom of the stack first. The date was December 21st, 1836. The writing was faded and difficult to decipher but I managed to make out a few words before it hit me. This was the handwriting of my mother, Maria. I scanned quickly through the pile and they were all from her. Next, I scoured the dozens of envelopes for dates finding the topmost letter to be dated January 19, 1859. That was only last month! A sick type of knot that had become so familiar lately began to form in my stomach. My first thought was that the two of them were conspiring against me. Had he recruited her to help him in his mission to have me committed to an asylum? But then, why did the letters go back to when I was an infant? Leaving the drawer open just as it was, I grabbed the money and the box of letters and retreated to my new quarters upstairs and quickly lit a lamp. I placed it on the floor beside me and spread out the letters in order from bottom to top and I began to read.

"My dearest Dan" began the first letter from back in 1836. Most of the words were too faded to read but it was her signature at the bottom. I opened the next letter and the next until I came to one that was more legible. I was reading things like "We cannot continue to see each other" and "Teresa is getting old enough to become aware" and "she could tell her father." The words bounced around in my head and I couldn't manage to arrange them in any logical way that was making sense. I read the letters throughout the night and by morning whatever faint light that had survived in my soul after seeing Philip murdered was now completely extinguished.

My mother and Dan had been lovers since I was a baby, and it had continued for the last twenty-two years.

CHAPTER 15

DISENTANGLEMENT

Morning arrived and the ramifications of my discovery were so complex that I wasn't sure I had the mental fortitude to spend another moment alone. I wanted to be with Laura. That was my guiding light. I changed clothes for the first time in three days and woke Henry in the Parlor asking him to accompany me in the carriage to fetch her. We went the one block to Mrs. Ridgeley's home, and I asked Henry to do the talking, unsure of my own ability to converse. He knocked and then announced that we were there to collect Laura and Bridget. Laura had seen the carriage pull up and she was already on her way down the stairs. When she saw me, she leaped into my arms and we squeezed each other so tightly that I was afraid I would hurt her. I kissed her face a dozen times and she pretended to wipe the kisses off with the back of her hand. I laughed genuinely for the first time in many days. I had never seen her do that before. Perhaps it was a new trick she'd learned while staying at the Ridgeley's. I thanked Octavia and her mother profusely while Laura said goodbye and patted each of the seven dogs on the head before allowing me to lead her out to the carriage. Henry helped Bridget in next and we were on our way home.

It was comforting having Laura and Bridget back home. I had left the desk in the library in disarray and at first sight, Henry thought we had been robbed. As he panicked, I clarified for him that yes there had been a robbery of sorts, but he needn't call for the law. His face was priceless as he tried to make sense of what I was saying and why I was not as frantic as he was. I thought to myself, I had been robbed of so many things in the last few days, Philip was the greatest loss and then there was my mother who would never be my mother to me again. My faith in humanity had been shaken to the core and the childhood I cherished for twenty-two years was pulled out from under my feet. Yes, there had been a robbery, but the robber already sat behind bars.

I didn't weep or fret that day. I felt absolutely nothing. I was empty. I had nothing more to cry out. The shell that I occupied walked and talked but my heart and soul had been suspended. I straightened the desk in the library and sat a moment looking at the morning edition of the daily news. "Tragedy in Washington," the newspaper headlines blared, and I thought that was a most appropriate description. It depicted in some detail the events of the prior day, most factual, some exaggerated. Firsthand accounts from witnesses were recorded along with their opinion of me and their thoughts on suggested punishments. I read that a final shot had been attempted to the victim's head but that the gun had jammed. This I hadn't known while watching across the square from the bedroom window. I couldn't read any more details of the murder, I'd seen enough with my own eyes. In the center of the page, I did notice the column reporting that the autopsy on Philip's body would be performed today and that the funeral would be held tomorrow, Tuesday, March 1st at his home on C Street. I decided at once, that one way or another, I was going.

Dan brutally murdered Philip in the street for something that he himself had been guilty of my entire life, not only adultery but a betrayal of the worst kind. I thought about the times he'd accused me when I hadn't been doing anything wrong at all, all while having an affair himself. The difference being that his affair was with my own mother. From the moment the anonymous letter from R.P.G. arrived he had allowed me to believe that he was the victim and that I was, what had he called me? "An insignificant speck of dirt." He played the part well of the poor devastated husband, and the public could pity him all they wanted. I didn't care to know anyone's opinion of me anymore. They could call me weak and immoral but from the carnage, I had now uncovered a new weapon and it was my turn to take control of the situation. If I had to say something positive about my ghastly discovery regarding my mother, it was that I now had a bartering piece. If I handled the situation carefully, I was almost certain that Laura could never be taken from me and that I would never be committed to an asylum against my will.

I needed Dan to know that I had discovered his dirty secret while still implying that I was willing to bargain with him on keeping it quiet. Reverend Haley returned that afternoon as promised, and I asked him to visit with Laura in the nursery to see if he could be of any comfort. She was aware that something very bad was happening, but she was too young to understand or to be told. I devised my plan while they spoke and when the reverend emerged, he commented that Laura was a bright strong child and promised to pray for her daily. It warmed my heart a bit knowing that he felt she was handling herself well. I then handed to him, my plan, an empty cigar box. He was baffled but willing to honor my request to deliver the box. Dan would know that I'd found the letters but seeing the empty box where he'd hidden them would tell him that they were now in my possession and that the tables had turned.

I spent the remainder of the day imagining what was happening at the jail moment by moment. He would recognize the box immediately I was sure; he'd presumably been storing letters in it for twenty-two years. When he realized that I had found the letters he would be furious. I hoped that he would not take a tantrum with the good reverend who of course had no part in it except the delivery. I was sure his parents had arrived from New York today. Perhaps he would try to contain himself for their benefit. It would take him some thought to fully grasp the possible consequences of my discovery. Over the course of the afternoon, he would realize that he stood to lose far more than I did. I was disgraced for sure, but as a Congressman, the public outcry against him would be humbling, and endlessly humiliating, especially if the letters were "leaked" and the papers spun it into a frenzy as they tended to do. It would mean the end of his political career, if being a murderer hadn't already, and being guilty of the same crime as the man he'd murdered, certainly would not help his defense at trial.

Reverend Haley was back before supper with Dan's response. He excitedly produced my bent gold wedding band from his purse and placed it into my hand. Dan would never bring himself to admit defeat directly, but the return of my ring told me exactly what I needed to know. The reverend was overjoyed with satisfaction that he'd somehow managed to facilitate a reconciliation, and in some ways, he had.

I invited the reverend to stay for the evening meal and as soon as he departed, I began composing my first letter to Dan. I carefully detailed my list of demands and tried to be as fair as possible considering I was no more an innocent victim than he was. In exchange for my silence on the affair with "Maria", he would sign custody rights of Laura over to me. He would allow me to keep the house in Bloomingdale where I would be going to live with Laura and Dandy as soon as next week. We would be provided with a monthly stipend to cover our basic needs. I also asked that whether found innocent or guilty he publicly forgive me *after* the trial. I understood that vilifying me would be his best chance at avoiding the gallows and I was willing to bear the burden of that much as penance for my own sin.

I considered stopping there and not upsetting the delicate balance of power that was being created. But then I thought of the multitude of times Dan had gone to New York on "business" where he was likely sleeping with her. My father traveled extensively, it was too convenient. It made sense now why she was always willing to step in on Dan's behalf against me. It made sense that she was often unpredictably distant and cold. I had sensed for years that some part of her resented me. She'd been forced to share her lover with me.

I thought of how she reprimanded me for being a spoiled wife and suggested that I didn't appreciate Dan enough. I thought of how Dan had stayed home, supposedly ill, from the costume ball while she was staying at our home. Had they gone to our bed to make love when I left, while his daughter, her grandchild was in the next room? This explained why I never had all his love. He couldn't possess her because she was married to my father and so he had settled for the next best thing, her child. I decided to add one last thing, "with my face concealed and utmost discretion," I wrote; "I will be attending Philip's funeral." He was just going to have to accept it.

Tuesday, March 1st, 1859

Reverend Haley arrived bright and early as I suspected he might, and I had my letter to Dan prepared and sealed for delivery. I had also prepared an envelope for the reverend with a thank you note and a monetary donation to his church. I wanted him to know that I appreciated his time and efforts on behalf of a couple that others would see as most undeserving.

I very deliberately chose my clothing for Philip's funeral. Ironically, I had plenty of experience with disguise when going to see Philip and today I would be seeing him for the very last time. I wanted to wear only the things that I had worn during our times together while carefully protecting my identity. The shock of the past few days was beginning to wear off and with that came the return of the intense grief I had experienced right after seeing him killed. I dressed alone without assistance from Bridget and as I pulled my black silk dress over my hips my eyes filled with tears as I remembered the way his hands felt helping me out of it. I missed his touch so badly. How was it possible that he was dead? I was determined to go, and I hoped that I could bear it in reality. My fingers trembled as I straightened the lace on the black shawl I wrapped around my shoulders. I decided on a simple fur hat and black veil that concealed my hair and face well. Last I slipped on my black velvet cloak and in my hand, I squeezed the brass key that Dan had sent to me from the jail. He may have intended it as a taunt, but Philip had held and touched the key in life, and I defied his efforts at wounding me by clinging to that key as a piece of Philip that I could still hold tightly.

I arrived at noon although the funeral was planned for two o'clock. I was hoping to have a moment to speak with Alicia if possible before the mourners arrived but as the carriage neared C Street, I could see that a long line had already formed stretching down the block leading to the Key home. I asked the coachman to stop a bit further away so as not to draw attention. From there I watched the crowd with a heavy heart. Well-dressed men and women stood amongst common folks and children. It was moving and heartbreaking to see the number of people whose lives had in some way been touched by Philip. I felt responsible for their suffering and the guilt was overwhelming. His poor little children were orphans. I wasn't even sure if Alicia would want to see my face. She might hate me and order me out of her sight, and I wouldn't blame her for it. Her brother, the fourth of the six she had, was dead, taken away too young.

I waited down the street until the viewing line had moved through the home and the 2 o'clock service had begun before I asked to be taken closer. I nearly changed my mind as the carriage stopped at the corner of C and Third Street, but I steadied my resolve and began to make my way toward the house. It was still and quiet and

I was afraid of being recognized and causing a scene, so I crept as quietly as possible through the open front door and blended into the crowd near the back of the parlor. The minister was reading a passage from the Bible and much sobbing and sniffling could be heard around the room. As everyone bowed their heads, I took an opportunity to glance to the front of the room where Philip was laid out in an ornate wooden coffin. I could barely see his face over the edge of the casket. His head was raised on a pillow and he looked so life-like and peaceful. It was terrible and wonderful to see him one more time and I was thankful that the gun had jammed before a shot could be fired at his head and ruined his beautiful face. I said a silent prayer and whispered, "goodbye my love, I'm so sorry."

I turned to go before I could be noticed and as I passed through the front foyer, I encountered Alicia's lady's maid, Sara. She didn't recognize me at first and so I pulled her aside and moved my veil so that she could see who I was. She gasped a little and I knew that she recognized me. "Please Sara, don't draw attention, I'm leaving now. After everyone has gone will you please tell Alicia quietly that I was here?" She nodded and I exited swiftly to the safety of my carriage while she stared after me in disbelief.

There was another carriage pulling up outside my home when we turned the corner of Jackson Place. I spotted my father stepping out first with Maria behind him. Apparently, they had just arrived in Washington, so I guessed things were about to get interesting. "My poor father," I whispered, realizing that he was still completely oblivious. I had been so caught up in my own tragedy that I hadn't considered the heartbreak that would befall my father learning of her betrayal. His wife and his friend, Dan had been having an affair going all the way back to living at the Da Pointe house together. When I was born, they were in their late teens and the letters revealed that Dan had tried to convince her to run off with him taking me along. She had refused and he'd nearly imploded with jealousy to the point where she had been afraid of him and convinced my father to flee the home they all shared. Dan had stalked her and moved as close as possible to a home near theirs.

A sudden alarming thought stopped me in my tracks. I fell against the back of the carriage seat and for a moment I felt woozy. What were the possibilities that Dan was my natural father? I thought over the words in the letters to consider that twisted possibility. She had referred to Antonio as my father many times and in reading the early letters I got a sense that they were not yet sleeping together until sometime the year I was born. I was relieved for that hope. I looked at my father organizing his belongings in front of my house and studied him carefully. I had heard my entire life that I was his spitting image. We shared many physical features and I supposed there was no way to know for certain, but I was confident upon reflection that Antonio Bagioli was my true father and I decided to never think of it again.

My father had already paid a visit to the jail to see Dan in person, I was taken aback that seeing Dan had been the first priority before seeing me and Laura, but then again, he didn't know what I knew, yet. I welcomed him with a warm hug and her with a cold stare and led the way up the front stairs and into my home. As they removed their outer garments Bridget offered hot tea and Henry carried their things to the upstairs guest room. I knew that my father was disappointed in me and that was the worst punishment I faced besides losing Philip. I was thankful to see the love still in his eyes for me as we sat together in the parlor.

"She" had gone immediately upstairs to find Laura. I wanted so badly to tell him everything, but I couldn't, not yet. I needed more time to think things through. His face showed his distress and he reported to me that Dan had asked to see Laura. I winced at the idea of sending Laura to that place to see her father. What would go through her little mind? Would she be terrified or was she too little to understand what she would see? I asked my father if he thought that was wise, after all, he had seen the conditions for himself.

"He is not in a rat-infested cell if that's what you imagine," he began. "In fact, he is relatively comfortable in a room adjacent to the warden's family's quarters. He is locked in yes, but he's got a window and a bed, books to read, a desk at which to write and of course Dandy is there with him as well. He wears his own clothing and I understand his meals are being delivered from home, yes? I don't think Laura would notice much since she won't be going farther than the front hall. It would do him well to see his daughter, Teresa, after all he's been through."

Immediately tears puddled in my eyes and ran down my cheeks. Never had I been so conflicted and so overwhelmed. It was all so much, too much. I was having trouble separating my emotions. I had caused this right? Or had it started long before, when I was a baby and my mother was sleeping with a man who manipulated me into marrying him, practically as a child?

I had never loved anyone the way I loved Philip. This I knew for sure, and yet I'd gotten him killed. That made me so angry with myself and was the source of my deepest pain. I felt terrible for Laura. She would never know a happy home with the love of a mother and father, but then again, had she ever? Had I? My father was about to have his life shattered as well, by my words but not by my deeds. Perhaps if I had never met Philip, he could have gone on in ignorance. I considered not telling him, letting him live in the false oblivion that he knew for all these years, but it was time for the lies to stop.

"Tell *her* to take her grandchild to see him," I said pointing in the direction she had left the room moments before. "I cannot bear to go, and you have already been. Henry will take them straight away and have it done with. Will you please stay with me, I cannot be alone now father," I pleaded?

I brushed and braided Laura's beautiful long hair while my father made the arrangements for them to go. I wanted to say so many things to my precious child at that moment but nothing I was coming up with seemed appropriate. I wanted to say I was sorry so badly, but she wouldn't understand. I wanted to tell her not to be frightened but didn't want to place the idea in her head if it wasn't there to begin with. I wanted to tell her to say goodbye to him, but she had no idea the plans I had made to leave the city, and it would only confuse her more. In the end, I told her to give her papa a big hug and to be a very good girl. I watched the carriage roll away and the knot in my stomach tightened as I imagined my tiny girl walking into that awful place with her vile grandmother at her side. Of course, she didn't know these things and I was thankful for the innocence of youth.

I wondered if Dan would find a way to warn her during the visit that I had found the letters. Her smug expression told me that she did not yet know. I almost wished I had gone along to see the revelation unfold but I needed this time alone with my father. He sat with his tea in the parlor looking at the newspaper and for a moment, I nearly lost my nerve. He had become an older man sometime in the last few years. His hair was gray, and his shoulders slouched. He was still handsome and strong, and I hated knowing the pain I was about to cause. Would he be angry? At her? At me? Would he refuse to hear me out, and walk out on me as well? What if he did nothing at all? Could I forgive him for that?

I began by apologizing for the way I had behaved with Philip. I stopped short of telling him that Philip had been the love of my life and that I didn't regret a single second we had spent together. That could be said later. I briefly summarized the events of the last few days in my own words and finally, I began to tell him about searching through the desk and finding the old cigar box of letters. I watched his expression change from surprise to skepticism and then to shock and hurt, as I continued to tell him detail by detail of my discovery. It was painful for me to explain how I had always felt a resentment from her, and I pieced together for him the details that I had already spent days doing so for myself. I explained and unloaded my words until he finally asked me to stop. He didn't want to hear any more. I moved closer and he allowed me to hug him tightly and I expressed to him that he had always been my source of constant comfort as a child and that I needed him now more than ever.

He asked to see the letters and I agreed to hand them over. Together we wept for the losses we were enduring, each in our own way. He questioned if I had told Dan what I knew, and I recounted what I had done with the knowledge and for a single moment, I saw a flash of pride in his eyes. It was no time to celebrate anything, but I did know then that my father was going to be alright in time and that we were going to get through this together.

A while later we heard the carriage approach and the front door flew opened and Laura bounded up the stairs to her nursery without a word. I was about to go after her when my father tugged my arm and motioned for me to look through the front window. Expecting to see her climbing down from the carriage we watched in disbelief as the carriage continued on with her still inside. She had clearly learned that the truth was out. Being the coward and the selfish creature that she was, she had obviously decided that she wasn't going to face the situation right now and so she had run away. With nothing but the clothes she was wearing, she was gone. Where she was going, I did not know. If she was going back to Dan, frantic, at this very moment, I did not care. I laid my head on his shoulder for a moment then left my father peering through the glass to have a moment to himself to ponder and to grieve.

In the nursery, I found Laura sitting in her tiny rocker cuddling her favorite doll and as I went to her, she stated: "Papa was crying, why was papa crying, mommy?" I reached for her and held her tight. In the bravest voice I could muster I explained to her that we weren't going to be seeing him for a while and that made him sad. I told her that we were going to be going on a trip back to our home in New York soon with her grandpa.

"And Dandy?" she asked. Of course, we were taking Dandy along I assured her, and I promised her that no matter what, she and I were always going to be together.

By Saturday I had managed to pack most of our belongings into trunks to send ahead of us to New York. I did not ask Bridget to come along. She was part of a terribly memorable few days and I wanted to leave as much of the past behind as possible. Dan and I had corresponded several times regarding the move and our unspoken agreement. Not once did he mention if he was aware that *she* had run off, nor did I ask. My father had stayed in his room for two days and when he emerged, he was anxious to leave Washington as well. He, Laura, and I were going to New York on Thursday morning by train. We'd decided together that he'd move into Bloomingdale with us for the foreseeable future. I needed him to help me with Laura and I did not feel that I was ready to be alone. He didn't want to return to the home he had shared with her and so it was decided. We needed him as much as he needed us.

The one matter that hadn't been settled was that of the dog. Dan had not acknowledged nor denied my request to take Dandy back to New York. I wasn't sure if that meant he was unwilling to give him up but by Wednesday he had not yet sent him home. I considered going myself to the jail to fetch him, but I had not seen Dan in person since the day of the shooting and I feared that doing so may disturb any sense of peace that I had managed to achieve in the past week and a half, and I dared not risk the setback.

My father offered to go for Dandy on Wednesday evening. I worried that this was unwise for the same reasons that I would not go but my father was determined. I did not ask his reasons besides the obvious of collecting the dog, but I imagine it had something to do with wanting to look into the eyes of the man who had been his friend and son-in-law, who had betrayed him in a most masterful and disturbing way. There was nothing more to say but sometimes it took seeing to believe, to dismiss any last ray of hope that it hadn't happened the way we imagined. Looking into Dan's eyes and judging his reaction would be a bit of revenge for my father. Besides, I was completely certain that Dan wouldn't dare deny his request to leave the jail with Dandy.

While he was gone there was an unexpected knock at the door. Certain it was yet another journalist prying for personal information, I ignored it at first. Henry had heard the frantic knocking and eventually gone to reply to the disturbance. I was in my bedroom packing my carpet bag for the following morning when suddenly Mary appeared in my doorway. I was flooded with emotion at seeing her face. I'd written her several times asking her to come and hadn't heard back. I was beginning to think that she'd turned her back on me too. I was overjoyed to see her but also nervous and unsure of what she wanted to say to me. I rose from the floor where I was loading my bag and she put her arms out to me beckoning me for an embrace and I practically flew into her arms and hugged her tight.

"Oh Mary," I cried. "I have been needing you so much. I know that you are angry with me but believe me when I say that you cannot despise me any more than I despise myself."

I had been keeping myself composed relatively well for a few days but seeing my dearest friend sent me into an all too common sobbing fit that I was helpless to control. We sat together on the loveseat at the foot of my bed and she gripped my hands tightly and we cried together until we were finally dry of tears and could once again find our voices to communicate.

"Teresa, I know you are leaving tomorrow and though I know you are bearing an unimaginable burden right now, I too am burdened, and I could not let you leave Washington without seeing you. Our precious children have known each other as family, I adore Laura with every fiber of my being, and you know that I considered Philip a good man and a good friend as well. I cannot believe he is no longer with us and his poor children, especially baby Alice. Never knowing her mother, and now an orphan. I can hardly allow myself to imagine her sweet little face."

She began to break down again and I reached for her hands once more, but she put them up in defense and leaned away from me. My heart was breaking for her, she was so distraught, and it was all my fault. She had even been so kind as to warn me of this perilous outcome months ago when I had confided in her about my relationship with Philip. "I'm so sorry Mary," I stammered not knowing what else to say.

"No!" She abruptly cried out. "You do not know what I have done. I am the one who should be sorry Teresa. I have come to beg your forgiveness before you go. I couldn't let you leave without telling you the truth.

The ever-present knot in my stomach tightened and a sense of dread washed over me as I considered her words. I'd had about all of the truth I could handle lately and thought nothing more could possibly surprise me now, but I was wrong again.

Listening to her jumbled confession between breaks of hysteria I managed to gather the gist of what she was trying to say and as I did, I felt myself beginning to shake.

"I thought I could trust Abraham," she bawled. "I said very little except that I believed that my good friend had found happiness outside of her marriage. I don't know why I told him, I think I may have wanted to imply that husbands need to take notice and appreciate their wives. With all the campaigning and politics, I too had been feeling neglected and I wanted to make a point. When he questioned me, I may have mentioned your names… but I swore him to secrecy Teresa, you have to believe that."

I nodded slightly as she continued on, "Please don't hate me, Teresa. It's sure to be my life's biggest regret, Philip was my friend too. I suppose I didn't think of it through Abraham's eyes. Dan has done so much for him, introducing him to President Buchanan, making it possible for him to have a real chance at winning the election next year, and becoming the next President. He values his friendship with Dan perhaps over his loyalty to me. He is so hell bent on honesty at all costs and though I begged him not to do it, Teresa. Abraham was the one who wrote the anonymous letter to Dan."

I held my breath as she spoke those words, afraid that if I tried to breathe, I might scream instead. She continued on about how

Abe had tried to give Philip a chance to come clean on his own first by writing him the encoded message that he'd received in the first yellow envelope. She claimed to have tried everything to stop him from writing the letter, but he could not be dissuaded.

"More importantly Teresa," she paused to look at me straight on, her eyes pleading with me to believe. "He did not know that Dan was going to kill Philip. He felt very strongly that Dan deserved to know about the affair, and I imagine he knew there would be consequences, a lawsuit, perhaps even a duel, but he didn't consider that Dan was unstable enough to murder a man on the street in front of the White House."

I wanted her to leave. I stood abruptly and walked to the window where I focused my eyes on the tree across LaFayette Square that Philip had fallen against as Dan fired shots into his body. I thought of all the blame there was to go around, plenty for everyone for sure. I did not know what to feel or how to respond and perhaps because I hadn't absorbed this new information yet I wanted very much to be alone. Facing the window but speaking to Mary, I expressed that I did not hate her and explained that I needed to be alone, but I had one last question for her. "Why did he send it anonymously and why did he sign it R.P.G?" I said quizzingly.

Mary stated flatly that Abe had agreed to send the letter anonymously so that our friendship would not be ruined. If he told Dan himself, then the source would have been immediately obvious. "He knows how fond I am of you, I hardly have any friends at all, but the guilt was too much for me when Philip was killed, I simply cannot bear the secret anymore. R.P.G. stands for a Republican Party Gentleman."

Behind me, I heard her rise to go and begin shuffling toward the bedroom door. She stopped at some point and turned back to declare sadly, "We are all scoundrels, me, you, Philip, Dan, Abe, all guilty as sin. I fear God will punish the lot of us one by one."

Thursday, March 10<u>th</u>, 1859

There was one last visit I needed to pay before I caught the train that would take us out of Washington forever. I woke before dawn and walked alone to the church of Reverend Haley several blocks away. I entered through the large wooden doors and looked around for a few moments. It was a lovely chapel with marble columns and rows of fine wooden pews each with a wreath, meant to depict a crown of thorns, carved into the aisle end. I slipped the envelope I carried into the donation box near the doorway and sat in the last row for a moment to rest and to reflect on the events of the last few weeks that had led me to this day. I hated Dan for what he had done but I hated myself more for having been a part of it. We were both guilty, both ruined, and Dan was going to have to take his chances in a court of law just as I was being judged by an entire nation of my peers. I had lost Philip. My heart and soul were permanently scarred, so did I really care what people thought anyway?

I removed the book of hymns from the back ledge of the pew in front of me and mindlessly flipped through the pages pondering these thoughts when I happened to open to the page of a familiar song. I read the lines carefully as I sat in Reverend Haley's church just as the sun was beginning to rise on Washington.

Oh, say can you see, by the dawn's early light,
What so proudly we hailed at the twilight's last gleaming?
Whose broad stripes and bright stars, through the perilous fight,
O'er the ramparts we watched, were so gallantly streaming?
And the rockets' red glare, the bombs bursting in air,
Gave proof through the night that our flag was still there.
O say, does that star-spangled banner yet wave
O'er the land of the free and the home of the brave?

On the shore, dimly seen through the mists of the deep,
Where the foe's haughty host in dread silence reposes,

What is that which the breeze, o'er the towering steep,
As it fitfully blows, half conceals, half discloses?
Now it catches the gleam of the morning's first beam,
In full glory reflected now shines on the stream:
'Tis the star-spangled banner! O long may it wave
O'er the land of the free and the home of the brave.

And where is that band who so vauntingly swore
That the havoc of war and the battle's confusion
A home and a country should leave us no more?
Their blood has wiped out their foul footstep's pollution.
No refuge could save the hireling and slave
From the terror of flight, or the gloom of the grave:
And the star-spangled banner in triumph doth wave
O'er the land of the free and the home of the brave.

Oh! thus be it ever, when freemen shall stand
Between their loved homes and the war's desolation!
Blest with victory and peace, may the heaven-rescued land
Praise the Power that hath made and preserved us a nation.
Then conquer we must, when our cause it is just,
And this be our motto: "In God is our trust."
And the star-spangled banner in triumph shall wave
O'er the land of the free and the home of the brave!

Nothing was going to bring Philip back. He had been taken from me because of our love, and because of the words in a simple anonymous letter. I didn't want revenge, or to confront any of the parties to this tragedy. All I wanted now was to be free; free from the city of Washington where Dan would stand trial and where Abraham Lincoln was going to campaign to be President. I vowed never to hear the marching bands that would play for him the "Star-Spangled Banner" while the blood of Francis Scott Key's son had barely dried on his hands.

PART THREE
ALICIA KEY PENDLETON

CHAPTER 16

THE TRIAL

If father were here, he'd know what to do, I thought to myself as I stared at the front page of the Daily National Intelligencer. I knew Dan Sickles personally, but I could never think of him again except as the man who had shot Philip. My oldest brother, Frankie, was living with my husband, George, and me for the duration of the trial. Since it wasn't proper for ladies to attend, I was getting updates throughout the days from him.

It was not going well for the prosecution and apparently, Mr. Sickles seemed more confident and smug as each day passed. Ironically, both my father and my brother, if either were still alive would have been in the seat of this new prosecutor, Robert Ould, and making a fantastic case against Sickles. This man, however, was inexperienced as a trial lawyer. He was appointed by James Buchannan as the new district attorney upon Philip's death. It seemed more than coincidental that Ould who never tried a major case on his own was here fighting, poorly, against a team of eight highly successful lawyers, and a system that was weighted toward protecting one of their own. It was no secret that Buchanan and Sickles had a close relationship but if no laws were being broken, there was nothing my family could do to challenge the appointment. Uncle Roger had investigated it very carefully. What we could do is hire, and pay for, legal counsel of our own choosing to assist Ould in seeking justice for Philip.

On that dreadful day, February twenty-seventh, of 1859, George and I were home having a relaxing morning tea after church services when we received word that Philip had just been shot and killed by Dan Sickles in the street near the White House. George had set out immediately and wanted to go after Sickles himself. Our cousin Benjamin Ogle Tayloe, who lived just next door to the National Club House where Philip, bleeding to death, was carried, was wise and calm enough to stop him. Together they guarded the body of my brother making sure he was treated with respect and honor. A crowd of hundreds had squeezed into the Clubhouse hoping to catch a glimpse and be witness to the gruesome scene. My cousin removed Philip's personal effects before they could be stolen from his body. George brought the items home to me that evening, but it took days before I could bring myself to touch them. His gloves and ring, his cufflinks, a crumpled letter and $14.02 that I would never spend.

Philip's two youngest children, James and Alice were in our home that tragic day, playing happily with our children in the nursery. I ordered the nanny to keep all four of them in there and occupied, hoping they wouldn't sense the commotion. My first reaction was disbelief, it was the Sabbath day, but as more information was relayed, I began to get a very clear picture of what had transpired. I was well aware of the relationship between Philip and Teresa. I'd probably encouraged it even, and now my brother was dead.

"I should have done more," I agonized aloud. I should have set him straight and told him I was worried about the dangerous situation he was involved with. Maybe I shouldn't have invited Teresa to Terra Rubra when Philip asked me to do so last summer.

That visit had encouraged them further. Perhaps he'd still be alive today and I wouldn't be watching the man who killed him get away with murder.

The truth is that Philip was a forty-year-old man and I could have done very little to dissuade him from being with Teresa, and I don't know if I would have even wanted to do so. I could almost hear his dismissal in my head, "Calm down Alicia, I've got it under control," he'd have said in his playful brotherly way. He'd been so unlucky in love and when he lost Ellen, I worried he may never be the same Philip I'd always known. He was a broken man and if it weren't for his children I wonder if he would have been able to go on.

After he met Teresa a light had come back on inside him. He was so much in love that it was almost uncomfortable to witness. A grown man behaving like a lovesick pup was mildly ridiculous, but it was so good to see him smile that I didn't have the heart to discourage him. Nor was it difficult to understand the attraction. Teresa was young, vibrant and had that special something about her that made folks clamor to make her acquaintance. I always enjoyed her company myself and a blind man could see that she was incredibly beautiful. Her gentle manner and youthful innocence made her even more endearing. I understood the appeal certainly, but why did he settle on someone who was married to another man. Philip was notorious for his good looks and style. He could have had his pick of nearly any available lady, but I suppose you cannot control what the heart wants. Besides, it was too late for that now.

Of all my siblings Frankie was having the hardest time accepting Philip's death. As the oldest brother, he had felt responsible for being the man of the Key family since father had passed away. The feeling of having failed us all somehow was plaguing his heart as much as losing his best friend. He'd been there when Philip was born and the two of them had always shared an extra special bond. Attending the trial was part of the healing process for him although I could see how much it pained him, both emotionally and physically, to set out each day. He wasn't as young anymore and I was learning that men tended to soften with age. His accounts from the courtroom were usually delivered around noon and I waited on them anxiously. He would report the scene in great detail, and I clung to his every word.

Dearest Sister Alicia,

I note several familiar faces in the crowd today. One of those belongs to Antonio Bagioli, Teresa's father. I've not met him in person, have you? I can see the strong resemblance to his daughter's features. He looks like a man who has been through enough for one lifetime. I imagined how I would feel if it were my daughter in Teresa's shoes and I sat here as her father. I assume he is ashamed for he looks heartbroken. I assume he is angry with his daughter from the look of bitterness in his expression. But mostly he appears sad. His eyes are red-rimmed and have bags under them. I imagine he's had very little sleep lately. The poor man stayed only a short time in the courtroom. Perhaps it is too difficult to face his son in law with the shame of his daughter's behavior on his shoulders.

Yours very truly,
Francis Scott Key II

From what I could gather, Teresa had gone back to New York with her daughter and was on the edge of a mental breakdown. I heard that her father had moved in with her and Laura at their old house in Bloomingdale and was helping them through this nightmare. While Mr. Bagioli was in Washington for the trial, a family friend was trading off staying with Teresa to keep a vigilant eye on the mother and daughter. Threats had been made on Teresa's life and she was not without threat to herself. Sickles had made it clear that he was finished with her, but a woman such as Teresa could not be left to fend for herself and her little child in a world that judged her so harshly, more so even than the man who'd committed the murder. I had pity in my heart for her and I knew that Philip would have wanted me to forgive her and to look after her, and so I decided after the trial I would visit New York.

She'd been to Philip's funeral. My lady's maid Sara told me in secret that Teresa had quietly shown herself and wanted me to know she'd been there. It was brave and stupid of her to come and I didn't know if I should be upset with her or proud. I liked her very much and she'd obviously taken care not to be seen but if she had been discovered, oh I can't even imagine it! Seeing Philip one last time had been important enough to her to take the risk and I did have to respect that. She loved Philip for certain. If things had been different, I'd have welcomed her wholeheartedly as a sister-in-law. One thing I couldn't figure out was how she had managed to attend the funeral without Dan knowing. Even from jail, he certainly would never have allowed her to go.

It was a terrible day saying goodbye to Philip. Sickles had caused the death of my fourth brother. My mother was as fragile as a child at his funeral having lost yet another son. Seeing her weeping was enough alone to make me want to strangle the life out of Sickles with my own hands. My Uncle Roger, the supreme court justice, had been able to console my mother, his sister-in-law, to some degree, and she was comforted when he promised to do all he could to see that justice was served, but Uncle Roger was facing struggles of his own in Washington.

There was bad blood between my uncle, Roger Taney, and a man named Abraham Lincoln, who had been stirring up attention in Washington for the last year or more. He was an inconsequential lawyer running for a U.S. Senate seat from Illinois. In my opinion, he was a bit of a backwoods type, and his wife Mary was strange as well. He gained recognition during his campaign speeches when he debated with Stephen Douglas and openly criticized my uncle and the Dred Scott decision of the Supreme Court, a controversial case arguing the Constitutional rights of slaves. Uncle Roger had penned the decision on behalf of the court and so he was the target of the criticism. To our relief, Lincoln lost the election, but our family was not happy to learn that Lincoln, who campaigned on ravaging my uncle's name, was now being considered as a nominee for the upcoming Presidential election.

Dan Sickles and James Buchanan despised Stephen Douglas, a friend of my family, who defended Uncle Roger. Douglas, a member of their own political party, who had won the Senate seat over Lincoln was extremely critical of Buchanan's presidency. So, although Buchanan was a Democrat, and Lincoln was a Republican, the President himself appeared determined to assist Abraham Lincoln with his political aspirations.

He and Mary had been spending more time in Washington than ever, and I avoided her as much as possible without being rude. I knew Teresa had a fondness for Mary and I had tried to warn her away from the Lincolns, but Dan was controlled by President Buchanan, who was determined to keep the Lincolns close. My Uncle Roger was becoming increasingly displeased with President Buchanan, and now Dan Sickles was on trial for his life and justified or not, he had taken the life of my brother, and Roger Taney's nephew. The lines of loyalty were being drawn, and the sides were becoming further divided.

Some would say that I could never understand such complex political matters. I was *just* a woman. The wife of a Congressman who could throw wonderful parties and arrange flowers but, understanding the business of Washington was for the men. I disagree. In fact, I would wager that most of the men in this city were seeking the opinion of their wives at home, George certainly did. The women I knew were all capable of thinking intelligently. We paid attention to the happenings and could tell you the players and the rules as well as any man. We often predicted outcomes long before the men, but our opinions we kept to ourselves, unless asked.

There was something about the way Frankie described him that made me feel a bit sorry for Dan Sickles. He was obviously a minor player in his own life and destiny. All the city's most powerful men huddled over him in the courtroom making his decisions and speaking on his behalf. It was easy to imagine that this was how it usually went for him, being a puppet on the string of whoever was directing the show at the moment. Frankie said Dan was always crying and moaning in some manner of discomfort. His sudden fits of howling causing the trial to be halted time and time again and for him to be taken out, practically carried by his entourage. It sounded pathetic really, and I wondered how he'd summoned up the courage on the morning of February 27th to confront my brother? I suspected he hadn't acted alone and was assisted in some way by his friend Samuel who was reported in every newspaper I'd read to have been present at the scene.

The biggest surprise of the trial to me wasn't that Sam Butterworth was never called as a witness, even though he'd been with Dan that morning and stood several feet away and did nothing as Philip was killed. It wasn't that Sickles pled not guilty to a crime witnessed by a dozen bystanders. The shock was when the defense announced that they intended to prove Dan Sickles not guilty by reason of "temporary insanity." What did that even mean?! He was insane for a moment in which he killed Philip and then returned to his full mental capacity shortly after?

It was preposterous. I, nor anyone else had heard of such a thing and the courtroom had reportedly erupted in mass confusion as the defense attempted to proceed with the opening statement. My thoughts drifted as I imagined the scene. I never expected for him to receive a death sentence, his ensemble of legal experts practically guaranteed that much. I *had* envisioned him in prison for life. If he were to be found insane, he could live out his days in a hospital somewhere instead, but if he was only insane during the moment of the murder but was now mentally fit did that mean he could potentially walk away a free man? That would not be an acceptable conclusion.

The judge accepted the absurd defense and ruled in favor of the defendant that a full account of the adultery would be permitted as part of the argument. From that point on Frankie stared Sickles down willing him to drop dead on the courtroom floor. He listened to our brother being called a "horrid adulterer" and "cuckold" and nearly had an outburst when it was stated that his death had been but a cheap sacrifice in righting a wrong. The longer the trial went on the more it became clear that there was going to be no justice served here. The public opinion, which according to Frankie was expressed loudly and daily by the spectators in the courtroom, was that the sinful Philip and Teresa had gotten what they deserved, and that Dan was but a victim who had no choice in the matter. It angered me that the judge allowed the court of public opinion to be so dramatically expressed in front of the jury, how could they not be swayed by it?

Our lawyers argued that the investigation had been poorly conducted. Philip's dead body had been handled by onlookers, my husband included, instead of waiting for the coroner, and the rented house on Fifteenth Street had been unlawfully searched. But the refusal of our own lead prosecutor to call Sam Butterworth into court to testify solidified in our minds that Buchanan was behind the scenes, calling in favors for Dan. Ould had to know that Butterworth was perhaps the only witness who could have given testimony on Dan's mental state at the very moment of the murder, yet he wasn't called in. Appeals to Buchanan to reappoint a more experienced district attorney were useless since he denied having any influence in the case at all.

Teresa had apparently written a confession letter and the defense intended to use it as evidence, but the judge ruled it inadmissible. I was thankful for that. My family didn't need to hear the details of their transgressions while still mourning his death. Several of my brother's personal effects taken from the house on Fifteenth Street were on display to the jurors. The defense was successfully chipping away at his humanity and painting the jury a picture of a soulless beast. Frankie wanted nothing more than to make a mad dash to the front of the courtroom and snatch his things away from their bloodthirsty eyes. He wanted to shout that they were all wrong about Philip and order everyone to go home. He yearned to be the protector he'd always been to Philip but of course, that wasn't possible, so we endured the trial while struggling to accept the inevitable outcome.

Teresa's confession was leaked nevertheless and printed in the next day's newspapers. I sat quietly at the breakfast table having a cup of tea and reading what I had hoped to avoid. It was scandalous material to be printed in such a public way. Frankie, who normally remained composed, was so upset by the contents that he stayed in his room all morning and asked not to be disturbed by anyone, even me. He did not go to court that day. Our family was being destroyed in front of me and I felt helpless to stop it.

I studied Teresa's confession that obviously to me had been written under duress. I shuddered as I imagined how that scene had played out. I retraced the facts back to the beginning. How had this whole terrible ordeal begun? I knew the nature of their relationship and I had hoped that Philip was practicing the utmost discretion when choosing to pursue a married woman. His love for her had clearly outweighed his respect for her husband. How was it that Dan had discovered the affair? Evidence showed that an anonymous letter had been delivered to him. The author had without restraint exposed and accused Teresa and Philip of adultery and provided specific details of the affair that were not delicately stated and were highly provocative to the recipient. The poison pen letter had been signed only R.P.G. and although various attempts had been made to find the source, it remained a mystery. It was a careless and cowardly way to address a perceived injustice and I resented its writer tremendously.

My brother's children were now orphans. What had they done to deserve such a fate? They had been sent to Baltimore to stay with my oldest sister, Elizabeth's family, the same night as the murder. It was not in their best interest to remain in Washington. Their father, my brother was gone forever. My mother, who lived with Elizabeth also, was beside herself with grief and having Philip's children near was soothing to her. All of us were suspended in time awaiting the outcome of this trial.

I missed my brother terribly. We were particularly close after Ellen died. I was helping him raise my nieces and nephew. I knew Philip's heart and he hadn't deserved any of this. People were committing ghastly acts in every corner of this city. I understood that Teresa and Philip's affair had perhaps been especially complicated, but sin was sin. His downfall came when another person took it upon themselves to destroy his life and write that terrible letter to Dan. I did not believe that anyone deserved to be killed in cold blood by another person. Even in a proper duel, both parties had equal preparations and the ultimate judgment was reserved for God. Dan Sickles was not God.

Frankie became anxious to leave the city and get home to his wife Elizabeth in Annapolis. I wasn't sure he'd ever return to what he called this "revolting swamp." The outcome of the trial had become painfully obvious to us. There was no reason to stay until the bitter end. Political alliances trumped the value of human life here and Frankie wasn't sure anymore if he could contain himself in a room of strangers who would cheer the decision of the jury to set a killer free. He left before the closing arguments. He offered his home as a place of solace for me as well. But I was staying here and would provide the most frequent updates available, I assured him. Washington was my true home. Growing up here and being married to a Congressman I'd adapted to the lifestyle in a way Frankie hadn't. One had to know how to protect their heart to live in the city and understand its dark side without being absorbed into it. I could handle the naysayers and I intended to restore our family's reputation by staying put. The Key family was in deep despair and needed a representative to preserve the appearance of our strength.

A week or so later, two months after Philip's death, I sent the most dreadful telegram to Frankie: not guilty, unanimous jury, acquitted of all charges, walking free.

CHAPTER 17

TALES FROM NEW YORK CITY

The summer passed quickly. I had gone through the motions of my life and somehow survived the worst of the grief of losing my brother Philip. I hadn't cried in days I realized, as we returned on the train from Ohio where we had been visiting George's family. I felt newly capable of taking on the world back in Washington. My plans included a visit to my cousin Benjamin and his wife, who had been so kind to me in the aftermath and then sorting through Philip's home and belongings to create a hope chest for each of his children that would hold items and keepsakes of their mother and father. I planned to keep the boxes for each of them until they married and had a home of their own. Children wouldn't appreciate fine china and linens or law books now, but as adults, I knew they would treasure owning things that had belonged to their parents. The poor darlings, I nearly cried again just picturing their sweet faces. They were so young to have to endure this heartache that I could barely handle as an adult.

My own children Francis and Mary were still very young, and they knew that something terrible had happened to their Uncle Philip, but as the months passed, they mentioned him less and seemed to be coping well as most children do. I thought of little Laura, Teresa's daughter, and hoped she was faring as well with her family tragedy. A trip to New York was at the top of my list of priorities. As soon as we were settled back in at home, I arranged it.

I wanted to visit Philip's grave again, alone. I was there only once for the funeral, so I planned a stopover in Baltimore on my way to New York. My sister lived not far from the train depot and as the train pulled in to the station, I saw six familiar faces outside the window and I nearly shoved other passengers from the platform trying to get to them. My mother was looking well, considering. I kissed her first and she wiped the tears from my cheek. I turned my attention to my sister Elizabeth and all four of Philip's children. My nieces had grown a bit since I saw them last in March. But my nephew James had changed the most. Gone were his wispy blond curls and his chubby cheeks. His hair had gone light brown. He had grown a few inches at least and was thinning out as he grew tall. He looked just like his father and as I hugged him tightly my sister caught my eye and nodded, acknowledging what she knew I was thinking. It was bittersweet seeing Philip's features in James. I missed him so much still and wished he were here to see his son turning into his likeness.

Little Alice, Philip's youngest, wrapped her tiny arms around my legs and held on for dear life. She and I had been very attached. I was the closest thing to a mother she had since Ellen died in childbirth. She was named after me and I had been with her most days for the nearly four years of her life.

I suddenly felt absolutely horrible. How could I be so stupid? She must have thought she'd lost me as well. In my grief and self-preservation, I had failed to see things through her eyes. She was too young to understand that I had not abandoned her. In my mind, she was safe with family, her grandmother, especially, who I knew would be giving her everything she needed. But in her mind, I was gone. I picked her up and held her close and she nuzzled into my neck. The tears poured from my eyes and I willed her to feel my remorse through my hug. Poor sweet Alice. I would never let go of her again.

"I go home," said little Alice. The group gasped and froze. I stared baffled at them waiting for someone to explain to me what the great shock was in Alice wanting to go home.

"She hasn't spoken a word since March," my mother explained gently.

How could they have kept this from me? I alternated between anger and shame a dozen times in as many seconds. I stared at my sister and then my mother.

"You were grieving Alicia, and you had your own family to worry about," Elizabeth continued. "I knew she would be alright eventually. I would have written you if it continued on. I'm sorry for not telling you sooner. I'm ashamed to admit that I've become so accustomed to her silence that it didn't seem odd anymore."

She looked so distressed as she tried to rationalize it. I knew that she too had been grieving and she bore the additional responsibility of having all four children and mother staying with her. I relaxed my stance and answered kindly, "I understand Elizabeth, it's not your fault. I should have checked in on her sooner. "Let's go home, right Alice?"

Staying a few days with family had been good medicine for all of us. I went to visit Philip's grave the next morning. Standing next to his headstone I began to cry. "Oh Philip, why did this happen to you? I know you loved Teresa, but it cost you your family. I'm going to see her when I leave here and I'm not going to hold that against her, I promise. You'd want me to check on her and Laura. She was my friend too, I owe her that much. You know that no one has been punished for doing this to you. That is the part that has been the hardest on us all. Dan walked away free Philip."

I kneeled on the grass beside the mound of still loose dirt and straightened the wreath that hung on his stone. I placed the bouquet of flowers I carried with the others and plucked off the imperfect petals until it was just right. "How can we let this rest? There must be something else we can do. Who hated you enough to send that letter to Dan? If you can hear me right now, help us figure this out. For the sake of your good name, let us help you have some justice." I kissed the tips of my fingers and touched his headstone one last time. "Goodbye Philip, we all love you so."

I decided to take Alice with me to New York. I couldn't leave her behind. Neither of us would have been happy and she and Laura had been playmates their whole lives. It might be very healing for them to see each other again. We boarded the train in Baltimore and Alice watched fascinated out the window the entire trip. I was queasy this morning and the rocking of the train was making it worse. I didn't know what I was going to say to Teresa, but I hoped that when I saw her it would come naturally. We made it to the Bloomingdale neighborhood just after noon and Teresa and Laura greeted us warmly. Teresa wept intensely when she saw little Alice was with me. I hadn't sent word ahead that I was bringing her and I'm sure it was a bit of a shock to see Philip's smallest child at her door.

Dandy pranced happily at our feet and welcomed us as well. Alice was happy to see them both and Laura seemed ecstatic to have her playmate. I imagine she'd had a difficult transition coming to New York under this dark cloud. The girls ran off to play, holding hands and talking excitedly as they bounded up the stairs.

Teresa offered a glass of wine, but I asked for tea instead. I didn't mention when I noticed she awkwardly prepared it herself and seemed not to have any servants. I wanted to ask her a hundred questions about her new life, her relationship with Dan, what exactly happened in Washington, and how she was managing on her own.

She spoke first saying "I am so humbled that you've come, Alicia. I don't deserve the benefit of your friendship and if you have come here to tell me how much you hate me then I will bear it." She blubbered a bit and continued, "I am so very sorry that you've lost your brother. I still cannot believe that he is gone. God has cursed me never to sleep again so I can spend all the hours of my wretched life thinking of my sins."

She did look as though she hadn't slept well in a very long time. "Stop there Teresa," I said putting my hand in the air and speaking to her tenderly like I would a child. "I have not come to hate you or to make you feel worse. I know that you loved Philip and you made him very happy for the time you had together. It's terrible for all of us but nothing will bring Philip back. I came because he would have wanted me to and because I wanted to come. For forgiveness. For the children. For friendship."

She turned her head and breathed a huge sigh of relief and gratitude hearing that I hadn't come in anger. She asked if she could give me a hug and when I said she could, she gave me the saddest, loneliest, most genuine embrace, and I could sense that she had probably not had physical contact with another human being, besides Laura I'm sure, in a good while. It absolutely broke my heart for her, and I let her hug me until she was ready to pull away. As hard as these past months had been, I realized that she was suffering still and possibly worst of all.

We talked for hours about Philip and how much we missed him. We reminisced about better times. I confirmed that Sara had reported her appearance at the funeral. We talked about where her relationship stood with Dan and she stopped short of telling me something, but I couldn't imagine what, and I didn't press it. I wanted her to say that she loathed him; that she secretly slipped arsenic into his best bottles of whiskey or stuffed poison ivy into his pipe, or that she burned anything that looked important that arrived for him by post. Instead, she began to cry describing the way that Laura pleaded for him to stay when he visited and that he brushed her off cruelly and seemed to be purposely causing his own daughter's emotional trauma as punishment.

"And what can I do? Nothing!" she sobbed. "He has the money. I'd have nothing if he didn't provide for us. Besides, I brought this upon myself, didn't I? I can hardly pass blame."

I felt for her. Our society allowed men to do as they pleased and hindered women from doing the same, it was an issue that constantly frustrated me. She and Dan were living separately but he was corresponding with her regularly. He'd been facing significant backlash for continuing to support Teresa. He had publicly forgiven her after the trial, to his own political demise, and I had read for myself the letter he published in the newspapers defending his decision. To most people, his forgiveness was a crime as heinous as the murder. How could he absolve his wife who had so disgraced his home, it was unheard of. If he could forgive her then what was to keep the next man's wife from conducting herself in the same manner?

As Dan fell out of favor with the public, Philip's murder was becoming more and more unpopular. Months after the fact, rumors circulated of corruption and belated suspicion of a fixed trial. Dan was being ostracized by the same community that had applauded him for the murder of my brother. It was disturbing to witness the fickleness of people.

Teresa added that her father was living with them, but she didn't mention her mother. I assumed her parents also had the Bagioli residence to manage. Her father had moved in with her as part of the agreement that allowed her to keep Laura. I was pleased to hear that she had managed to secure custody of her child at least. Imagine having to turn your child over to a monster who'd just recently committed a murder. She and her father, Antonio had been doing fine together she claimed. Money was tight but there was food on the table. He regularly went into the city to teach his music lessons, but she hadn't left the house more than a few times since March. When she tried, she had faced cruel taunting and was now afraid to venture out alone.

No one, except for me, had been to visit from her "old life" and she desperately wanted to hear about the goings-on in Washington. Had the theater been repaired since the fire? Was there anything new on the menu at Gautier's? How were Octavia Ridgeley and her mother? I could tell that she missed her life. The fact that things would never be the same had obviously taken its toll on her spirit and through her smile, I could see the pain. In some ways, her life had ended along with Philip's.

Life in Bloomingdale was monotonous for a woman who had once hosted lavish parties for the President of the United States, and it was odd to hear her expressing enthusiasm over a hen that was laying well. She reached for a small brown glass medicine bottle on the shelf beside her to show me. The doctor had prescribed her Laudanum, a tincture of opium. She mixed it into her wine and offered to pour me a bit as well. I declined but listened as she marveled at its benefits and explained that its ability to suppress an aching heart was just as effective as it was in suppressing an aching bone.

She brightened momentarily when she mentioned the recent funeral of a woman named Fanny. Apparently, this Fanny had been a thorn in her side for some time and she had just died of syphilis. She pointed to the newspaper obituary that she had cut from the Herald and pinned to her wall. I didn't know what this woman had done to her, but Teresa seemed satisfied that she no longer walked about the streets of New York.

She offered her home as overnight accommodations, but we had arrangements to stay at the Astor House. She hid her disappointment as much as possible, but I could tell that she didn't want us to go. I was glad I had come. It provided the resolution I needed to not harbor any resentment against her, and it reminded me that she was still the good person and friend that I'd believed she was in Washington.

"Before you go," she began cautiously, "There is something I need to tell you."

I had sensed there was something she had wanted to say earlier, and I was glad that she was ready to come out with it.

"You were right all along about Mary Lincoln," she said looking despondent. "You told me not to trust her and I should have listened to you, Alicia. She was such a good friend to me at the time and I was sure you were mistaken about her.

"She knew about Philip and me," she anxiously confessed. "I told her around Christmas time. She was happy for me Alicia! Yes, she told me that it was dangerous and stupid, but she was my friend and she was Philip's friend as well. She could see that we were in love and though she didn't encourage it, she swore that she would tell no one and she was glad for our happiness."

My thoughts were trying to keep up with her words and I didn't see yet how that made me "right."

"She betrayed me, Alicia." She continued. "The day before I left Washington, she came to my home. She was plagued with guilt and sorrow and she admitted to me that she had told Abraham about the affair between Philip and me. She hadn't done it for spiteful reasons, it just kind of…slipped," she sighed heavily. "I didn't know what to say to Mary that day. She was my friend. I had trusted her completely and she betrayed me. She betrayed us all. She misjudged Abraham's reaction, and when he learned the secret, he became determined to intervene. Dan had done so much for him and his sense of loyalty to him was fierce, perhaps even more so than his loyalty to Mary. And she never even warned me," she said quietly.

Teresa explained how Abraham had conducted his own small investigation and was clearly torn on what to do because he had first written an encoded message to Philip letting him know that he'd been discovered. I thought of the odd note in the yellow envelope stating, "it is known," that was among Philip's possessions returned to me the evening of his death. He'd been hoping that Philip would be nervous enough to confess on his own at that point and deal with it man to man. He hadn't allowed much time for that though because the next night he had contrived the "anonymous" letter and had it delivered to Dan. I learned he'd signed R.P.G. to stand for Republican Party Gentleman. She explained how Mary had begged him not to send it and tried to convince him to mind his own business, that she would lose her best friend, but a sense of duty and brotherhood won out and the letter was done.

The pieces were falling into place now and I was in complete shock. I knew from the first time I met Mary that she was evil, and I angrily said so to Teresa who was still sitting across the table from me but staring at the floor.

"I'm not defending her I swear," Teresa uttered. "But I know Mary had no idea what the consequences would be. Philip was her friend. I know Abraham never imagined that Dan was unstable enough to murder anyone. He must have known that Dan would be angry and defend the honor of his name and family, but I have to believe he thought it would be handled quietly and privately. He was wrong, and now Philip is gone, and Mary is convinced God will condemn us all."

She was crying quietly now. What began as a pleasant visit had suddenly ended on a terrible note. It was time to say goodbye, the carriage had arrived to take us to the hotel. I gathered Alice and our belongings. I thanked Teresa for her honesty even though I needed more time to consider her role in the sequence of events. As we rode, with tears in my eyes, the magnitude of what I'd just learned began to sink in. If it weren't for Abraham Lincoln and his God damned noble air, Philip might still be alive, and this precious girl sleeping on my lap would still have her father. I suddenly remembered my words at Philip's grave. Obviously, he had heard my plea and his redemption was in my hands.

CHAPTER 18

FAMILY TIES

On the train ride home, I was ill again. Perhaps I'd been traveling a bit too much the past few months. I brought Alice back to Washington with me and I planned to rest while I decided what to do with the new information I'd learned. The new session of Congress would begin soon, and George would be preoccupied with business and I needed to begin preparations for Christmas. The first one without Philip. How could we have joy during the holiday season when there seemed so little to celebrate.

Alice thrived back in the comfort of our home with her cousins and she hadn't gone silent again. I supposed we could celebrate that small victory. She was a darling girl and I loved her dearly. I had just adjusted to the concept that I now had three children, when I discovered that I was soon to have four. Apparently seeking comfort in my husband's arms in the months after Philip's death had led to the unexpected blessing of a new baby. I had been feeling ill for weeks and it had taken a while for me to realize that it wasn't motion sickness or stress that was causing my discomfort. Not until my clothes became tight did I recognize the symptoms for what they were. I was still not myself obviously, and as much as I felt excited about having another child, I hoped I was capable of caring for him or her properly at a time when I felt incapable of so much.

I didn't go straight to Frankie with the information I'd learned in New York. He was much too emotional still and I feared he could do something rash and put yet another of my brothers in a dangerous predicament. No, he was not ready to hear the truth. The writer of the poison pen letter was one of the last unanswered questions of Philip's murder and this bit of information had to be guarded carefully. It was not, however, a burden I wanted to bear alone, and so I went to visit my Uncle Roger. I arrived at the Courthouse and asked the clerk to inform him that his niece Alicia wanted to see him. He was in deliberations and I sat a long while on the hard, wooden bench waiting for him to be free. He finally appeared and invited me into his chambers where the accommodations were much more comfortable.

"To what do I owe this pleasure dear," he asked jovially. He was my favorite uncle. He had been a good friend of my father from childhood and then fallen in love with my Aunt Anne. We spent many summers together at Terra Rubra over the years and I'd always known him to be a good-humored man and one who was fond of us children. My Aunt Anne died several years ago but I knew that Roger would always consider me family and being a Supreme Court Justice, I decided he was most likely to have a calm and intelligent response to this volatile information. He knew the unsavory side of the Lincolns better than anyone and he would be least likely to discredit the revelation or to doubt its probability before hearing me out.

With tears in my eyes I explained how I'd been to see Teresa in New York and as I unveiled her confession, his kind eyes became hard and his expression changed considerably. He recognized immediately all the intricacies of the situation and why I'd come to him first. "Blasted Devil," he shouted and pounded his fist on his hard desktop startling me and making me forget where I was in my sentence. "I'm sorry dear," he immediately apologized for his outburst. "Abraham Lincoln is no friend of mine and politically I detest the man if I'm honest, but this is personal, Philip was my nephew for God sakes. How can he live with himself; walking about the streets of Washington as if he knows nothing of Philip's murder and taking no responsibility for his part in it? Letting the public admire him for his honesty and integrity all the while he is practically a murderer himself. It's criminal and disgraceful, to say the least. Election year is nearing Alicia, and I fear he will become President and it will be the duty of my position to swear him in."

"I fear the same," I agreed sadly. "How can our family endure seeing him lead our country? It would be too much to bear Uncle. What can you do? What can we do?"

We discussed the possibility of going public with the information but with the current political tension, the whole thing could be turned around as a baseless partisan attack and Philip deserved better than that. He deserved real justice, not to be just another pre-election scandal to undermine the vote. It was not the time. We wondered if Dan himself even knew this truth of the author, or if he was just as clueless. It was hard to say. I agreed with Uncle Roger to keep this between the two of us until the time came that something worthy of Philip's memory could be done.

Baby Jane arrived on a Monday morning and she was an angel from birth. A beautiful, calm, sweet baby with my brother's eyes and I knew looking at her that she had been sent by Philip to look after Alice and me. Never had a baby brought more joy to a suffering family. My mother and all my siblings came when she was born and for the first time in a very long time, there was a peace in our hearts. Baby Jane brought our family back together and through her eyes, Philip was with us as well. Alice formed an immediate bond with her and called her "my baby Jane," from that moment on. In such a difficult time, it was a miracle in and of itself that this tiny child could heal such a large hole in our hearts.

The following year, much to my displeasure, Abraham Lincoln was elected the sixteenth President. March 4, 1861, was one of the worst days in my recent memory. The Lincoln inauguration was taking place just a few blocks from my home and as a Congressman's wife, I was expected to attend. No one, but Uncle Roger and I knew the truth and I felt deep empathy watching him standing face to face with Abraham Lincoln in front of the Capital as he asked him to place his hand on the Bible to take the oath of office. It must have been extremely difficult for him to maintain his composure staring into the face of a man who had not only made it his agenda to oppose him politically but who he knew to be partly responsible for the murder of his nephew. There amongst the thousands of visitors, my heart ached as I heard "Chief Justice Roger Taney" say the words that Lincoln would repeat and therefore become our Nation's leader. There was a stoniness in both of their eyes and though most remarked on the reason as being purely political and a result of an extremely bitter campaign, I knew that it was also personal. There was a moment before the ceremony that words were exchanged between the two of them but from the audience, it was impossible to interpret. Poor Uncle Roger, I wanted to hug him at that moment, and as for Lincoln, a hug was not what I had in mind for him.

At the Inauguration ball that evening, a moment presented itself where I could give Uncle Roger that hug. He quickly and quietly revealed that he had managed to unnerve Abraham just before the swearing in. He'd purposely uttered the same warning that Abraham had written encoded in the message to Philip and that I had shown to Uncle Roger. He was a very clever man for sure and he'd said to him only, "It is Known." From the flash of recognition in Lincoln's eyes, my uncle knew that he grasped its meaning instantaneously.

Almost immediately war erupted in the country between north and south and between Taney and Lincoln as well. Assassination rumors against Lincoln were rampant and I feared that Lincoln had his own plans to silence my uncle. I lived in fear every day that our secret would be his demise. I nearly told Frankie everything. I'd even sent a telegram for him to come to Washington after Uncle Roger had briefly visited my home on an evening in May to say that he feared Lincoln had likely ordered his arrest. They were engaged in a struggle for power that on the surface appeared to be due to a situation unfolding in Baltimore. But for the two of them, the stakes were much higher. If arresting my uncle was the plan, he had failed, but it sickened me to receive an urgent telegram from my sister Elizabeth saying that her oldest son Frank had been arrested. He was a newspaper editor in Baltimore and along with most of the city government, he'd been sent to Ft. McHenry as a prisoner by the orders of Lincolns secretary of war. Lincoln was relentless and if he had failed to offend my uncle directly, it appeared he'd stooped to going after other members of the Key Family instead.

My nephew now sat prisoner at the same fort that my father watched being defended when he'd written the anthem that had brought so much notoriety to our family. Was there no end to the irony and the suffering for my family?

Then a letter arrived from Bloomingdale, NY.

Dearest Friend, March 1862

I think fondly upon your visit to us in New York and I hope that you are well in Washington. This terrible war is most depressing and Dan is now serving as a General for the Union. I fear for his safety each day. Our dear Philip is blessed in some ways to have avoided this atrocity, for he was much to kind and gentle to be subjected to such a brutal conflict. I am writing to let you know that I recently received a letter from Mary. I know not what you have decided to do with the information I shared with you last, but nevertheless, I wanted to keep you abreast of any developments. She is not well you see. I'm concerned for her health and well-being. She has lost her dear son Willy. A ball was held at the President's house on February 5th and she and Abe argued before the party. She is convinced that the devil is in the White House, and because of what Abraham has done to Philip, that God is refusing to protect them. She pleads with him daily to repent for his sins and to seek forgiveness from God and the Key family but he is a stubborn old fool and instead, he challenges her mental stability and threatens her with the asylum. That evening, Mary's children Willy and Tad were upstairs feeling ill and Dan himself was present at the downstairs ball this night. She saw a dark figure emerge while Abe and Dan were conversing and it disappeared up the stairwell, and it scared her so. That night Willie took a turn for the worst and she sat at his bedside day and night praying for a miracle but within two weeks Willy was dead and Tad was nearly so. Mary says she confronted Abe saying that he had taken the life of Francis Scott Keys son and now he was paying for it with the lives of her sons. She demanded he repents immediately to spare Tad's life. He agreed to do so though I don't know in what form. I cannot imagine what ensued for the next few days in that place. Mary must have been mad with grief and worry for Tad. He is such a sweet fragile child you know. But he's alive Alicia.

Tad has recovered and so I am left to the conclusion that Abraham has decided to ask forgiveness and I wonder if you have had any word from him as of yet?

Most Sincerely,
T.B.S.

Of course, I had not heard of a single correspondence between the Lincoln's and my family and I had no expectation that I ever would. Teresa may feel that there was a bit of humanity left in those people, but I felt otherwise, and I was certainly not counting on an apology transpiring any time soon.

Terra Rubra in the springtime of 1863 was just as beautiful as always, and I was looking forward to spending a few weeks there with George and the children, away from the war-torn Capital. The most recent session of Congress was especially draining for George considering that the country was several years into a war that did not appear to have an end in sight. The Lincoln administration sure did know how to create destruction and mayhem and I for one was hoping that with the election next year that he would be voted out, and the country could begin to heal. It was here at Terra Rubra that I begged George to accept the nomination for vice presidential candidate in the next election. He was an anti-war Democrat and he knew the sentiments my family held against Lincoln. I had no doubt that he could lead us out of this terrible situation and although I never shared the uncovered details of my brother's tragedy with my husband, there was enough hatred of Lincoln that he'd earned on his own, and I hoped that would be enough to motivate George. My husband was well respected and had earned himself the nickname Gentleman George in Congress. This country needed a gentleman in charge again. I suspected that both North and South had grown weary of the slaughter and were ready to dismiss Abraham Lincoln and see him out the White House door. My George was unsure of the implications, but his friend and comrade George McClellan was also a Democrat but, in favor of the war, and the presidential nominee, and so between George and I, we only hoped he could be convinced in favor of peace.

My mother, Polly, was particularly pleased to have the family together at Terra Rubra again. Even Uncle Roger had made the trip. He was in Fredericktown for the summer and this was his first stop. Our arrival was next, and then Frankie and his wife Elizabeth. My sister Elizabeth joined us a few days later with her family including Philip's three oldest children and it was wonderful to have them back together again with Alice. It was almost like old times and besides the infantry marching past our farm now and then and the occasional cannon blast, it was just as I remembered it. It seemed following Pipe Creek was a common route for the troops heading to Pennsylvania and so we provided as much as we could to the passing men that summer. Water from the wells, food, and any other supplies that we could find. It was a terrible thing to see men with no shoes and bleeding feet attempting to stay in line with a march and it pained me to imagine if my own son was old enough to join the fight. This was my vantage point of the Civil War and I detested it more each day.

Three visitors arrived at the farm the following week and though they seemed vaguely familiar I couldn't place them until mother offered the proper introductions. "I don't know if you'd remember your father's cousin Eliza," she questioned me? "Eliza passed away long ago, and you were pretty young back then. Well anyways, this pretty lady here is her daughter Susanna. She is the same age as Philip was and they played together all the time here as children. Best of friends they were, isn't that right Susanna? Oh, the good old days," she said lifting her eyes to the sky and pausing a moment. "Do you remember when you and Philip climbed to the top of the old silo and couldn't find your way down? We searched everywhere for the two of you before Uncle Clem finally heard you both shouting from up there and climbed up to get you down himself! Oh, my my, the things children do," she reminisced sweetly.

Cousin Susanna and her daughter Mary were staying a few days on their way through to Baltimore. I didn't remember them at all, but family was family and I welcomed them as so. Mary was sweet and very pretty. She was just eighteen years old and thrilled to be spending some time with her beau. A nice kid named John Surratt who'd come up all the way from Southern Maryland to escort the ladies from Germantown where they lived, to their destination safely. It was good to see new love. It looked even brighter and warmer in a world that had become so dark and cold with this war.

Mint tea was being served in the garden before dinner and we all congregated there enjoying the warm June sunshine. Mary and I were discussing her beau John, while the men were discussing, of course, the war. I recalled bringing George to Terra Rubra for the first time as my fiancé. Things had turned out well for us and I hoped the same for two of them.

Frankie, George, and Uncle Roger grumbled about Lincoln for a while, each listing their own personal grievances and remarking on the unfortunate state of the Confederacy. The idea of them sitting here so close to the Mason-Dixon line was a bit ironic, to say the least. John Surratt was listening carefully but not contributing to the conversation, when Frankie asked him directly where his loyalties stood on the matter. Apparently, the kid had been saving a few thoughts up for this moment and once he got talking, it was a wonder if he'd ever stop. His family owned a Tavern in Southern Maryland and his father had built the area around it into a small town with a few homes and a post office. "My daddy died last year though," he paused in his story.

"I'm sorry to hear that son," Frankie offered.

"Nah, don't be. He was a no-good drunk," John continued, looking around nervously. "But our Tavern is a place known for bein' friendly to the confederates you could say. I quit school when this doggone war started up and got to know some of the boys passin' through there. Next thing I knew I was running packages and messages for 'em. My brother went to fight down South, and I took over my daddy's job as postmaster when he died. Only this real nosy Yankee detective keeps coming around investigatin' and firin' people from our post office. He's about due for another visit I reckon, and I'm sure he'll have my job this time, he's been tryin' for years to find a reason to do it. He works straight for the government, tryin' to sniff out spies and make everyone real miserable. I sure hate that guy. Why can't they worry about themselves and let us worry about our own, that's what I'd like to know? It's enough to drive ya crazy."

He stopped for a sip of tea and I thought he was through, but on he went, "I do what I can to help out my momma and my sister. Lord knows Mr. Lincoln ain't gonna do nothin' for them and so I ain't doin' nothin' for him neither, but I will make deliveries to Pennsylvania from time to time for the south if asked to do so," he winked and tapped his jacket pocket.

So besides escorting his girl and her mother to Baltimore, he was also carrying out a mission up this way. I figured in my mind before commenting.

"Why I do believe you are our first confederate spy Mr. Surratt," I chimed in and the table erupted in laughter.

CHAPTER 19

A CIVIL MATTER

The war between the states waged on through 1863 and the country was in shambles. Brothers fought brothers and families were being destroyed in every state of the now divided nation. My husband decided to accept the offer of the vice presidential nominee, and it gave me great hope to imagine that he would help to end this terrible war. Mr. Lincoln, it seemed had become obsessed with not allowing the South to secede taking America's most profitable industry, cotton, with them. He appeared to be willing to sacrifice as many men's lives as necessary to achieve that outcome. Hardly a person could be found at the beginning of this war who stood behind him in his crusade. The Southern states were standing firm on their decision and the Northern states, even though they wanted to share in the ample income being generated by cotton grown in the South, were reluctant to send their own sons off to fight for it. I certainly wouldn't want to send my child for that cause. But Lincoln was astute, I'll give him that much. He saw through the minds of the people and into their hearts. While almost no one cared about the government's money, Lincoln cleverly focused instead on the one emotional issue that was on the hearts and minds of many, slavery. He saw a deeper cause that the North would be willing to fight for and he somehow managed to combine his desire for success with their desire for man's freedom. Suddenly the war had taken on a new meaning and Northerners couldn't sign up fast enough. It was clever indeed. While we always had servants in our family, personally I was revolted by the institution of slave trading, I know that Abraham Lincoln had once agreed with my father and Uncle in supporting the colonization society and was critical of the abolitionists. His tune changed when it suited him, his attacks on my Uncle Roger and the Dred Scott Supreme Court decision had shown the dark side of this man's heart. He may have convinced the general population that his intentions were selfless and compassionate, but he certainly wasn't fooling me. I yearned to tell anyone who would listen what I knew of Lincoln and his poison pen that took my brother's life, but with the bloodshed and tears he'd caused so many families now through war, my brother's death was merely a drop in the bucket.

On July 2nd, 1863 Washington was afire with rumors that Mary Lincoln was dead. My lady's maid, Sara had heard it from her friend whose father was a gardener at the White House, and she was the first to tell me. She'd come running into the parlor where I was visiting with Nelly McClellan talking of our husband's bid for the Presidency. She was red in the face, flushed and struggling to catch her breath and immediately I was gripped with fear. I was terrified for a moment that something had happened to one of the children and as I jumped from my chair hot tea spilled down my dress front burning the skin underneath through my corset. I nearly fainted with relief when she announced that Mary Lincoln had been in a carriage accident near the soldiers' home. My children were still upstairs and just fine but apparently Mrs. Lincoln was not so lucky today. I sat back down in the chair across from Nelly and we listened as Sara told us all she knew so far of the accident. "Just awful dear, thank you for letting me know Sara. You are excused," I'd said as she finished her last sentence.

When she'd gone, Nelly who was staring at my now ruined dress remarked, "what an incredible waste of a lovely cup of tea."

We shared a glance, both understanding that neither cared for Mary and yet being Christian women, neither wanting to state it aloud. Of course, it was a tragedy for anyone to die in such a way and I truly felt for her son Tad who was still so very young. I thought briefly of the letter from Teresa and wondered if there wasn't indeed some sort of cloud over the Lincoln family. Perhaps Mr. Lincoln *was* being punished for cowardly masking his role in Philip's death.

As the afternoon ticked by, reports were printed that Mary Lincoln was *not* in fact dead. There had been a terrible accident, and upon leaping from the runaway carriage, Mary had struck her head on a rock and laid unconscious for several hours. Eventually, she was discovered and taken to the Army hospital nearby where she was revived and treated for cuts and bruises as well as the head wound. It sounded like a terrible ordeal and I summoned all the goodwill I could manage to say a prayer for her recovery. It was not possible to completely forgive Mary for her careless chin wagging that had set in motion the events that led to Philip's murder and I would never admit it to anyone, but now that she was no longer dead, I didn't feel as much sympathy for her at all.

Weeks later a new letter arrived from Bloomingdale, NY

Dearest Friend,   August 1863

I hope this letter finds you well. I've been a bit under the weather myself with a bothersome cough and I fear I may be allergic to Laura's new best friend, a cat she's named Peanut. The things we endure for our children. It's not been a good month for many and I'm not sure if you've heard but Dan has been severely injured and is in Washington now recovering. A cannonball struck him while fighting in a place called Gettysburg and his leg had to be removed. Poor Dan, he reports that he is in so much pain. A little pain would be fine with me, but not too much! I'm only being mischievous because, though it's been four years, he is still responsible for taking Philip away from us and I will never forget that. Abraham and Tad have been to visit him you know. It seems Dan and Mary are both struggling with a difficult recovery. Of course, you heard the news about Mary, but Alicia, I note only to you, that Dan was injured the very same day as Mary's accident, July 2nd and practically at the same time. Is it possible that this was a mere coincidence? I find it very odd and deeply troubling. I assume there was no plea from Abraham for your forgiveness since I've not heard from you. Mary has just written to me again and she is not herself at all since the accident. She spoke of revenge and all sorts of crazy things that make no sense at all. She urged me to confront Abraham myself to make him confess and save her from his evil deeds. She is convinced if he does not repent, she will be dead by the winter. It seems to me she mistrusts her own husband and she spoke of him harshly in a way I've not heard from her before. She also claims, and forgive me for this elaborate tale, that she has spoken to her son Willy at a séance. Willy told Mary that unless she can find a way to soften his father's heart that they will not leave the White House alive. You know how seriously she takes a supernatural message and from reading her words even I have been unnerved regarding my own well-being. It seems she thinks we will all continue to be punished including me and anyone else who has knowledge of this never-ending nightmare and so I apologize in advance if I've somehow cursed you too.

Most Sincerely,
T.B.S.

"Cursed me," I thought aloud. That was nonsense...wasn't it? I tried for a few days to ignore the uncomfortable feeling that had been plaguing me since reading Teresa's letter. Surely Mary was still grieving from the trauma of having lost two sons, but she was also suffering from a head injury so why was I letting her threat chill me to the bone.

We were long overdue for a visit to Annapolis to see my brother Frankie and his wife. I realized now that it was time to share the truth with him. I needed his support and his logical nature to help convince myself that this idea of a curse was foolish. He had grieved long enough, and I prayed his reaction would be less hostile by now. My hope now was that he would not be too angry that I'd kept it from him so long.

I packed one trunk for myself and one for the four children and we set out first thing the next morning. George would accompany us to see to our safety but with the war still raging and an intense campaign happening, he would have to return immediately to Washington. I planned to stay for a few days at least and I hoped that Frankie would not be upset I hadn't given much notice of our visit.

The ride to Annapolis was hot and miserable. August could be brutal in Maryland and before the halfway point the children were sweating and restless. We had already stopped several times to water the horses and stretch our legs and once to picnic along the way. The heat was setting my nerves on edge as much as thinking about what I was going to say to Frankie. The incessant bouncing of the carriage and constant whining of the children was making me irritable. George finally commented on my foul mood and playfully suggested that I ought to stay with Frankie until it passed. I smacked his hand away as he reached for mine. I was not feeling playful at this moment and the trip was the longest in recent memory. I almost welcomed the fishy smell and salty air that greeted us as we neared the Bay town and not soon enough we arrived at my brother's home and the children vied to be the first off the carriage.

I knew immediately upon arriving at Frankie's that something was terribly wrong. The curtains were drawn, and it was eerily quiet. The screeching of the seagulls overhead was the only source of sound. Not that I expected a parade or any such thing. Frankie's children were grown and just he and Elizabeth lived in the house alone. But the house was closed up tight and it was the hottest part of the summer. Had they gone off somewhere? Surely, he'd have telegrammed back if so. I knocked at the wooden door and called his name several times before finally the door creaked opened just slightly and there stood Frankie looking white as a ghost and with swollen eyes and strong whiskey on his breath.

"George darling," I called over my shoulder. "Would you please take the children down to the dock to see the Chesapeake Bay, it should be lovely this time of day." I pleaded with my eyes for him to catch onto my meaning and in typical George fashion, he knew exactly what to do. I turned my attention back to the doorway where Frankie still stood blinking at the sudden onslaught of daylight. Pushing the door open the rest of the way, I invited myself inside and followed Frankie back to his chair where he'd been posted, by the looks of the nearly empty bottle on the table beside him, for some time.

"Frankie, look at me. Talk to me. Where is Elizabeth? What's happened." I pleaded with my brother. He said nothing but pushed an envelope across the table to me at a snail's pace and I tried to make out the writing as it inched closer in my direction. It was addressed to Mr. and Mrs. Francis Key. He refused to speak and so snatching the letter myself, I moved to the window where I could read by the bit of daylight still coming in. It was a long letter, dated July 1863 written in neat penmanship and my eyes instantly searched the bottom of the page for a signature to see who sent it. Brigadier General John H Morgan. I did not know that name at all. My heart sunk as I read the first line. "It is most distressing that I write to report to you the sad news that your son William has fallen."

My nephew William was their youngest child and had just turned twenty-eight years old. He'd been a surprise addition to the family coming nearly ten years after Henry and Elizabeth. Even into adulthood, we called him "Baby Willie" and oh, how he hated that name! I swiped at my tears with one hand and held up the paper in the other. Last I'd heard, William had gone to fight for the Confederacy and ended up somewhere in Tennessee. The letter described the circumstances of William's death and though I wanted to understand, it was difficult to read such devastating news.

On July 9th, the company had successfully crossed the Ohio River from Kentucky into Indiana and were marching toward a town called Corydon prepared for a fight. Along an isolated stretch, the brigade was ambushed, and shots rang out from a nearby field. The unit returned fire and when order ensued, William laid dead in the road. A renegade band of farmers had fired the shots randomly into the passing troops and William had been the unlucky recipient of a lead ball through the chest. He'd died instantly as had the shooters in the return fire. Nearing their point of enemy contact, they'd left his body behind by the roadside. Upon the successful battle in Corydon, several of his men notified the General that the fallen soldier on the road was William Key, grandson of Francis Scott Key. Morgan had immediately ordered his body to be retrieved and given a proper burial which was done in the town of Corydon. The letter detailed the exact location should we wish to inter his body in a family plot and offered his deepest regrets for our misfortune.

This was more than misfortune, I thought. Abraham Lincoln and his damned war had gone on too long and someone had to stop him. I hoped that George and George would be the ones to do it come the next election. Horrific reports of a bloody and savage battle were still coming from the place Teresa had mentioned in her letter where Dan was injured, Gettysburg. Fifty thousand casualties the headlines blared. The newspaper offices were overrun at first with customers demanding clarification, thinking that surely there had been a misprint but as the days went by and names surfaced, the devastating reality sunk in. Almost no family I knew in Washington had been spared a loss in Pennsylvania and rarely did a family even have a body to bury or mourn over. The tragedy of the war had come home now in a most heartbreaking way and my nephew wouldn't be coming back.

I rushed to Frankie's side and threw my arms around him. How much pain could one man bear? "I'm so sorry," I repeated over and over until he pushed me away. He was beginning to sober up slightly and I could see the recognition in his eyes that I had arrived. I hoped that he would be coherent enough now that he could answer my questions and so I tried again. "When did the letter arrive Frankie, and where is Elizabeth?"

He finally managed several slurred words, "Elizabeth's gone to her father's house to tell the family and I am drunk."

"Yes, I see that. I'm staying with you. I need to tell George what's happened and ask him to take the children back to Washington. I'll be right back." In the short distance between the house and the shore, I thought of how to explain this to George without upsetting the children. Their fingers splashed happily at the water's edge as I approached and it made me smile to see them having a good time, innocent of all the world's ugliness. I whispered to George quietly and tears filled his eyes, but he remained stoic and calm for the sake of the children.

"I have an idea," he offered. I could think of nothing else to say and so I was more than willing to let him take it from here. "Children," he called kneeling to their eye level and waiting as they gathered around. "We have just received a telegram and I'm afraid there is a problem back home. Cook did not realize that we were leaving today, and she has spent all day making the largest batch of ice cream you've ever seen."

Their eyes were wide, captivated by this mental image. "Sara says cook is crying and very sad that all of the ice cream will melt and be wasted." He looked so sorrowful that I almost felt sad a moment too until I remembered that he was telling them a tale. "I don't like to think of cook so sad and all of that ice cream…it's probably melting now. I wonder if we turned around to go straight home quickly if we might make it there in time to save the batch and cooks feelings by celebrating with a midnight ice cream party? Mommy can stay here and visit Uncle Frankie and then be on her way."

YES! was the resounding opinion, of the children who then insisted on completing their father's noble mission. They bounded back to the carriage each racing to be the first inside and Alice turned to wait for little Jane toddling behind and doing her best to keep up. He was a genius man, my husband, and a wonderful father. If he could inspire four cranky children to repeat the long journey we'd just finished, then I had no doubt in my mind that he was going to make an excellent Vice President. He reminded me to telegram ahead immediately and explain to cook and Sara to prepare an emergency ice cream feast, sparing no expense. With a grateful smile, I kissed him and hugged all the children goodbye. I hoped that they would sleep for him most of the way. I wished them well on their quest to save the ice cream and waved until I could no longer see their little hands waving back.

CHAPTER 20

HATCHING THE PLAN

The next morning Frankie woke late and stumbled into the kitchen where I had a pot of coffee ready for him. He looked like he wished he hadn't woken up at all. I was completely torn on what to do about my purpose in coming to see him. He was already so distraught and overwhelmed by William's death. If I told him, would it add to his misery sparking anger or would it divide his thoughts? Perhaps having an older, less fresh wound to fixate on would help him cope with this one. I needed to get him awake and moving before I decided for sure. I asked him when he expected Elizabeth to return and he thought that she would be home by the evening. I suggested that we tidy the house for her and perhaps store away anything that might be difficult for her to see right away, such as the letter. Williams most personal belongings could be put in his untouched upstairs bedroom. We should also have a bit of supper ready in case she feels like eating I thought. I imagined she hadn't had much in the last day or so. If I could focus his attention toward taking care of Elizabeth, I hoped it would give him strength and motivation to get through the coming days.

He cleaned himself up and shaved off his scruff and was looking better already by the time I knocked at his bedroom door to hand him the shopping list I'd created for him. I asked if he felt he could manage a walk down to the market to get a few things. The fresh air would do him good and I wanted to open all the doors and windows to air out the strong stench of whiskey before the day became oppressively hot.

He was gone only a few minutes when the gravity of William's death overtook me. Perhaps being alone in this house right now was a bad idea for anyone. Peeking into his upstairs bedroom I was flooded with memories of Baby Willie. He was ten years younger than me and often times, as a girl, I was put in charge of watching over him at Terra Rubra during the summers. He was as precious as babies come and a lively little boy. I remembered him getting into everything! Most of the time I was the one scolded for the messes left in his path, but he was worth it. Looking after Willie was my first experience caring for a little one and from him, I learned that I wanted to be a mother myself one day. I picked up a small framed picture from his bureau and looked into his eyes one last time before closing the door and saying goodbye to my sweet nephew.

Frankie took longer than I expected and while he was gone, I had cleaned every room in the house and managed to start a fire in the kitchen hearth to begin preparing supper. He'd gone for a long walk through town and it had done wonders for his appearance. We sat together to peel potatoes at the long wooden table. I was as impressed with his domestic skills as he was with mine and it was nice to have a little something to laugh about. This was my chance if we were going to talk alone. Elizabeth would arrive sometime in the next few hours and I wasn't going to add this to her burdens. Frankie was strong and he needed to hear what I had known for so long.

"I have something important to tell you, Frankie," I began hesitantly.

"As long as it's not about William; I'm not ready," he replied softly.

I promised him that it wasn't, and his shoulders relaxed a bit, but I premised by saying that it was still something difficult to hear. "It's been over five years since we lost Philip. Sometimes it feels like a lifetime ago and sometimes it feels like yesterday. Nothing can bring him back, we know this much," I paused waiting for acknowledgment. "But there is something that I learned a long time ago that I shared only with Uncle Roger. I wanted to tell you, but I was too scared. I feared you would take matters into your own hands and do something foolish. I've lost four of my brothers and I could not bear the thought of losing five. Please don't be too angry with me Frankie."

"Nothing can surprise me anymore Alicia. Come out with it," he said flatly.

"You know I visited with Teresa years ago in New York. She confided in me a secret about Philip's murder and it changes everything and nothing at the same time."

I explained to him how Teresa had confided in Mary Lincoln about her relationship with Philip. His eyebrows lifted in interest possibly beginning to see where I was going with this.

"We know of course that Dan Sickles fired the gun, and he will have to answer God. He is still ultimately responsible for his own actions. But…the letter Frankie, the mysterious letter that set everything into motion. Haven't we always wondered who disliked Philip enough to write Dan in such an inflammatory way? Well, it may not have been a hatred for Philip personally that prompted the letter, but rather for our family as a whole. Who do we know that has opposed us and caused us grief for no apparent reason for years starting with Uncle Roger?"

Frankie stared ahead answering immediately, "Abraham Lincoln."

"Mary told him," I sighed, "and he exposed it. I want to believe that his intentions came more from a loyalty to Dan than a disdain for our family. Dan had been very good to him you know. He was indebted to Dan. According to Teresa, no one knew the volatile and unstable nature of Dan's behavior, except for herself, and she truly believes that Abraham had no idea that Dan would murder anyone. I actually believe that as well. He may be a diplomatic weasel but not a murderer. However, he should have gone to Dan directly, in person where he could have evaluated his reaction and perhaps softened the blow a bit. Sending an anonymous letter was cowardly and not only that, but he never come forward to accept the responsibility for it. He let Uncle Roger stand there, face to face and deliver the oath of office without once admitting or expressing sympathy to our family for Philip's death."

"I can't believe we didn't put it together ourselves," was Frankie's aggravated reply. "I knew the Sickles and Lincoln families were quite friendly, didn't you? Of course, Teresa would have shared secrets with Mary, and don't wives have a way of sharing any bit of gossip with their husbands?"

We both sat back staring at each other and wondering what we could have done differently and if it would have made a difference, but of course, the past is done and although we may have figured it out sooner, it wouldn't have saved Philip's life. But William's? That was an entirely different question.

"If Abe had come forward straight away, it may not have ruined him," Frankie analyzed. "But if *we* had discovered the truth sooner after Dan's acquittal, we may have been able to expose Lincoln's secret involvement and discredit his whole 'Honest Abe' image. He may have been, like Dan, ostracized from public life. The public disliked a coward as much as a murderer. He likely would have lost the election if we had exposed him during the campaign. It wasn't as though he'd been a popular choice to begin with. If he was never President, then would William be sitting here with us now?"

My eyes filled with tears pondering that sickening question. "He can't get away with this," I avowed.

"No, he cannot," agreed Frankie.

"What should we do? What can we do," I pleaded, hoping he had an answer?

"The election is a year away and George McClellan and your husband *must* win," he said. We mustn't allow him four more years in office. The war has got to end, and the killing must stop. We need some way to discredit that man, to show the people another way that doesn't including butchering our children one by one, we must simply find it."

"I think I may know someone who can help." Frankie rubbed his chin thoughtfully. "We will need assistance to obtain the kind of information that we can use to sour his chances at re-election. Do you remember at Terra Rubra last spring, our cousin Susanna and her daughter Mary Hunter? The young man with Mary, I think his name was John, John Surratt," he recalled. "He had connections, he didn't say exactly who, but he knows people who despise the North and have as much against Abraham Lincoln as we do. He also works as the Post Master in his little town and I wonder what kinds of letters and documents cross his desk that could be of use to our cause. I think I will pay him a visit."

Chapter 21

Surrattsville

As soon as William's body had been sent home to Washington and buried, Frankie began making plans to depart for Surrattsville. I'd wanted to go along but he felt that it could be unsafe and did not want my face shown there. Surrattsville was in the Southern portion of Maryland, a half day ride from Annapolis. He easily found John working at the town post office inside the tavern and the young man recognized Frankie immediately. John showed him around the small town his family had created, from the carriage house to the gristmill and to the inn where he invited Frankie to stay for the night. He'd dined that evening with the Surratt family and had the pleasure to meet John's sister and his mother, Mary, who he noted was kind and hospitable. He remarked that Mary was also the name of our cousin to whom he was attached and asked if things were well between them. John said that things were well indeed, and they had a chuckle over becoming family someday soon. When evening drinks were served, Frankie took the opportunity to discuss his reason for the visit with John. He told me that he'd explained everything to John, from Lincoln's feud with Uncle Roger, to Philip's murder, and to the letter that linked it all together. He'd also sadly shared the news of Williams death and John had expressed deep sympathy for his loss.

John alluded to Frankie that he was still working behind the scenes for the Confederacy and so Frankie proposed our plan to him bluntly. We want information he'd told him. Something to ensure that Lincoln would be disgraced and not win another four-year term as President. Of course, this was already the goal of the South, and John had been trying for years to obtain this type of negative publicity to discredit Lincoln. But Frankie had gone there armed with information and solid leads. We'd met with Uncle Roger, and he'd managed to obtain a list of Abraham Lincoln's family and friends back home in Illinois, with whom he might be more informal and careless in his correspondence. John having contacts of his own throughout the postal system in the North could keep a very close eye on those interactions. Sooner or later, Lincoln would slip and say something unsavory. All Frankie asked was that if he came across anything at all, that he come to Frankie first, instead of to his contacts in the Confederate Army. It was personal, a family matter and wasn't John soon to become a member of the Key family himself?

For the next months, John sent frequent updates on his progress or lack thereof. Lincoln was being very careful in his written words and hardly anything at all had been discovered by John or his contacts in the North. But it was not lack of trying, in fact by opening and expertly resealing every letter that came through his post, he discovered a good supply of sympathizers in the North for his comrades in the South. With that, the network could be expanded and this, in turn, pleased John's Confederate commanders.

During Thanksgiving 1863, our family was gathered at my home in Washington celebrating what had just been declared a federal holiday by our *dear* Mr. Lincoln. The turkey was roasting, and the table was beautifully set awaiting our last guests. There was a knock and Frankie being closest to the door answered. It was a telegram being delivered to Frankie himself. He read it casually and placed it in his jacket pocket. At the first chance to catch me alone for a moment, he let me know that the telegram had come from John. He'd been dismissed from his job as postmaster of Surrattsville. We exchanged nervous glances hoping that this had nothing to do with our request of him and that he hadn't mentioned our name in the process. I'm sure he knew we would be together for the holiday and it was smart to think of sending the telegram then. He was coming to Washington on Monday and would we be available? He also mentioned that perhaps we could arrange for our cousin Mary to be visiting then as well.

He arrived Monday afternoon with an early-season snowstorm on his heels. As he stepped into my home, I felt the strong whoosh of air fighting to come inside with him. It had just begun to snow, and the skies were dark and grey above. The wind was still swirling the flurries about in the street and it had not yet settled into a coating on the ground. I sent for a warm drink right away and led him toward the fire in the parlor where he could warm his hands. As he turned the corner to enter the doorway, his girl, Mary jumped out and surprised him! He was nearly incapacitated with shock, but he recovered quickly and swept her off her feet in a warm embrace. They were so excited to see each other. I was glad I'd taken the opportunity to ask her to come. We'd sent a carriage Saturday morning to Germantown, twenty miles away in Maryland, where she and Susanna lived, in hopes she'd be free to return to Washington in it. We weren't sure if she'd care to come at all, but she'd been overjoyed to receive an invitation to the city. She'd quickly packed her things and showed up here by the afternoon bursting with excitement. It was a lovely weekend getting to know our cousin better and she was such a dear girl. The children especially took to her and she was wonderful with them. I could see that she would make a good wife and mother.

John Surratt was a good kid and I was pleased to think that he would become a part of our very large extended family. Mary went upstairs while we were conversing. She'd been tied and fancied up until she could hardly breathe trying to look her best for the moment

John saw her. Now that he had, in order to do any talking or sitting for that matter, she was changing into something less restrictive. It was probably best for her to know as little as possible anyhow. If John wanted to enlighten her on his current situation, then I'd prefer to leave that up to him.

John settled in and when we had finished with the small talk and holiday greetings, he began to explain, "I lost my job as I said already. This Baker fella who keeps showing up in Surrattsville, finally come back around, and this time he was lookin' for me. A while back I put in for a government job and they didn't like something I said on my application. So, he said I was bein' fired for disloyalty. Fired me as postmaster in my own town, in my own tavern even, good gracious. Them Northern fools think they can do just about anything they want."

"That's just terrible," Frankie and I both began to say. "I know you needed that job to help your mom and sister get by. I hope that this war will end soon and then you can go back to it." As delicately as possible I questioned, "This doesn't have anything to do with our arrangement, does it, John?"

He assured us that no, this was a long time coming before he ever met us. "Don't worry," he said confidently. "I might be many things but I ain't no snitch. My momma taught me that since I was a little kid. Even if they turned me upside down in tar and feathers, I wouldn't speak a word. I'm not givin' up though, they can't take away any job they *don't* know 'bout. It's just, I gotta be extra careful now with that one. I go all over the place gettin' messages and supplies delivered and I don't doubt if they plan on havin' me followed," John finished up saying as Sara brought a tray of tea.

"Well son," Frankie offered. "Please don't take any unnecessary risks on our behalf. If you come upon something then we'd still appreciate that, but your safety is what's most important. Your mother and sister need you."

It was 1864 and election year had come upon us swiftly. My husband was working harder than ever to gain supporters who wanted peace. Lincoln was losing momentum and three years into this war between the states, tensions were higher than ever. I worried that the stress was all too much on my George. He and George McClellan were ahead by nearly all estimates, and no candidate in recent memory had won a second term. Lincoln himself seemed to be preparing to leave the White House. The war was raging, and it seemed remarkable that an election was still being held at all. The Southern States were not being considered in the vote and so a bit of a second war between states was happening in the North as both party leaders competed for the remaining constituents. The strain of campaigning to be in the White House was exhausting. I wondered if actually living there was even more so, and I hoped it would be worthwhile in the end.

March came and I received a message from Frankie saying that he was coming to Washington. He said nothing else and so I anxiously awaited his arrival. He arrived at my home in soaking wet clothes and frozen to the bone.

"Frankie!", I said. "Have you gone mad? Don't you care that this is how we lost father? He insisted on riding in foul weather and it killed him, and now you've done the same! Come inside and change out of those clothes and go to the fire. I'll get the warm water to thaw your fingers and your face. Cook will make you some hot coffee right away." The mother in me took over and I scolded him whilst running about collecting blankets and barking out requests to cook from across the house.

While he was thawing out and I'd finally calmed down, I remembered to ask what was so important for him to come in these conditions. He had a very good reason indeed. He'd received a telegram from John Surratt saying to meet here again the next day and saying only "I've got something."

John arrived on schedule and we exchanged pleasantries for as long as we could stand it before whisking him off to the parlor for a private discussion. It was unbearable waiting and Frankie and I anxiously ushered him into a seat and waited for his reveal.

"I reckon you've heard how they ain't sendin' our boys home no more if they capture 'em up North. Up till now, we been exchanging every so often, their boys for ours, but they decided they don't wanna do that no more," he explained. "Well, that ain't goin' over too well if you imagine. They even got kids from my town."

"How is that going to help anything John," Frankie inquired impatiently. "We need Lincoln out and when that happens then they can all go home, right? Unless there is something more to what you are saying."

"Oh, there's much more." He began. "I know some folks who decided to take matters into their own hands and they'll need help. My friends David and George came askin' if I wanted to help bring the boys home, so of course, I said yes right off. I didn't know exactly what that meant, but I was gonna do what I could for 'em. Well, turns out they got big plans. They are workin' on the details right now and I do think it can be done. They are gonna catch old Abe Lincoln himself. And they ain't giving him back till they send all our boys home."

"Are you crazy, John?!" Frankie said. "You are talking about kidnapping the President for God's sake. You'll never get away with it, and you'll hang, all of you."

"See, I thought so too when I first heard," he replied. But there's some very important minds, if you know what I mean, in on this thing and after hearin' it through, I think it just might work. They ain't gonna hurt him of course, we even got a doctor who's willin' to take care of him while we got 'em just in case he needs one. Doc's name is Mudd. So, I got to thinkin about your situation and I know it don't guarantee nothin' bout the election, but since he's gonna be with us a while, I thought maybe in his time with us, he could be persuaded into writin' up an apology to your Uncle, Mr. Taney, and write up a little confession for your family. You can do what you want with it after, put it in a newspaper, or just take peace in it for yourselves. But I come to ask for somethin' too."

Frankie and I exchanged glances. I wondered if we shouldn't toss Mr. Surratt out into the street for even coming here and saying this kind of thing out loud. We were practically accomplices just for listening to it. Then I thought of Uncle Roger. He wasn't well and he'd dedicated his life to serving on the Supreme Court and for very little appreciation. He had performed his duties even when it meant facing the man who contributed to his nephew's death, the man who had caused his own personal desecration and still swearing him into the highest office in our country. Suddenly I wanted very much to give Uncle Roger that confession. An apology for these things could go a long way in unburdening my uncle in his late years. Not to mention Philip's children, they deserved to know the true story of their father's death and without proof, they could never proudly defend his name.

"We'll do it," I blurted out to John, and Frankie turned white as a sheet and stared at me as though he thought I'd gone mad as well. I pressed on, "What is it we can do?"

John looked at Frankie uncertain if he should continue but Frankie just nodded and said nothing. "Well, we ain't got enough money to do everything we need to do. We need money for bribin' a few folks at checkpoints and such. What I come to ask you though is 'bout Dr. Mudd. I don't know many rich folks and he is a downright costly part of the plan. Would you all be willin' to provide some funds to pay the doc in exchange for your confession from Mr. Lincoln? I'll see to that part my own self, I promise."

"And you are not going to hurt the man, nor mistreat, or torture him either?" Frankie said finally speaking up. "When is this meant to happen? Won't he suspect we are behind it when you ask him to write the confession? How will you find him alone to do this thing? What if he refuses to write it?"

"I know you got a lot of question but I'm tellin' ya that it's all been thought of. Probably the less you know, the better. As for him confessin', he may suspect ya, but I'm gonna tell him that I found out on my own by readin' through his wife's mail and that I'm hopin' for some reward money from the Keys by solvin' their mystery. I'd be bluffin' though, I never did read her mail, but he don't know that. Besides, what's he gonna do? If he calls ya out, the letter he writes confessin' will go public, he won't want that."

"Does your girl, Mary, know what you are doing John," I asked hoping that he would say no.

"Nope, no women. Not a single one but you Mrs. Pendleton, and no one in the gang ever hears your real names either." John continued, saying that he would never subject his girl or his sister or mother to that type of burden of knowledge and I believed him.

We agreed to offer a sum of money when the time came for the plan to be carried out. I hoped that we weren't making the biggest mistake of our lives. Frankie and I vowed to tell nobody, even Uncle Roger of the plan. For better or worse we had managed, in one afternoon, to become accomplices to kidnapping a President.

CHAPTER 22

REGRET AND REMORSE

In early Fall, I had unexpected visitors. John Surratt had come to call one evening and brought his sister Anna and his mother Mary along as well. While I was happy to finally meet them, I wondered if the visit also had to do with updated plans for Mr. Lincoln. The latest I heard was that things were still moving forward. I tried to have a brief word alone with John, but the opportunity had not presented itself. The family had just moved from their town of Surrattsville to a townhome here in Washington several blocks away. Her husband had purchased it as a rental property years before he died, and though it needed a bit of work it was large enough to house the three of them and take on boarders to help with finances. It seems that the Tavern in Surrattsville had become too expensive to maintain alone and so Mary was renting it to a man who'd come from Washington. Mary, being new to the city, asked for any advice I could offer on obtaining boarders. She was worried about renting to any questionable characters, especially with a young daughter in the home. I didn't know a thing about that, but I did refer her to a friend in the Daily Evening Star newspaper office who could help to place an advertisement. I mentioned that my cousin Mary must be happy that John lived a bit closer and would probably be wanting to visit far more. His mother's eyebrows lifted, and I wondered if I had accidentally shared a little too much information.

John explained that they'd broken up recently. I apologized for bringing it up, but John was quick to say that he fully intended to win her back. Apparently, she was a bit more prepared than he was to settle into family life. He confidently said, "she loves me though. I just need to take care of some stuff, then I'll be ready," he insisted. His mother looked doubtful and his sister rolled her eyes, but he just grinned back at them. I could see that he was bound and determined to make good on that promise. I hoped that his "stuff" didn't take so long to finish up that Mary grew tired of waiting for him. I thought they made a good match and I'd wanted to see it work between them. John had already met her family and now here he was introducing his family and it would be a shame to see them split up.

Uncle Roger passed away on October 12, 1864, peacefully in his sleep. I supposed he couldn't bear to see if Lincoln would win the November election. In hindsight, Uncle Roger could perhaps have changed the course of events if he had lived just a little longer. Sadly, I was unable to provide the apology from Lincoln before he died.

The tables had turned by late October, and the election was decidedly leaning toward favoring Lincoln. He'd found a way to include the soldier's votes, and the soldiers were now adamantly dedicated to Lincoln and the Northern cause. Telling their families back home to vote accordingly had done the trick and on November 8, 1864, George McClellan and my husband accepted defeat gracefully as Lincoln was voted into office for four more years and would be sworn in by a new chief justice.

After that, the kidnapping plan began to move ahead quickly. It made sense that they had waited for the official results from the election to confirm that Lincoln needed to be dealt with. John visited several times between November and December, each time with an update and to be reassured that we had the funds available to pay Dr. Mudd when the time came. I tried to tell myself that the money was going to a good cause, paying the doctor who would see to President Lincoln's health and well-being. When Uncle Roger passed away, we had considered pulling out of the plan completely and were just about to break the news to John, when Abraham Lincoln himself, had the nerve to show up at my uncle's funeral. Had he no shame? Hadn't he caused our family enough grief? I could not believe that he showed his face there and I stared him down with looks that could kill, but he pretended to be oblivious. He even nodded and tipped his hat to Frankie. There was no way we were pulling out of the plan now. This smug, pompous man deserved what was being arranged for him.

John's latest report as of December 24, was that the preparations were nearly complete and that several more men had been recruited for the operation. I had never met this Dr. Mudd in person, but I guessed he must have been a distinguished gentleman when John mentioned that Mr. Mudd had brought a well-known actor from Washington into the group. He obviously knew important people, and this gave me more confidence that this plan wasn't doomed to be a complete disaster. The men already involved, including John's own friends George Atzerodt and David Herold, were dazzled upon meeting the actor, John Wilkes Booth. Even his sister had asked Booth for an autographed picture. John didn't seem particularly impressed by his fame and seemed more concerned that with him came others, and the group was beginning to get a bit large. His mother had allowed George and David, who John knew from School, to board at her home but was quickly irritated with the rowdy bunch. George only lasted a few days before Mary asked him to leave for being a drunk. It sounded as though things were quite interesting over at the Surratt Boarding House, famous actors and all.

Frankie and I had prepared and hidden the money away for weeks until I finally received a message saying that the time had come. I assumed John would be coming to collect it very soon. Half out of curiosity about this boarding house with its vast array of characters and half wanting to see his mother again to get the gossip on John and Mary's breakup, I decided to deliver the package of money to John's house instead.

Poor Mary Surratt was such a lovely woman trying to raise two children on her own. She invited me in to the second-floor parlor and offered to make coffee. She apologized for the sparse furnishings. She'd not brought much of the furniture from the Tavern along. There was a lovely piano and a few cushioned seats at least. I told her I didn't mind a bit and even envied it. Sometimes, I wished to get rid of some of my furniture to have the free space. She seemed glad to have someone to converse with, and I listened thoughtfully about the troubles of being a landlord. Several times she had let rooms to her son's friends, including one man named Lewis Powell who seemed to be suffering from amnesia. She told me how she remembered him introducing himself as "Mr. Wood" and she'd been confused when he came back again calling himself Mr. Powell, but John had begged her not to make a fuss when she confronted him about it. She didn't care for John's choice of friendships much and blamed herself for having moved from a small town to the big city. She was particularly worried for her only daughter Anna who found most of John's friends handsome and charming.

Mary had an uneasy feeling about Mr. Booth and even though he was well mannered, she warned her son that she did not like something about the man. She'd even pulled Mr. Booth aside to warn him, "I told him, Mrs. Pendleton, if he were up to no good, that he better keep John out of it and to take his secret meetings and hushed conversations elsewhere."

"Please, you must call me Alicia," I replied. We discussed John and my cousin Mary's breakup and she attested that it had gone bad soon after they'd moved to the city. He was preoccupied with the war, and I pretended to be surprised when she confided in me that he was involved with some sort of secret ring that was running messages all over the place. She was worried for his safety. and young Mary was worried too. When she asked him to stop doing it, he refused. She'd broken it off with him until he picked a more suitable profession. I could understand; being in any way associated with secret dealings was very scary. I should know.

I left a brown paper package tied in string for John claiming it to be letters I'd picked up while visiting Mary, I hoped she was not the kind of mother who would sneak a peek into her son's business and discover the money.

After that visit with Mary in the new year of 1865, I had no appetite, nor was I sleeping peacefully, and my guilty conscience finally got the best of me. I couldn't sit by any longer, this was a mistake, Dan Sickles was responsible for my brother's death. Abraham Lincoln was guilty of bad judgment and a poor choice of comrades. The war was nearly done, it seemed from all accounts, and the only worthy outcome I imagined from it had been all but accomplished, slavery was exceedingly close to being abolished. If Abraham was captured now, would his mission continue to be the objective of the union? It was far too noble of a cause to abandon when so many lives had been sacrificed for it already.

There was one other person who had been harmed as much as the Key family by Abraham Lincoln's choices. Teresa had lost Philip too, and on top of that, she had lost any semblance of the life that she had known. Perhaps she could help decide if revenge was justified. She displayed a softer stance on the Lincolns and maybe I needed her to balance my anger and help me make the right decision. I couldn't tell George anything, after all he'd been through, he'd had enough turmoil for a lifetime. Determined, I opened the drawer to my husband's desk looking for some inconspicuous looking paper to write on.

Dear T.B.S.,

I leave to your discretion information that could change the course of history. The burden is heavy and I provide you the option to share this information with another who may prevent a grave danger to our president. A band of rebels await the opportunity to capture him, not to inflict harm, but to bargain with his release. If you see fit to have mercy, then implore him to keep vigilant and take precautions for his safety. If you choose to remain silent, as will I. Please forgive that I do not wish to reveal myself to you, far too much is at risk. I wish for you to be well and remain well.

Most sympathetically

I signed the note P.F.A, once for Philip, once for Frankie, and once for myself. I took the train to Baltimore under the premise of visiting my sister and posted the letter anonymously to Teresa there, so it could not be traced back to Washington. The next weeks were agony, bracing myself each morning for the unthinkable, and hoping that the letter had made it into Teresa's hands and that she would influence the outcome. If she chose to warn Mary, who would warn Abraham, then I would accept her judgment. The note was meant to protect, but the ultimate decision was in the appropriate hands of the greatest victim of all.

The rain was pouring down on a cool April evening when a loud banging woke me from a deep sleep. George snored beside me not stirring at all. I almost started to shake him awake then thought to have a look out the window down to the front steps first. I tried to peer through the wavy glass and frustrated I cracked the window a bit and felt the raindrops hitting my head as I leaned out slightly to have a look. A wet and terrified looking John Surratt stood on the top step at my front door staring back at me. I rushed to find my robe and slippers before hurrying downstairs to let the poor boy inside. He was breathing heavily and white as a sheet. He took off his soaking outer clothes and shoes and I grabbed a blanket that he could wrap around himself to warm up.

"Tell me what's happened John, are you hurt? Is anyone hurt," I asked anxiously?

He launched into a story that sent chills down my spine and I was frozen to the floor where I stood as he explained that the kidnapping had been attempted several times in March but failed when Lincoln didn't show up where they anticipated him to be. I inwardly breathed a sigh of relief. I was certain now that Teresa had received my letter and I was comforted that in the end, she chose forgiveness, my respect for her was solidified. The kidnapping had failed but there was a huge problem.

"Booth's gone mad," he exclaimed. "He's taken complete control of the plan and the entire gang has gone mad along with him! Seems I'm the only one who's still got any sense! Booth found out that Lincoln's goin' to Ford's theater soon and tonight we was working up a new plan on how to capture him. Next thing I know, Booth starts talking crazy sayin' it wasn't gonna be good enough to just catch him anymore. He wants him dead! Not only him either, more people too. I was waitin' for the others to stand up to 'em but no one did. They downright agreed to it. I didn't say a word but when we got out of there I went off my own way and I ran straight here. I didn't know where else to go."

He was shaking and practically in tears. "I don't want no part of it. That wasn't the deal and I ain't killin' nobody, especially a President." Booth is crazy you know, he'll do it too. Besides, you seen the papers today, right, they sayin' the war's 'bout over, the boys will be comin' home, but Booth ain't stoppin'. What am I gonna do?"

I gave him a light hug around his shoulders. I wanted him to stop talking so I could think and so I hushed him like a child and walked him into the parlor and shut the door. My mind was racing so fast and I was more panicked than I let on. I wished Frankie was here. He would have a cool head and know what to do. But he was in Annapolis and John was here in my parlor. I first suggested that we go to the authorities, but a member of the Confederate Secret Service couldn't exactly walk into a police station and start talking without stirring up a bee's nest for himself and there was no way to explain my involvement whatsoever, so that was out.

"Can we find a way to prevent it," I asked him next. "Could we stop it altogether; warn Lincoln not to attend the theater? Can you talk to the others and try to make them see that they can't do this?"

"Booth's got 'em under a spell or somethin' and nobody is gonna listen to reason. I don't trust a one of 'em. It won't matter if he don't go to the theater, he'll find 'em anyhow. If a man like Booth finds out you might interfere with his plans, you'd likely end up as dead as Abe Lincoln, or worse he'd go after my ma or my sister. They don't know nothin' and I can't tell 'em nothin' or they gonna be in even more danger."

We talked through the night. The plan had become bigger than we could manage, and by morning we decided that the best thing was to get John out of town or even out of the country as soon as possible. He was going to pretend to play along with Booth if necessary while we made the arrangements. John slipped out briefly to avoid being seen by my husband, but as soon as George was off to work, John returned.

I'd sent a telegram to Frankie when the sun came up and asked him to make haste to Washington. He arrived the same day and I was thankful to have someone to share this burden with. I was terribly afraid and trying to be strong for John, who sat nearly catatonic in my parlor most of the day. When Frankie finally walked in, I cried and cried on his shoulder.

The problem that stumped us was that if John disappeared without telling his mother, she would go to the ends of the earth to look for him and could possibly blow his cover trying to find him. A mother desperately searching for a missing child does more thorough research than a detective agency. We also feared she would confront Booth, whom she didn't like at all, and he'd turn his temper on her for John's disappearance. We all agreed that his sister should know nothing, but that his mother had to be brought in on it. She only needed to know enough to understand John's disappearance while being as careful as possible not to incriminate her.

"Do you still have the money John," asked Frankie. "The money for Doctor Mudd?"

"It's hidden out at the Tavern along with some guns and other stuff," he replied. "It's there for Booth and the gang to pick up on his way outta here. I bet the Doc don't even know the plans changed, he don't live near here. He's gonna be in for a real big shock."

Frankie laid out the plan in detail and we both listened very carefully. "John, you must go home and act completely normal. Pull your mother aside privately and make sure no one can overhear. Tell her that she is right about Booth and that you have become involved over your head. Do not give her the details even when she demands them from you. Tell her that you have help, someone who is working on getting you out of town a while. Does she know that there is money in the package Alicia left for you?"

"No, she didn't open it, she thinks it's letters," He looked pale and I hoped he hadn't made himself ill running here through the rain last night.

"Good," Frankie continued. "Ask her to help you get some things together for your trip. Ask her to retrieve that brown paper package and one of the smaller revolvers from the Tavern. Tell her you want to take "Mary's letters" with you. You can use that money to get you by for a while. You cannot show your face at the Tavern, it will make you look guilty, understand? Tell her to move the rest of the guns to a new hiding place and to make sure those guns are ready to use just in case Booth shows up. He's going to be angry when the money is missing, and he may terrorize the folks there looking for them. Have her leave word with someone she trusts about where she puts them, maybe her tenant. Can you do all of that John?"

"Yes sir, I can do it. Once I get hold of the money, then where do I go," he asked Frankie.

"Come back here late this evening, after George has gone to bed. If you encounter Booth at any point, act normal, pretend to be on board. Take only what you must, pack light. I'm going to have some papers made up for you today while you're gone. You and I will leave at once for Annapolis. I know someone who's got a fishing boat there and he'll take you to Maine, you should be able to get yourself into Canada. From there you are on your own," Frankie frowned. "I wish I could do more, but I don't have any trustworthy associates up there. I suggest you disguise yourself, memorize your new name and seek refuge in the churches, to begin with. Time is of the essence, you must be long gone if, or when, Booth makes his move."

When John came back that evening, he had done as instructed. He also pulled from his sack a letter and asked if I could see that my cousin Mary got it. He asked if I could do my best to help her understand what happened and I promised that I would. "You can read it if you like," John said handing it to me with the saddest expression I'd seen in a long time. My heart broke for him and for young Mary and I hoped that they would find each other again one day. I peeked inside the letter and scanned the first line, "I'll be coming back to you darling, wait for me." I could read no more through my tear filled eyes.

CHAPTER 23

THE COST OF FORGIVENESS

Frankie delivered John safely to the boat in Annapolis and saw him off from the pier. We'd helped him change his appearance to look like a battle-worn union soldier and his story was that he had been released from duty and was on his way back home to Brunswick, Maine. John was nervous but thankful to Frankie and me for helping him escape. He really was a good kid, despite the war, and it was a shame that he'd gotten caught up with such a wicked man as John Wilkes Booth. Leaving his family, his home and his girl was surely one of the most difficult choices of his young life. Perhaps nothing would come of Booth's plan to assassinate Abraham Lincoln and John could return sooner than later. I hoped so for both John's sake and for Lincoln's, but deep in my gut, I had a terrible feeling that it was too much to hope for.

I was anxious each minute of the next few days, consumed with listening for the sound of gunfire ringing out somewhere in the city, but not wanting to witness the exact moment that Abraham

Lincoln would be murdered. Hope filled my heart on April 10th when news trickled in that the Army of Virginia had officially surrendered yesterday in a place called Appomattox, indicating the end of the war. I thought of Teresa and was grateful that maybe she had thwarted the efforts of the kidnapping long enough to see this day. My brother was still gone but Lincoln was not and if the war was over, surely, he was out of harm's way. Neither he or my brother deserved to die, especially at the hands of deranged lunatics.

Alas, it had been futile. My heart was broken when the headlines that I dreaded seeing, appeared days later in the morning newspaper. April 15th, 1865, Abraham Lincoln, shot last night at Ford's theater, died this morning at 7:22 a.m. from a gunshot wound to the head. The manhunt was already underway for John Wilkes Booth.

It took no time at all for John Surratt's name to surface in the investigation, and he too was being hunted. I said a silent prayer that we had gotten him far enough away to safety. David Herold was the third most wanted. Each man's capture offered large rewards. Lincoln was not the only target of the attack, which John had mentioned to Frankie and me. In fact, one of the victims had been attacked in the very same building where my brother had been carried to die, the National Clubhouse. Nothing like this had ever happened before and it seemed the police had arrested half the city on suspicion of involvement in the murder. Even poor Mr. Ford, the theater owner was held behind bars. I recognized several of the names in the papers as men mentioned along the way by John. But the most shocking news for me was two days later, on the seventeenth, when it was reported that Mary Surratt had been arrested and was being held for conspiracy to the assassination. I was devastated to read that the police had raided her boarding house, the same place I'd had coffee with her weeks ago. They claimed to have evidence that showed she was involved in the plot. I knew this wasn't true and my heart ached for her knowing how scared she must be. Why were they doing this to her? They insisted on her guilt and publicly destroyed her name. Not a person in the city had sympathy for her after how the reports portrayed her. She was being exhibited like a token, proving progress in the investigation. Why would they be so cruel to a woman? I was instantly ill when a realization washed over me…They targeted her because they could not find her son, John Surratt.

Abraham Lincoln's death was mourned throughout the country, flags were lowered, black shrouds covered windows and doors, an entire nation was grieving. I wanted to be made of stone and not be too distraught over his death, but the truth is that I was devastated. I never wished for him to die or to be murdered in front of his wife. I wanted him to admit what he'd done to my brother and to understand the pain he'd caused our family but not by execution. There had been enough death and sorrow already; now a widow was left behind, another child with no father, and those entangled in the truth, plagued with guilt.

The day Mary Surratt was hung, I did not leave my bed. She stood military trial as a civilian and endured the harshest treatment inflicted on any man, as the lone woman accused in the conspiracy to assassinate President Lincoln. The nation was shocked to hear her sentence. No woman had ever been put to death by the United States Government. I followed the reports carefully. The evidence against her was circumstantial and witnesses caught up in the hysteria offered testimony that was utterly ridiculous. Throughout it all, she never wavered on protecting her son. Any responsibility she could take from his accusers, she took it, even when it was untrue, to absorb their hatred for her son. Had she known and offered to turn over his whereabouts, leading to his capture, I believe she may have been set free, but she would not. She was willing to take the punishment for him rather than feed her son to the wolves.

On the worst days, I blamed myself as the cause of Mary's death. If we hadn't helped John escape, he would have stood trial and been hanged in her place. If I hadn't insisted on seeking revenge for Philip would Abraham Lincoln still be alive? Would my name be brought into this tragedy at some point and I would be hanged as well? These are the things I thought on a bad day.

On a better day, I reminded myself that Mary would have died a thousand deaths to protect her son and his freedom was probably the one comfort she had left in her final moments. Dan Sickles killed Philip and Abraham Lincoln encouraged it. Neither of them were held accountable for my brother's death and so the responsibility of solving the mystery and vindicating his name had fallen on our family. John Wilkes Booth was a madman, and even if he had no accomplices, I knew in my heart that he still would have killed the President. The only person in the world who knew of our involvement was, hopefully, hiding in Canada and was deeply in love with and planned to marry a member of my own family so the likelihood of being exposed was slim.

The internal struggle was exhausting, and I felt sure that Abraham Lincoln had experienced this same kind of inner turmoil after Philip's death. I never liked Mary Lincoln, but I was immeasurably sorry for her loss. With two sons and a husband dead and her youngest son in fragile health, she must have felt that her life was over while still in her forties. I wondered if Teresa still heard from her and I suddenly wondered what Teresa thought of this news from her home in New York. I wrote to her and asked if perhaps I could visit again. I was beyond holding a grudge against anyone anymore and writing to Teresa, who had written me so many times over the years getting no response, was my first step toward being a kinder more forgiving person.

To add to the growing list of sorrows Teresa had written back promptly to inform me that she was sick and that I should not visit for fear of becoming sick too. Consumption had taken hold of her body and the cough that she'd been fighting for years turned worse and she was weak and having breathing difficulties. Laura was staying with Dan's parents as a precaution and Teresa's father had become her round the clock nurse. She also wrote "I always thought of you as a dear friend. I hope you can forgive me and Mary Lincoln. I have been told the terrible news of Abraham's death and it is so sad to see what devastation life can behold. We should all try to love each other a little more. Thank you P.F.A.

With Love, Teresa."

My breath caught in my throat as I realized what she was saying. She had known who the warning letter was from and it was to remain our secret.

These were the final words I would read from Teresa. She passed away within a few weeks and another person had vanished from my life. I didn't travel to attend her funeral for fear of crossing paths with Dan. Even with his missing limb, he was the person it would be hardest for me to forgive. I would need time to work up to that one. I did write to Laura though to express my sympathy and to tell her that she was always welcome to visit us and that she and Alice were old enough to exchange letters as well if she wished to stay in touch. I wondered what would become of the poor child.

Lincoln's death was hard enough to bear, but the day I was sorting through papers left in boxes in my attic was one that will haunt me for the rest of my life. Uncle Roger's belongings had been hastily gathered upon his death last October and sent wherever there was room to store them, and that place at the time had been the top floor of my home. I was determined to clean house and lighten up a bit for spring which was in full bloom. As I sat and thumbed through pages of paperwork, I came across an ornately decorated sheet of paper folded in thirds with the wax seal still unbroken. It was an odd thing to find in the box of boring legal documents, so of course, I opened it.

Discovered far too late now, a letter had been written freely by Abraham Lincoln to Uncle Roger. The letter was lost, unread, for many months in the chaos of my uncle's death and emptying his home, preparing it for new tenants. Lincoln hadn't come to the funeral to gloat after all, he hadn't known that his letter never made it to Uncle Roger and laid unopened in a stack of papers that sat in my attic. Perhaps he came to pay his final respects, thinking he'd made amends, and was at peace with their relationship, as strained as it had been.

What my Uncle would have learned, had the letter reached him in time, is that Mr. Lincoln was weighed down by a heavy conscience, and his wife's strong insistence that they were under a curse, was beginning to eat away at him. Thousands of soldiers died fighting his war, he'd lost two sons and his youngest child Tad was never well, and he feared for his fragile state every day. Apparently, Tad's survival was a strong enough reason to consider Mary's ravings as possible and he decided to make as many amends as he could.

He wrote that he had always respected Roger Taney as a Supreme Court Justice and was sorry that as a young politician he had not realized that it was a personal attack on Taney to condemn the Dred Scott decision. It had launched him into the spotlight and his ego could not give it up. He blamed the politics of war for the ongoing feud. Then he went on to say that being sworn in as President had been one of the worst days of his life. He'd not wanted to meet eyes, and he knew the exact meaning of Uncle Roger saying, "It is known." Each time a wrong decision turned deadly, or each time one of his family members fell ill or was injured, he'd thought of Philip and regretted the decision he'd made years ago sending the letter to Dan.

He went on to say that he could not change the past but that he was deeply sorry for the grief he caused our family. He pleaded for forgiveness from my uncle, saying he could not bear to be sworn in again, should he be re-elected, by Justice Taney without first repenting. As a tribute to my father and Uncle Roger in Philip's honor, Lincoln described his plan to adopt the words "in God we trust" from the last stanza of my father's poem, The Star-Spangled Banner, on coins minted in the United States from here forward, he said, and he hoped that Uncle Roger would accept it as his way of showing deep remorse and respect for the Key family. The tears streamed down my face when I held the letter, reading it over and over and knowing that it was too late.

I read it once more out loud to myself: "In God We Trust." I made my way quickly downstairs and rummaged through my coin purse and produced a silver dollar, and there it was, "in God we trust," the half dollar too, a quarter, and a two-cent piece all bearing the words of my father's poem that was so revered to this day. Sorrow and gratitude overwhelmed me all at once and I collapsed to the ground clenching the coins tightly in my hand and crying tears of sorrow, joy, regret, gratitude, forgiveness, anger, and every other emotion all at the same time.

Immediately I wanted to visit Frankie to show him the letter. I asked for the carriage and packed a few things and I was off to Annapolis within the hour. Frankie was already in bed when I arrived and since it was only 6 p.m. I had been confused when Elizabeth let me in and spoke in a soft voice, "Frankie isn't well. I was just about to send for you and here you are." She looked at me puzzled and asked how I had known to come.

"Fate, I suppose," I replied as she led me to the bedroom. Frankie was ill indeed. He shook with chills and fever and Elizabeth replaced the wet rag on his forehead with a fresh one. I asked if the doctor had been to see him and found he had left just minutes before I arrived. The doctor diagnosed Frankie with brain fever and told Elizabeth to make final preparations and call family to his side. I sat beside him and spoke his name, but his neck was stiff and he could not turn to see me. He squeezed my hand instead, acknowledging my presence and I held fast to his hand and asked Elizabeth for a few moments alone with my brother. She needed to send messages to their children and family, and she was glad for me to stay with him so that she could see to the telegrams.

"I didn't come here because you are sick Frankie," I whispered.

"Dying," he corrected me.

I couldn't say that word and it felt like a slap to hear him speak it. I continued, "I found something today in Uncle Roger's things and I wanted to show you right away." I held the fancy paper in his line of sight so that he could have a look. "Abraham Lincoln wrote a letter to Uncle Roger."

I explained that the seal had been unbroken, it was never read by our uncle. Reading him the letter I watched his expression change, his eyes darting back and forth as he digested the information I was feeding him. It was a good thing and a terrible thing to comprehend. Perhaps it had been less painful to be angry at Abraham for our brother's death. Thinking of him as a mere human being who made a terrible mistake only compounded the sense of loss that had occurred since February 27, 1859, when Philip was shot. A single tear rolled down Frankie's cheek and I used his rag to dab it away. It hadn't changed a thing to know the truth, but I could sense Frankie's peace and we were comforted knowing that we had done all we could for Philip and for Uncle Roger, and for father. I knew that I had also done what I could for Abe Lincoln. If they were together right now, I hoped that they were looking down on us with pride and not disappointment. I planned to ask them just that someday; we would inevitably meet again.

The following year a letter arrived with overseas postage markings. It was unsigned and in unfamiliar handwriting but upon reading its contents I knew exactly who had sent it. Our hidden fugitive had made his way across the Atlantic Ocean. He was well but missed home terribly. Word of his mother's "misfortune" had cut him deeply. He was careful with his choice of words and I appreciated the precaution. He had never dreamed that something like that would have happened and he would never forgive himself for it. The last sentence read "Best to you and Frankie." He clearly hadn't heard that Frankie had passed. So much could change in a year and he'd left no way of returning a letter.

He was not in the dark for long, because weeks later the headlines boasted that the fugitive, John Surratt, was arrested in Egypt and was on his way back to America to stand trial. I wasn't sure how much more my heart could take and without Frankie or Uncle Roger to turn to, I had never felt so alone. I prayed and prayed that John would not be coaxed into revealing my name. He had stated years ago that his mother taught him never to snitch and I hoped with all my might that he honored that code still.

The laws had changed after Mary Surratt was hung. Unfortunately, it was too late to save her, but it could save her son. Civilians were no longer allowed to be tried before a military tribunal. It was deemed unconstitutional and that citizens were entitled to a trial by a jury of their peers. The trial lasted two agonizing months and the details coming from the courtroom terrified me daily. I bit my fingernails down to nubs and paced hundreds of miles in my bedroom. His lawyer had admitted his knowledge of the kidnapping plot but denied participating in the assassination. Witnesses were brought from as far as Montreal to testify to his whereabouts during the time of the murder. With most of the co-conspirators dead and very little solid evidence against him the jury had not been able to reach a unified verdict. Beyond the murder charge, the time limit for charging him with other possible crimes had run out and John, with a hung jury, was released and walked away a free man.

I nearly jumped up and down with happiness when this decision was announced and it felt like finally, the revenge and the killing had come to an end. John quietly disappeared for several years and I knew that he was taking care to protect me from association with his name. He was a smart and loyal man and my only displeasure came from fretting that he and my cousin Mary would not be reunited and that we would not become family after all. The war had ended, and the country was in the process of healing and reconstructing itself. George launched a second attempt at the presidential nomination, and I would be lying if I said I was sorry he'd lost. Finally, no one I knew was President, and I was immensely thankful for that.

George took a job as President after all, but it was of a railroad company in Kentucky, not the United States Government. Life in Kentucky was far from the life we lived in Washington and the children and I enjoyed the peace and tranquility of our life there. The only reminder from home that disturbed me was in learning that poor Tad Lincoln had passed away. He had succumbed to the illness that had caused his frail state, at the age of eighteen. He was laid to rest with his father and two brothers. Mary, it was reported was not handling the loss well and had been hospitalized for her own protection. I couldn't imagine the pain of losing a husband and three sons. Who could blame her for being deranged after the death of her "baby" Tad? As much as I hadn't been fond of her personally, I felt for the woman and sent flowers anonymously to the hospital where she was being cared for and to the church where the funeral for Tad was held.

To my tremendous surprise, three years after John had quietly slipped away, an invitation arrived in the mail. A wedding invitation for Mr. John Harrison Surratt, Jr. to wed Miss Mary Victorine Hunter. I couldn't believe my eyes and I was thrilled to receive such wonderful news. Best of all, the wedding was being held at Terra Rubra next summer. I was going home!

The wedding was a splendid day for the Key Family. It was wonderful to be reunited at the place we all thought so fondly of and missed. The beauty of Terra Rubra never failed to take my breath away upon approach. The colors and the landscape reminded me of a painting that should be hung above a mantle and I made a note to myself to look into the possibility of having that done.

My four children were all there, and Alice was overjoyed to see her brothers and sisters when they arrived from Baltimore. All of them were approaching adulthood and I was especially impressed with my nephew James, Philip's only son. He had endured the painful childhood loss of both his mother and father and had managed to become a smart, handsome, and successful young man. He studied law as his father and grandfather had, but his interest was in business. He spoke of his dreams of owning his own hotels and theaters in New York City and was well on his way to making those dreams come true.

The outdoor wedding reminded me of so many that had been held there before. Beautiful bouquets of fresh flowers were placed nearly everywhere. Chairs were set in neat rows with ribbons draped along the backs in the brides chosen shade of violet. A center aisle with white rose petals covering the ground was prepared for the bride to walk down. Impressive white columns stood tall at the end of the aisle and they were wrapped with beautiful vines of morning glory that must have been specially grown around them for this occasion. The orchestra was staged to the right and worked on tuning their instruments to play perfectly for the ceremony. I took a seat next to James so that we could chat while waiting for the wedding to begin. He was twenty years old now and taller than I by far, but I still thought of him as Philip's little boy, and he had grown into the spitting image of his father. He smiled when I told him so, and it looked like he wanted to say something.

"You can say what's on your mind James," I assured him. "I promise you can't scare me away. Your Aunt Alicia is made of iron." He chuckled as I knocked on my own knee to demonstrate my strength.

"It's just that, no one wants to talk about my father to me," he frowned. "I'm twenty years old and I still have to read old newspapers to get information on what happened to him back then. I know the facts, he was shot by Dan Sickles in Washington. He was having an affair with the man's wife. Her name was Teresa. But I want to know what really happened, did you know those people Aunt Alicia?

What were they like? What was my father like? I know it's a painful subject, but I really need to understand."

I sat back in my chair and tapped my chin trying to think of what to say. He was so sincere and while his eyes were pleading with me, for a brief second, I saw Philip in them. It was time. He was a grown man now and this was his family story. He deserved to know it and after all these years of carrying the secrets myself, it was time to pass the truth on to a future generation. I looked him straight in the eyes and could see that James was the right person to tell. He was his father's son and if anyone could empathize with Philip's story, it was him. "Well James," I smiled. "Do you have a few days? It's a very long story." He smiled back, a dashing Philip-like smile, and I assured him we would have that talk.

The orchestra began to play, signaling that the wedding was beginning. I hadn't seen John in years since the night he left for Annapolis with Frankie. In the meantime, he'd gone from a skinny kid into a grown man and he was a more handsome groom than I imagined he would be. After the ceremony, we came face to face in the receiving line, and we both had tears in our eyes. There was an unspoken and unbreakable bond between us, and I loved him like one of my own brothers. He kissed my cheek and squeezed my hands tightly, and despite my quivering voice I managed to say, "welcome to our family."

CPSIA information can be obtained
at www.ICGtesting.com
Printed in the USA
BVHW031323300719
554660BV00001B/41/P